Growing up in a publisher's home in South Africa, FIONA SUSSMAN fell in love with language and the written word at an early age. This was during the apartheid era, and witnessing the brutal regime at work sensitised Fiona to the issues of injustice and racial prejudice. Fiona now lives in New Zealand.

fionasussman.co.nz
@FionaSussman

By Fiona Sussman

Shifting Colours
The Last Time We Spoke

The Last Time We Spoke

FIONA SUSSMAN

Allison & Busby Limited
12 Fitzroy Mews
London W1T 6DW
allisonandbusby.com

First published in Great Britain by Allison & Busby in 2016.
This paperback edition published by Allison & Busby in 2017.

Ka Mate Haka - Right of Attribution
The publisher and the author recognise Te Rauparaha as the composer of Ka
Mate during the early nineteenth century, and a chief of Ngāti Toa Rangatira.

A CIP catalogue record for this book is available from
the British Library.

10 9 8 7 6 5 4 3 2 1

ISBN 978-0-7490-2064-4

Typeset in 10.5/15.5 pt Adobe Garamond Pro by
Allison & Busby Ltd.

The paper used for this Allison & Busby publication
has been produced from trees that have been legally sourced
from well-managed and credibly certified forests.

Printed and bound by
CPI Group (UK) Ltd, Croydon, CR0 4YY

To those living in the shadow of a violent crime

Turn your face to the sun and the shadows will fall behind you
— Māori proverb

The author states that any resemblance between fictional characters in this novel and any persons dead or living is purely coincidental. The surnames of some of the characters do not have a genealogical basis.

Beginnings

1989

'What will become of the monster?'

Thirty pairs of eyes grew wide. Felicity Taylor started to whimper and Garth Mullins rammed a finger up his freckled nostril, examined his haul, then sampled it.

'Garth!' Carla said, fixing him with a frown and shaking her head, strands of her ink-black hair escaping the order of a tortoiseshell clasp.

The class of new entrants sat cross-legged on the square of cranberry carpet. It was a humid February morning, and despite all four sash windows being open, the air was still and thick, and the children restless. Even the Loch Ness monster drooped from the roof, its cardboard tail buckling, its green scaly body sagging. And Garth's behaviour was worse than usual. The school year had barely begun, yet Carla already had a good idea of the little personalities in her charge.

'He's going to kill them all,' the freckly boy shouted, his hands clawing at the air, his teeth gnashing.

Felicity was now in full-blown wail.

'Garth, what about our quiet voices?' Carla said, opening her arms and beckoning to the pale, strawberry-blonde girl. 'Come here, love. It's just a story.'

Felicity Taylor wriggled onto her teacher's knee and buried her head into Carla's neck, her nose cold against Carla's skin. Carla turned the page, her silver bracelets jangling.

'I don't think our monster is quite that bad. Hilary and Owen, eyes this way.'

'He is! He is! He's evil, Mrs Reid.'

'Let's find out then, Nathan.'

Carla started to read again, her eyes darting from page to audience in playful exaggeration. 'Deeper and deeper into the murky waters he slid—'

There was a knock at the door. The class let out a collective gasp as the principal, Miss Carr, stepped into the room. Instantly shoulders were pulled back and arms folded.

'Lovely manners, James Tahu,' Miss Carr said, her eyebrows dancing independently of each other.

The chubby lad grinned. Carla winked at him.

'Sorry to disturb you, Mrs Reid . . .' The children scrutinised their principal's bronze lipstick, sharp green shoes, and laddered stocking, 'but there's an important call come through for you in the office.'

'An important call?' Carla felt a rush of apprehension. She eased Felicity off her knee and stood up.

'Don't know what it's about,' her boss whispered. 'Just said important. Something confidential.'

Carla hesitated.

'Off you go, then. I'll mind your class.'

Carla hurried from the room and started down the corridor.

She broke into a run, her red pumps clattering on the lino. Was it Kevin? Something on the farm? Please God her father hadn't had another fall.

Five C was just returning from music when Carla rounded the corner, the kids spread across her path in a noisy amble.

'Excuse me. Can I get past? Excuse me,' she said, weaving through the slow slouch of bodies. 'Thank you. Can I get through?'

'This is not a Sunday picnic, class. Move along!' came the shrill Irish tones of Esther Creighton bringing up the rear.

Carla smiled in grateful acknowledgment, then hurried on, leaving Esther open-mouthed as the opportunity for a corridor gossip slipped by.

She was out of breath by the time she heard the familiar *tap tap tap* of Daphne at the word processor. The secretary stopped and peered over her glasses as Carla burst into the office. On the desk lay the black telephone receiver dislocated from the rest of the instrument.

'Catch your breath, honey,' Daphne purred, slipping a Mint Imperial into her mouth. The room stank of cigarette smoke.

Carla picked up the phone. 'Hello?' She could hear a hum of voices in the background. 'Hello?'

'Carla.' The voice at the other end was familiar. 'Sorry to disturb you at work, but I thought you'd want to know.'

Carla's gums prickled.

'Your test results, they're back. It's not Giardia after all.'

Carla closed her eyes. 'More serious?'

'Well, you're . . .' Her doctor's voice was smiling. 'Carla, you're pregnant.'

'I'm what?' Carla began to tremble. 'Are you . . . I mean, that's impossible!' Eight years of trying. Her mind spun through it all.

The doctor kept talking, Daphne kept typing, and Carla wept and laughed at the same time.

When she finally replaced the handset, Daphne was waiting with a box of apricot tissues and her tell-me-all eyes. But Carla wasn't ready to talk. Silence would keep her baby safe. She excused herself and wandered back through the narrow corridors, past rows of hooked schoolbags spilling lunch boxes and books onto the floor, past frosted doors and serious silhouettes, past years of anguish and effort and resignation. And just before she reached her classroom, she turned and headed out into the sunshine.

The playground beckoned. Carla climbed onto the paint-peeled jungle gym, scaling the scarred yellow bars till she was teetering on the very top. Kevin was going to be a father. She flicked off her shoes, letting them drop to the ground. Her toes curled around the cool metal. Her father was going to be a *nonno*. She closed her eyes and stretched out her arms sideways, letting the cool fingers of breeze caress her. Then she jumped, her skirt billowing out to trap the freedom. She tumbled onto the grass and fell back on the damp earth, a twig snagging in her hair. 'I'm going to be mother!' she shouted, gazing up into the blue. 'I'm going to be a mother!'

Then she saw them, her students' faces pressed hard up against the classroom window – noses flattened, fingers pointing, hot breath misting up the glass – and behind them, squinting, a bemused Miss Carr.

1991

'Fuck, Debs, I'm pregnant,' Miriama Kāpehu said, flicking off the top of a bottle of DB Draught and taking a long swig.

'You what?'

'I'm pregnant.'

'Choice, girl,' Debs said, eyeing her friend's flat midriff with a mix of respect and suspicion.

'It's not bloody choice. Joel will lose me soon as he finds out. And I can't go back to the olds now. Not after running away with a man with a patch,' she groaned, shaking her slight shoulders to imitate his staunch stance. 'I'm stuffed.'

'Teach you for letting him poke you without protection, girl,' Debs said, snorting with laughter.

Miriama lay back in the dry grass and looked up at the sky littered with shredded clouds. 'Got a smoke?'

Debs passed over her half-smoked cigarette. 'How far gone?'

'I dunno.' Miriama inhaled deeply. 'Three months, maybe.'

'Three months! Too late for Family Planning, hon.' Debs broke a twig in two and used the sharp end to clean one of her fingernails. 'I knows this woman who does the business. Cost you 'bout a hundy to get rid of it.'

The two girls lay beside an upturned supermarket trolley in the middle of the empty lot, contemplating Miriama's predicament.

'Hey, you can't have the whole smoke,' her friend said, grabbing back the glowing stub. 'It's my last one.'

A week later, in some house in Drover Street, in a dank-smelling bedroom with peeling pink wallpaper, Miriama lay back on a grey plastic tarp. It stuck to the backs of her thighs and left a crisscross pattern on her bottom. She spread her legs, and a woman whose name Miriama never got to know stuck a knitting needle through the mouth of her young womb. But it was a hundred dollars wasted, because the *koru* of cells didn't let go. It held on, refusing to be annihilated. Perhaps it was meant for greater things . . . Grasping at life through bleeding and infection, it continued to grow, and six

13

months later, on April 1st, like some rude joke, it made its way into the world, tearing Miriama asunder.

'Aah, he's beautiful,' cooed Debs. 'Joel's gonna be stoked!'

To Miriama's surprise, Joel had been pleased about the pregnancy. He'd seemed almost excited at the prospect of becoming a father, at night rolling into the deep dip of their bed to put his ear to her growing belly.

'I thinks it's a Lenny,' he once said, his black curls tickling her taut tummy.

'You can't call him Lenny,' she protested. 'I had this really ugly uncle called Lenny. He had hundreds of warty bumps all over his face. Anyway, it's gonna be a girl.'

'Nah. It's a boy. He jus' told me,' Joel said, tapping her popped-out *pito*.

'No, he didn't!'

'See, you just said he!'

Miriama knew Joel wanted a son, but she was carrying high and everyone told her that meant it would be a girl.

They finally agreed on the name Benjamin Joel if it was a boy. Benjamin, after Bennie Edmonds, Joel's best mate in the gang. Miriama didn't like the idea of naming her son after one of the mob – it was a bad omen – but she gave in because she was sure she was having a girl, and then they'd call her Aroha Jude. Aroha after Miriama's mother, even though they hadn't seen each other in the longest time, and Jude after Jude Dobson, the pretty presenter on *Sale of the Century*. Miriama hoped her daughter would be pretty too.

Now she wiped the matted hair off her forehead and sank back into the pillows. The midwife, a round, rosy woman with warm hands, placed the baby next to her. Miriama took a closer look. A shock of black hair stood to attention on its crumpled brown scalp, and little popsicle-stick fingers poked out from under the soft *pink* blanket. Well, she thought she was having a girl, didn't she!

Miriama's breathing started to pick up. It wasn't that she was out of puff or anything. Rather, it was a sort of panic growing inside her.

'I'm gonna be a good mom, Debs.'

'Course you are. The bloody best.' Her friend laughed. 'Now don't be so serious. You look like you seen a ghost.'

Miriama slipped her pinkie into the baby's tiny creased palm and five little fingers rolled tightly around it, giving her goosebumps all over.

She spent three nights in the National Women's Hospital because of all the stitches down below. It was awesome. She'd never stayed in hospital before and it was how she imagined a hotel would be – food delivered on a tray three times a day, a jug of fresh water every morning, and a hot shower whenever she wanted. And Joel was so chuffed at getting the son he'd ordered, he swaggered into the ward that first night holding the biggest bunch of flowers she'd ever seen and wearing a grin as wide as the world.

On the day of discharge, Debs ordered a taxi, and Miriama was driven home like proper royalty, sitting there in the back seat with baby Ben wedged between her and her best friend.

But when they got home, Joel was there with his crew. They'd been on the booze all day.

'Come 'n' party,' he said, grabbing her round the waist.

'I've just had a bloody baby!' she flashed, wriggling free.

His eyes darkened. 'So now you got your fuckin' baby, you think you can jus' turn your back on me?' he roared. 'Well that's not how it's gonna be. Not with tits this size.' His hands moved up under her shirt and squeezed her swollen breasts. She winced as two damp patches bloomed over her blouse.

A few of the guys sniggered; others shifted uncomfortably.

'Get off me!' she cried, driving an elbow into him.

Joel's top lip curled back over his teeth, and he swung her round, the Moses basket pirouetting with her.

'I said, come party,' he hissed, his sour breath hot against her cheek.

Debs lunged forward and grabbed the basket with baby Ben inside, just as Joel grabbed a fistful of Miriama's long black hair.

'Jesus, man. Give her a break,' Debs screamed.

'Shut the fuck up, woman, or I'll give you a reason to moan.'

Later that night Miriama got up to give her baby a feed, but her milk had gone and she couldn't fill the screaming, wrinkly kid. It cried all night until Joel told her if she didn't do something he'd shut the baby up himself. So she took the little one onto the street and they walked up and down until dawn.

From the first day home, it was so hard having a baby.

Chapter One

CARLA

16 years later

Napoleon snorted and snuffled and nudged at Carla, smearing a glistening ribbon of saliva across her gumboot.

'That's all for now, greedy-guts,' she said, retrieving the upturned bucket and tilting it toward the pig. 'Look, nothing left.'

Napoleon stuck his snout in the pail, gave a resigned grunt, then reversed into Carla, jamming her between his bristly body and the railing.

'After a cuddle, eh?' she said, patting the kunekune's rotund belly. Then, with the swing of a leg, she hoisted herself over the fence. 'Got to get on, old fella. Lots to do.'

At the backdoor she pulled off her gumboots and padded into the kitchen. The aroma of caramelised tomatoes enveloped her. She peered into the oven; the lasagne was browning beautifully. Another ten minutes and it would be done.

As she scrubbed her hands in the sink, Carla gazed out of the open window, the breeze riffling her blue-black hair, the evening light airbrushing her weathered complexion. There was nothing exceptional about the vista, framed first by the rectangle of window and then the line of weeping willows bowing into the scene. Yet she never tired of it – the sweep of lawn, the copse, the grey-green pond. She loved how the land fell away, unfolded and breathed, the view transforming with each season as the year tinkered with its canvas.

When she looked carefully, she could just make out Kevin's silhouette on the far knoll, shadowing the herd as it lumbered down the slope ahead of the closing day. 5:50 p.m. She smiled. Perhaps, after all these years – twenty-seven to the day – she had finally succeeded in making her husband punctual.

Carla gave an involuntary shiver and slid the window shut. Jack would be arriving shortly too. How she looked forward to these brief pockets of time when she could play at being Mum again and fuss over him until Kevin would chide, 'Give the poor lad some space. He's a grown man, for Pete's sake.'

Untying her apron, Carla found herself for the second time that day heading down the hall to her son's room. It was just as he'd left it almost a year ago, complete with George Benson posters and model airplanes. Even his tennis racquet still stood at ease in the corner. She and Kevin had planned to convert the room into a study of sorts – a place where she could guiltlessly leave out her sewing machine, and Kevin, his piles of paperwork – freeing up the cluttered dining room for its original purpose. But they hadn't got around to it. To change the room was to admit that a phase of life was over. While Jack's corkboard remained cluttered with scribbled memos, exam timetables, and sporting certificates, the promise of his return remained real.

She tugged at the well-worn duvet, straightening a ridge of the creased brown fabric. Then she opened Jack's wardrobe, and in a *Narnia* moment, the smell of her boy – cricket greens,

Blue Stratos, earth, and leather – drifted out, rewinding time.

The ringing phone trespassed on her reverie.

'Carla, Deirdre here. Not interrupting dinner, am I?'

'No. Not for a while yet, Dee. Kev's still out on the farm.'

'I received your message and—'

'Yes. Look, thanks for returning my call. I was just wanting to ask whether there were any teaching positions coming up.'

'At long last, Carla Reid! So it's taken an empty nest to finally woo you back.'

Carla laughed. 'Actually, it's . . . Well, we could use a little extra cash right now.'

'Couldn't we all,' replied the school principal. 'Look, we've no permanent posts available at present, but I'll put your name down on the reliever's list in the meantime; something more long-term is bound to come up.'

Carla felt the muscles down the back of her neck loosen.

'It'll be good to have you back, Carla. Really good.'

Carla replaced the receiver. Dusk was falling fast, robbing the kitchen of light and wrapping a faded evening around the homestead. There wasn't really sufficient time to achieve much before tea, despite the growing list of jobs that challenged her from the refrigerator door, so she decided to pour herself a drink instead.

She positioned a stool against the kitchen cupboards, clambered onto it, and reached for a glass on the uppermost shelf. Kevin hadn't taken into account her height, or lack of it, when he'd installed the kitchen.

Her hand found the last surviving tumbler from a set of eight she and Kevin had collected on their only trip abroad together – a trek around the Yucatán Peninsula twenty years earlier. It was a chunky blue thing with bubbles of clear glass trapped in the thick cerulean rim. They'd lugged the set around Mexico for six weeks, Kevin cursing her impetuous purchase all the way.

Carla twisted the ice tray and frozen cubes clattered onto the bench, one sticking to her fingers and tugging painfully at her skin as she shook it off. She unscrewed the bottle of whisky and poured, ice blocks crackling and screeching as she drowned them in the amber liquor.

She was about to take her first sip when she heard footsteps behind her. She swung round, the drink slipping from her grasp. Shards of blue glass and whisky sprayed across the room.

'Jack!'

Her son was standing in the middle of the room, his head bowed under the low ceiling beams, his eyes wide with alarm. In his hand was a bunch of purple irises.

'The door was open. I wanted to surprise you.'

Carla sucked in a warbled breath. 'Well, that you certainly did, son!'

He screwed up his face apologetically. 'Sorry, Mum. I'll get the dustpan.'

'No, leave it! I'll do it in a minute.' She grabbed him by the hand. 'Now, let me take a good look at you, my handsome boy.'

He looked so grown-up in his jacket and tie, no resemblance to the grubby youngster she'd battled for years to keep clean, the streams and paddocks his playground.

He grinned and wound a lanky arm around her, pulling her in. She inhaled his sophisticated city scent.

'Happy anniversary, Mum,' he said, handing her the flowers.

It was just like Jack. He'd always been such a considerate kid, even as a six-year-old spending his pocket money on trinkets for her at the Ag Day fair. Years flashed before her – the emptiness and heartache, then the giddy news, the hope, and finally, unbelievably, a baby. That first night in the maternity ward, Kevin asleep in the La-Z-Boy beside her, their child moulded to his chest and a tall vase of deep purple irises on the windowsill.

The sound of barking dogs intruded.

'Seems Dad could use a hand,' Jack said, glancing out of the window.

'You'll want to get out of that suit first. Have a shower.'

'Later, Ma,' he said, peeling off his jacket and hooping the tie over his head as he made for the back door.

Carla stood watching as her son made his way across the paddock, the half-light smudging his outline till he'd been erased altogether. Reluctantly, she bent down and began picking up the fragments of glass, a thread of disquiet ruching her mood. She felt the loss of the tumbler more acutely than she'd have expected. In a strange way, it felt as if some tie with the past had been severed.

Suddenly a sharp pain sliced through her ruminations and a bubble of blood sprang up on the heel of her palm. She cursed and hurried to the bathroom, leaving a thin crimson trail behind her.

Dinner had been in the warmer for some time when she finally saw father and son, with their identical gait and tall-man stoop, sloping towards the house. Jack now had at least two inches on his dad. They appeared to be in earnest conversation when both stopped a short way off from the back door. At first Carla thought they were merely catching their breath – that incline could be punishing at the end of a long day. But the men remained there for longer than a breather, till even the bantams nearby had resumed their foraging.

Kevin spotted her at the window and gave a quick smile, spreading out a hand to say they'd be in in five.

Father and son had always got on well, despite their quite different personalities. Kevin was all Anglo-Saxon – a man of few words and even fewer emotions. Like a trusty old tractor, he had a quiet consistency about him. There were no surprises or breakdowns, but no glamour either. Jack was more volatile. He had a touch of Carla's Italian heat in him – his impulsiveness landing him in trouble on more than one occasion. Fortunately, his charm usually won out. Now he had a serious girlfriend – surprisingly his first – however, he hadn't yet introduced her to them. From what Carla could glean, the young woman was training to be a speech therapist and shared Jack's passion for tramping and the great outdoors. Not surprisingly, Jack's phone calls home had dwindled of late.

Therefore shall a man leave his father and mother, and shall cleave unto his wife . . .[1] Sunday's sermon echoed in Carla's head. Their son had been lent to them; a daughter was for keeps.

Lately, Carla hadn't been able to keep this undertow from sweeping her thoughts to that taboo place in her mind, the place she'd successfully kept buried for so many years. What if Gabby had lived beyond those few thin weeks? Carla and Kevin would have a grown-up daughter now too.

The light had drained out of the day when the three of them finally sat down to eat. Carla was glad for the early autumn nightfall, the darkness lending the dinner a more formal tone. She'd lit the candles and drawn the drapes, swathing the old kauri room in a cosiness, and had even folded the napkins into the shape of fans, just as they did in restaurants.

'Any chance of thirds, Mum?' Jack asked, eyeing the last burnished square of lasagne.

'It's for you to take back to the flat,' she said, moving the dish out of his reach.

'You're a hard woman,' he teased. 'How'd you put up with her all these years, Dad?'

Kevin smiled, but his eyes held onto a more sombre expression. Carla wondered what he and Jack had been discussing out in the yard.

'Keep some space for dessert,' she said, uncovering the apple pie. 'Ay! Fingers out of it!'

Jack was scraping the last of the custard from the little red jug when he stopped and looked up at his parents, his brown eyes unexpectedly earnest. 'Dad. Mum. I've been thinking. About the farm and all. It's a lot of work for the two of you.'

Kevin cocked his head to one side and looked at his son from under a heavy brow. 'Bit a work never did anybody any harm, boy.'

'I know. But you and Mum . . . You aren't getting any younger.'

'Thanks very much!' Carla said with a chuckle. 'I'm not in a wheelchair yet.'

'I just mean that you don't want to be getting up at four in the morning for the rest of your days, do you?'

Jack had grown his hair longer since leaving home, allowing the natural wave to reveal itself. He reminded Carla so much of her own father, with his liquorice-black eyes and caramel complexion, his drive and determination, his stubbornness. Her father hadn't been much older than Jack when he'd hidden from Mussolini's Blackshirts in the sewers of Turin before escaping with his bride on a boat bound for New Zealand.

Kevin clicked his tongue. 'It's not as hard as you make out. Rangi and Rebecca are good value. In fact, they're the best share milkers we've had. Anyway, won't be long before I can sleep in till six,' he added, 'and you'll be doing the hard yards.'

Jack slid his hands under his thighs, his neck sinking between hunched-up shoulders. 'See, Dad, the thing is . . . I'm not sure that's what I want to do any more . . . I like living in the city.'

Kevin put down his fork and wiped his mouth with his serviette. He stared at the placemat in front of him. Carla shut her eyes.

Jack swallowed. 'I don't know if I want live on the farm for the rest of my life. The bank's offered to sponsor me to go to uni next year, get a degree in finance.'

She opened her eyes and looked across at Kevin. Jack's job at the bank was only meant to be a stopgap, a way to earn some money for his big OE. The 'Overseas Experience' was a rite of passage for so many Kiwi kids – a way to see the world and satisfy their wanderlust before settling down. Jack was supposed to return to the farm. That had been the five-year plan: come home, work beside his father, one day, take over.

'University,' Kevin repeated slowly. 'Well, that's . . . I mean, if that's what you want. So they've offered to sponsor you, eh?'

Jack pressed on, as if getting a rehearsed speech out of the way. His words were tentative and his demeanour strangely wooden, as if his audience was foreign to him. Jack playing at being an adult, thought Carla. She wanted to reach out and shake him. Reverse the years. Rewind his words.

'It got me thinking about you guys and the farm. I've been wondering whether you should consider diversifying. Say, get into ostriches or alpacas? They're a lot less work than dairy, you know.'

Kevin swayed back and forth on his chair, his forehead creasing into deep ruts, his sunburned arms pushing back against the table.

'And when they're established, you could downsize the dairy side of things.'

Oh, Jack! Carla rolled a thumb over the back of her other hand, stretching the skin till it hurt.

But Jack kept going, words now sliding off his tongue with careless ease. 'You'd have time to travel a bit. Mum's always talking about wanting to go to Italy. You guys should enjoy life a bit, instead of always working so hard.' He shot her a sideways glance.

Carla sat back, allowing the evening to wash over her and packing her disappointment away carefully. Jack had been gone only a handful of months and already she missed sharing in his world, an intimacy she imagined his new girlfriend now enjoyed. The plan for his return to the farm had made the emptiness tolerable.

She looked over at Kevin, her rugged man who worked the land, cared for his family, and shunned the draw of the city. Beneath that tough carapace lurked a sensitive and shy Kiwi bloke who even enjoyed listening to poetry, and who desperately loved his son, though would never tell him. Jack's decision would be unfathomable for him.

'The bank, eh,' Kevin said, with a sigh, pushing his thumb and forefinger into the corners of his eyes.

'Look, Dad, we'll talk about it another time. I shouldn't have brought it up tonight,' Jack said, suddenly backtracking. 'On your wedding anniversary and all.' He turned. 'Hey, Mum, you still make the best apple pie ever.'

Carla smiled too widely.

Kevin took the cue and said in a gravelly voice, 'Yes, a great feed, Carl. You know what they say – *Kissing don't last, good cooking do*. Not that you aren't a fine kisser too.' With that, he pushed his chair back and hoisted himself up. He'd kept lean and strong on the farm, but already arthritis had crept into his knees and toyed with his steadiness.

'How about a port?'

For a moment he looked so vulnerable standing there, his shoulders a little rounder, his conviction threadbare.

'Good idea. Let's have it out on the deck,' she said, unlocking the French doors and inviting the navy night in. 'It's so mild.'

'I'll stick with beer,' Jack said, disappearing into the kitchen. Carla followed.

'You realise you've just dashed your father's dreams?' she said, coming up behind him as he peered into the fridge.

Jack turned, his face collapsing. The second she'd said it, Carla wished she hadn't, but the words were out, her disappointment selfishly articulated.

'They're all finished,' Kevin called out from the lounge. 'You might be lucky to find one in the garage.'

For a moment, mother and son stood staring at each other in the ice-blue light of the refrigerator.

'He means the beer,' she said. Then quickly, 'Jack, I'm sorry.' But he had already turned and was walking away down the hall.

The moon hung like a Christmas bauble in the sky, silvering the barn's corrugated iron roof and transforming the drooping branches of willow into lametta. Carla sank into the slack of a canvas deckchair and sighed. Kevin handed her a drink and pulled up the chair opposite. He'd brought a pack of Peter Stuyvesant outside with him. They sat in silence, the still night interrupted only by the haunting cry of a morepork. There was a new intimacy between them, a shared loneliness the day had imported.

'Twenty-seven years, Carl. A pretty good innings,' he said, patting her thigh. 'Remember that first dance at the Freemason's hall? You arriving late. All eyes on this honey-skinned beauty.'

'You didn't look too bad yourself, Elvis,' she said, forcing a laugh, 'except for those awful gold bell-bottoms you kept having to hoist up!'

'Bloody costume was too big,' he said with a chortle 'God, how come I got a look in? Reckon it was that disco ball . . . Blimmin' hypnotised you.'

Carla leant across and kissed him on the cheek.

'Your poor dad,' Kevin continued, shaking his head. 'Must have thought he was selling his only daughter down the river. Mind you, this rugged Kiwi bloke with two left feet didn't turn out so bad.' He laughed, but it was a hollow laugh – a valiant effort to varnish his defeat.

She placed a hand on his. 'It'll work out fine, Kev. You'll see.'

'Mind if I light up?' he asked, rummaging in his pocket for matches.

She didn't begrudge him the occasional cigarette. 'Just don't go offering Jack one.'

Kevin inhaled, the red tip glowing fiercely. He flung his head back and exhaled into the black. 'Do you feel trapped here on the farm?' he asked, staring at the night sky.

'Now where did that come from?'

'Maybe Jack's right. I mean we've hardly travelled.'

'Stop it, Kev! Our life is good. Really good. You know what our Jack's like. Always full of crazy ideas. Where's he got to, anyway?'

Then she felt it, cold on her neck. She lunged forward, shrugging her shoulders to distance herself from it. 'Jack, you silly boy, I'll—'

'Don't fuckin' move!' The voice, rough and unfamiliar, split open the mellow night.

Carla froze.

Kevin's face was a kaleidoscope of expression – surprise, melting into horror, then fury. Struggling to lever himself out of his chair, he bellowed, 'Now look here, what the hell do you think you're doing?' His face was puce, his body trembling with rage. 'Put that down!' He lunged forward.

Then there was a dull thwack and Kevin dropped heavily to the ground, his temple glancing off the corner of the patio table as he fell.

'Kevin!' Carla screamed, but before her voice could spread across the night, a hand had trapped it. The smell under her nostrils was strange and foreign. She had an overwhelming urge to vomit.

'Shut it, bitch! Or the motherfucker won't stand up no more.'

Blood tracked over Kevin's ear and collected in swollen red spheres on his chin before dripping onto the kwila decking.

Chapter Two

CARLA

'A one-eight-seven, bro. A fuckin' one-eight-seven!'

'No use if we don't get no dough, man. Check out the rest of the joint.' Furious footsteps disappeared down the corridor. Doors slammed. Glass shattered. Close to Carla, only inches away, a pair of sneakers with fraying red and black beading, circled, paced, lashed out. The laces were undone. Wiry black hairs thinned into smooth brown ankles.

Carla lay face down on the entrance hall floor, the musty smell of the kilim rug filling her nostrils. Her skirt was riding high; she wanted to pull it down. Bubbles coursed up and down her windpipe, searching for a way out. Her lips were burning where the masking tape had strained and stripped off slivers of skin.

Sixty-two, sixty-three, sixty-four . . . All she could do was count out the thumping beats of her heart, her mind jammed like a frozen computer screen.

'Where's the cash, you motherfucker? The money! The fuckin' money!' The voice crashed around Carla – a young voice made bold by a bandanna. Someone had pressed the fast-forward button. Carla couldn't keep up, couldn't process the words.

The eyes behind the voice were bloodshot, hyped, wild. 'Maybe I gotta take payment from someplace else.'

'No! Leave her alone,' Kevin cried, fumbling in his pockets. 'We don't keep much money at home, you must believe me. You can have anything. Everything! Just don't hurt my wife. Please—'

Carla could scarcely recognise Kevin's voice.

Ooof! The pipe wrench swung, forcing wind from his mouth and backside simultaneously. She started to count heartbeats again.

'Want another hidin'? Now where's the money, mister? You got a safe?'

Objects rained down around Carla and ricocheted off the floor – her lipstick, her Liberty diary, a packet of tissues, passport photo of Jack . . .

Jack! He would have been in the garage when the thugs burst in. Hopefully he'd gone for help. Please God! Carla lifted her head, trying to intercept Kevin's bloodied gaze and caution him not to allude to their son. But Kevin wasn't looking her way. He was cowering in the corner.

She'd only ever known Kevin to cry twice. After their daughter Gabby died, he'd sobbed softly behind a locked bathroom door. And when Pasha his favourite sheepdog was crushed under the tractor he'd let slip a few tears before putting her out of her misery.

'Hey, bro, nothin' more here,' the other voice shouted. 'Let's take the electronics and beat it before the pigs come.'

Carla held her breath, the Lord's Prayer scrolling through her mind.

'Nah. I'm hungry for some pussy.'

'Forget it, TT. Let's get outta here.'

'Fuck off, Ben.'

A hand grabbed Carla's bottom. She screamed, but as in a dream, no sound escaped.

'No!' Kevin's voice resounded through the laughter that filled the endless moment.

'Settle, boy, we jus' gonna service the missus. You gotta learn to share. Ain't that right, bro?'

The cold woke Carla. The terracotta tiles had driven an aching chill through the fibres of the kilim rug into her skin, her muscles, her marrow. Her brain registered only this most basic sensation – cold – otherwise, it was blank, as if a thousand volts of electricity had passed through, deleting neural pathways and wiping all trace of thought and fragment of memory. She tried to cough. Her throat felt stuffed full of autumn leaves.

Squinting downwards, she saw the shadow of her swollen, cracked lips. With her tongue she traced their bloated outline. Dried mucus and crusted blood stopped the fine vermillion creases and filled her nostrils with an alien stench.

One of her eyes agreed to open; the other remained shut.

Something off to the right caught her attention. She turned her head – the action delayed a few seconds behind the intent. The early morning sunshine had transformed a piece of broken glass into a prism and a rainbow of light now arched over the room.

A small clay pot came into view, then receded. Carla screwed up her obedient eye and pulled the pot back in focus. A lopsided sphere of clay engraved with stick figures – a lion, an elephant, a monkey. It was almost familiar . . . Synapses fought to connect,

31

her mind desperate for an anchor. Then the relief of recognition! It was the pottery bowl Jack had made when he was eight, his first attempt at throwing clay. The bowl had been presiding over the entrance hall for the past decade.

Grasping this recollection served to bridge a chasm, providing thought with a route back into Carla's consciousness. Like a flash flood, reality rushed in and she dropped her head back onto the floor, reeling from the information that now placed her firmly back in time and place.

Her body started to convulse with fear and pain. Metallic tears trickled into her parched mouth. Her big toe pointed sharply downwards in spasm. She tried to lift her head again, but the morning leant on it as the sharp light of dawn escaped the confines of the prism to wash over the room.

'Kevin! Jaaack!' Carla's voice lurched into space like a stretched cassette tape. 'Kev?'

She moved her head to the left. Her good eye scanned the room. It stopped at a twisted mound of clothes and limbs. Kevin – his bruised body at right angles to the wall. Motionless.

'Kevin! Kev! Can you hear me, Kevin?'

Nothing but the memory of her warped voice filled the ensuing silence. Her eye moved frantically on, searching for Jack. She didn't expect to find him. He would have been in the garage when . . . He'd have escaped and raised the alarm. A complete circuit of the room. No Jack. She swallowed, relief sticking in her parched throat.

She had to reach Kevin. But she couldn't move. Not even lever herself up. Her hands were missing. Where were her hands?

It took a moment to understand that they'd been bound so tightly behind her back she'd lost all feeling in them.

After several false starts Carla managed, like a frog doing breaststroke on its back, to manoeuvre herself haltingly across the room. Her muscles were burning and her arms stinging where the tiles rasped off slivers of skin.

About halfway over her body suddenly seized and refused to obey further commands.

'Come on!' Carla cried aloud, writhing on the floor like a dug-up earthworm. Kevin was so close.

Like an Olympic athlete just metres from the finish line, she demanded complete concentration from every part of her body, her pain miraculously dissolving into the focus, and with one final burst she was upon him.

She dropped into the small of Kevin's back and sank her face into his shirt. It smelt of stale sweat and dried fear. How she loved to snuggle up to him on a Sunday morning, moulding to his craggy contours and helping herself to his toasty heat. Now his body was cold and unyielding.

A heaviness spread across the room like dry ice. Carla lay there under the weight of this new reality, her will to live leaking from her body.

Click. A distant, but distinct *click*. Then Mozart swept down the corridor and into the room. Mozart? The sound swelled, growing louder and louder until the room was steeped in music.

Panting and perplexed, Carla gave over to it, the notes peeling back her fear to make way for other emotions, and her crying rose from a place she had never visited before.

Four beeps grounded her. *Beep. Beep. Beep. Beep. Good morning. This is the five o'clock news on Thursday the twentieth of March.* The radio alarm!

Only when Carla's sobbing had subsided and her gasps and

gurgles were no longer loud in her ears, did she notice Kevin's chest. Barely perceptible – she had to be completely still herself to see it – but there for certain . . . the gradual rise and fall of his ribcage as wisps of air threaded into and out of his lungs.

Chapter Three

BEN

They pulled into a deserted service station. Despite being at least an hour from the action, Ben's heart was still hammering in his chest, and his head bursting with a crazy cocktail of people and panic. Everything was mixed up – the thrill, the buzz, the bad bits. He felt as if he was inside one of those extreme arcade games.

Through the store window he could see a lone petrol attendant behind the counter. The guy was dressed in his regulation uniform and sporting a twist of white fabric on his head.

'That dude with the turban,' Ben said, turning to Tate, who was searching the footwell for the fuel cap lever. 'He's a Sikh.'

Tate ground his teeth in reply. The sound – like chalk screeching across a blackboard – made the skin under Ben's ears crawl.

'Let's get us up some pies,' Tate grunted. 'I'm fuckin' starving.'

Now that he thought about it, Ben was hungry too.

Tate got out, leaving the engine running. They'd nicked the Toyota from an Albany car yard, after abandoning the farm vehicle. It was low on fuel.

Ben fiddled with the radio dials, scanning the airwaves until he found something he recognised. '*Snap Yo Fingers*'. He bobbed in time to the beat and chewed on his fingernails. Next minute, Tate was sprinting across the forecourt, hoodie up, pockets bulging.

'We're outta here!' he shouted, jumping in the car.

So he hadn't paid.

They sped off, the smell of burnt rubber rising up through the car.

'Dumb move, bro,' Ben said, looking back through the rear window at the Sikh already on the phone. 'Just lost our lead time.'

Tate put his foot flat and the Toyota picked up speed –140, 150, 160 kilometres an hour.

'You should've seen the joker's face when I walked out,' he said with a grin. 'He's like, "Hey, you forgot to pay, sir."' They both laughed.

Then Tate was doing a screeching U-turn and doubling back.

'What the—?' There'd been too many surprises. The night had already unravelled way beyond Ben's expectations.

'Chill, bro,' Tate said, swerving into a parking lot behind a public library. 'We'll hang here for a while, till the pigs are off our scent.' Which they did – scoffing pies, drinking cola, and sharing a joint.

Tate was already completely stoned. He'd been on the fries for two days leading up to their big night, and with weed and booze thrown in, it was no surprise when he suddenly crashed, his long, lean body slumping over the wheel.

Ben hung in. He didn't do crack, and even on marijuana he reacted differently to others. Sure, it rounded off the sharp edges in his brain, but never made him sleepy, just mellow, as if he were travelling on a never-ending sigh. It also made everything super intense and clear, as if his brain had put on spectacles, or someone had shone a bright light into the dark drawers of his mind.

He was twelve the first time he'd tried a joint. There'd been a party at his house and he couldn't sleep because of the noise. When he got out of bed to go to the toilet, he bumped into a woman wearing pointy cowboy boots, a purple poncho, and shimmery gold Stetson.

'Wanna try some, kiddo?' she'd said, offering him a toke.

He did. And soon all the bad things in his head started to shrivel up like weeds after a dose of Roundup. A few puffs of the joint were better than any CYF's counsellor, and definitely easier than running away from home. He was hooked from day one. It wasn't cheap, but he always shared what he got with Lily; his sister needed it more than he did.

One time, when one of his mum's squeezes – Ben couldn't remember which one it was – had beaten her up really badly and she was lying on her bedroom floor like a bruised grapefruit, Ben had offered her a puff. Though she was nearly out of it, she still managed to be wild at him for smoking the stuff. She gave him a slurred talking to, using big responsible-parent words, then took the joint off him and smoked it all. The two of them had ended up leaning against the bedroom wall laughing and laughing, despite his mum's lip being split and her nose a bloody mess.

Tate was snoring loudly. Ben looked across at him. The spray of red on his jeans had darkened to a splatter of black. Ben tilted his seat back until he was lying flat. He looked up at the ceiling and traced the thick seam in the roof fabric as it dipped under the sun visor, ran along the edge of the windscreen, and looped over the rear-view mirror. For some bizarre reason he couldn't stop thinking about the Sikh gas attendant. It was dumb to be thinking about him of all people, considering what had already gone down that day. But the guy reminded him of one of his old schoolteachers. Mr Singh. Ben would have stayed in school if all his teachers had been like Singh. He was a big fellow – over six foot – with a woolly black beard, dark eyes, and a twist of cream fabric forever on his head. Ben smiled when he thought of Singh's socks. The guy wore the same clothes day in and day out: brown suit, beige tie, brown lace-ups, and then these wild lettuce-green socks.

Rumour had it that Singh had worked in the courts before turning to teaching. You could tell he hadn't been in the job forever; he didn't have the same dry expression the other teachers did. His face was as fresh as a full-price watermelon. And he always looked like he wanted to be there in front of his class.

Once, Singh had come upon Ben doodling instead of doing a maths worksheet. He'd picked up Ben's drawing, looked at it for the longest time, then held it up for the rest of the class to see. 'You've got talent, Ben Toroa,' he'd said in his deep rumbling voice.

Ben was on a high all day, despite getting a detention, and for a while after that wanted to be a Sikh, although he wasn't sure about the whole turban thing.

Swearing gives to the inarticulate the illusion of eloquence. One of Singh's favourite sayings popped into Ben's head. He scratched his head irritably. 'Fuck you!' he cursed, his voice ricocheting off the inside of the car. Tate stirred.

Then Ben heard the scream of a siren. His breathing picked up and he slunk lower in the seat The noise grew louder, and louder, then started to fade.

'Hey, TT. TT, wake up, man,' he said, shaking his mate.

Tate opened his eyes, two milky-white marbles covered in fine webs of red.

'Time to get out of here.'

They decided to abandon the car and call George, who collected them in a stolen Nissan, and the three of them went for a spin across the Harbour Bridge before heading back to Glenfield just as the grey light of dawn was climbing up over the dying night.

Beyond

The wind finds me, its sun-baked notes carrying dune dust from the Hokianga, salted spray from Cook Strait, and pungent bursts of crushed wild thyme from some southern slope. So many treasures carried on the wind's caressing breath. It brings me Rotorua's sulphured steam rising from the bubble and burst of a molten earth; a lone tui's captivating call; the rattle and clink of pipi shells tossed into a sack. It brings skeins of vibrant colour from Hahei's teal-green waters, and the damp, dark coolness of forest and fern – redwood and kauri, kiokio and mamaku. I sense the stolid patience of four fishermen on Tolaga Bay wharf, and taste the sweetness of some forager's honeyed harvest. Such riches! Yet I cannot enjoy them. Not today. For this breeze has brought me more . . .

'You have lost another son,' it cries on a gust. 'Aotearoa, New Zealand, you have lost another son.'

I am giddy with the news. It sucks up all the air and light, as if reversing the creation, rejoining Ranginui, Sky Father, and Papatūānuku, Earth Mother, and squeezing out all that is life.

Another son of Kupe has fallen from my basket, the woven flax now limp and loose. Where will it end, this unravelling? Where will it end?

Chapter Four

CARLA

Carla heard the voices and went rigid. They'd come back! The thugs had come back. She held her breath.

'Curtains are still drawn.' A man's voice. 'That's odd; the dogs are still in their cages. They don't look like they've been fed yet.'

'Rangi, something's not right.'

Carla breathed out. It was Rangi and Rebecca, the share milkers! She lifted her head and tried to call out, but her voice was hoarse and would not climb over a whisper.

'They probably spent the night with Jack in town. Or maybe Kev's alarm clock finally packed up.' A hearty Rangi chuckle.

Carla tried to call out again, but only a thin murmur spilt from her mouth.

'C'mon, chook, let's get on with the milking. Kev deserves a day off.'

'Hey look. Jack's Beetle.' Rebecca's voice. 'He must still be here.'

'See, told you we shouldn't be bugging them. They probably all had a late night. Wasn't it Kev and Carla's anniversary yesterday? I'm sure Kevin said so.'

The voices started to fade.

'He---e---lp!' Carla's voice scraped and clawed at her throat.

'You hear that?'

'What?'

'Someone calling.'

The footsteps came closer, then there was knocking at the front door. 'Yoo-hoo! Anyone home?'

Carla looked about frantically. There was a kitchen stool off to her right, just within reach of her foot. She lifted her leg and swung it at the stool. A wild pain exploded in her ankle as she connected with the wood. The stool teetered, rocked in space, then settled.

'Carla? Kevin?'

Carla tried again, this time dropping the stool. It landed with a thud on Kevin's crumpled frame. He gurgled.

'You hear that, Rangi? There *is* someone inside. I got a bad feeling about this. Let's call the police.'

'Slow down, chook. I'll see if I can get in. The bathroom window's open.'

'But Rangi.'

'What?'

'The front door. It's not locked.'

Carla fixed her eyes on the door. The handle was slowly depressed.

Rangi and Rebecca's voices shrunk to a whisper. 'You stay here. I'll—'

Suddenly a crack of golden light fanned out across the room. Carla squinted. In the doorway was Rangi's solid silhouette.

'Jesus, Becks! Call one-one-one.'

* * *

Carla was shaking uncontrollably, despite the blanket Rebecca had wrapped around her.

'A pillow! Kevin needs a pillow,' Carla spluttered. 'And another blanket. He's so cold, Beckie. Where's the ambulance? My Jack? It's taking so long.'

'Soon, love. Soon,' Rebecca said, stroking her arm.

'Kev! Kevin, can you hear me?' Carla barked in a hoarse whisper. 'Can he hear me? Is he breathing? He's still breathing isn't he?'

'I think so,' Rebecca said, looking at Kevin's motionless frame.

Rangi put down the phone receiver and knelt down beside Kevin, putting his ear to Kevin's chest. His frizz of brown hair obscured Kevin's grey face. After what felt like forever, he nodded.

Carla's body loosened. She tugged at Kevin's shirt with a bruised and trembling hand. 'Kevin Reid, you stick with me.'

Then she remembered. 'Becks, what is a one-eight-seven?'

'A what?'

'One of them said . . . I think he said he'd done a one-eight-seven.'

Rebecca shot Rangi a bemused glance. He was still on the phone to the emergency services, one ear to the receiver, one tuned in to the conversation between his wife and Carla.

'Excuse me, ma'am,' he said, again interrupting the operator. 'She's saying one of the intruders said something about a one-eight-seven. That's right. Yeah.'

Rangi's skin blanched and motley circles of cream rose through his toffee-coloured complexion. He lowered the receiver, his eyes wide. But Carla's unanchored thoughts had already floated on to new territory.

'Thank God he was in the garage,' she mumbled. 'Thank God. I mean, just for a beer. We shouldn't tell him about Kevin. Not yet.'

43

'Who?'

'Jack!' Carla said impatiently. 'He raised the alarm. Didn't he?' Then she tilted her head, her eyes darting skittishly over jumbled thoughts. 'No . . . He couldn't have, because you—'

Rebecca opened her mouth and closed it again. Carla looked from Rebecca to Rangi, then back to Rebecca. 'You . . . I heard you out there. You thought we'd slept in. And you said Jack's car was still here. So where is he? Where's Jack?' Her words were tripping over each other as they tried to keep pace with her thoughts.

Carla heaved herself off the ground.

'Carla, wait!' But she was already staggering down the corridor, her blood pressure struggling to catch up. She shambled past Jack's room – his mattress upturned on the floor, the cupboards gaping. She passed the toilet – a potent pool of yellow stagnating beneath the shiny white bowl. And her bedroom, where disembowelled drawers had been flung across the carpet, their contents strewn in frenzied disarray. Books stood on their heads, jackets buckled and spines ripped. Carla's jewellery box lay open, the lid unhinged, the baize compartments empty save for a lone brooch clinging on by a bent clasp.

Then she was in the passageway to the garage. The door seemed so far away, as if she were looking at it through the wrong end of a telescope.

The walls began to close in and the floor felt as if it was shifting under her. Carla lurched forward, her movements clumsy and uncoordinated.

In front of the panelled door she paused, swaying unsteadily, then slowly she lowered the cold brass handle.

The door sighed open and a hot, meaty cocktail of pesticide, lawnmower fuel, and old blood winded her.

The refrigerator door stood ajar. For a moment, this irritated her. In the ordinariness of life, it should have been shut. Then she saw the dented beer can lying unopened on the ground, and the bloodied shovel.

Her eyes crept warily along the concrete and stopped.

Carla stared blankly at first, caught in that brief hiatus like when sliced skin has just been parted. Then, as a new wound colours red and the nerve receptors resound, so comprehension dawned.

Rebecca caught up with her. 'Oh God, no!' she cried out, bringing a trembling hand to her face.

Alien noises bubbled out of Carla's mouth. She squeezed her eyes shut, but in vain. The snapshot had already been taken and would be the screen saver of her life from this moment on.

Carla crumpled in a heap beside her child, sucking in air with whooping gasps. Then she lifted Jack's head onto her lap and with the corner of her skirt, began to wipe clean his face with meticulous maternal detail – his neck, his ears, his forehead. 'It's all right, my boy. I'm here. It's alright.'

Rebecca turned and ran from the room, the sound of her retching mingling with the wail of approaching sirens.

Chapter Five

CARLA

'Jack needs me,' Carla screamed, fighting to free herself from the ambulance officer's grip. 'I won't leave him. Don't!'

'Mrs Reid, we need to get you and your husband to hospital. I understand how you feel,' the young man tried.

'No, you don't. Can't . . . possibly.'

A siren severed the fracas, whirring in the background as an ambulance with Kevin on board retreated down the driveway.

'Carla, love, come now,' Rebecca said, taking Carla's hand and caressing it. 'We need to get you medical attention as soon as possible. Here, the blanket is sliding off you. You're shaking. Lie back.'

'But Jack. What about Jack?'

'I know.' Rebecca's voice shuddered. 'But they've sealed the scene. None of us can go back in. I'm so sorry.'

Carla sank back on the gurney and the paramedic secured a broad leather strap across her legs.

Another thought swam into her consciousness. She sat up. 'The cows. Who's going to milk the—?'

'Rangi will sort everything. Now just you lie down. Come on, love.'

Carla gave over to Rebecca stroking her hair. The ambulance officer shot Rebecca a grateful glance.

'Becks, my mouth. It's so dry.'

'I'll see if—'

'She can't be having anything to drink,' said an apparition in a blue boiler suit, as he glided past them. 'Not till they've taken swabs.'

The driveway was jammed with unfamiliar traffic – vehicles crammed onto the front lawn, and people fluorescing in uniforms Carla had only ever seen on television. Cameras flashed, dogs barked, and emergency lights revolved. A white van was trying to reverse, the large satellite dish on its roof breaking a branch of the ash tree as it lurched backwards.

Rebecca climbed into the back of the ambulance with Carla. Someone closed one of the doors. Carla lifted her head and looked through the remaining rectangle of light. A band of red and white plastic – *Police Emergency, Police Emergency, Police Emergency* – barred her from her home. She closed her eyes. A paramedic was crouching beside her, taking her pulse. His gloved hand felt peculiar. It reminded her of the game 'Dead Man's Skin' they used to play as kids, holding two forefingers together in a steeple while someone rubbed their own fingers over it.

She heard a voice rising above the noise of the idling engine and howling siren. The ambulance door banged and a shadow swept over Carla. She opened her eyes.

A large man in a blue uniform was sitting down on the stretcher opposite, his frame dwarfing Rebecca. His eyes met Carla's – speckled grey eyes that sloped away under heavy folds of lid. His charcoal hair looked recently cropped, the blunt bristles not yet mellowed into shape, and his jaw showed the shadow of a day's growth. Already wide across the shoulders, he was further bulked out by a bulletproof vest. His hands were big and each nail ended bluntly in a straight white line.

'Mrs Reid, I'm Detective Inspector Steve Herbert.' His solid voice promised safety. He placed a hand on her bare arm. It was warm. 'I'm very sorry.'

He would be heading the investigation, he told her. Working round the clock to catch the killers – the people who had invaded her home, her life, her body.

And so the wheel of justice creaked, groaned, and began to turn.

As they made their way through the dawn to North Shore Hospital, Carla tried to answer as best she could Detective Inspector Herbert's careful questions. Already blank spaces censored her memory. Like a schoolchild sitting her first exam, every answer seemed so important. As if Jack's very survival depended on her accuracy.

But Jack was dead. *Nothing* could bring him back. Dead was for ever.

Her arrival at hospital brought more people, more questions, and more people – house surgeons, registrars, nurses, forensics, victim support – a blur of uniform and process. And through it all, DI Steve Herbert was there in the background, a quiet reassuring presence.

Carla lost track of time. Windowless fluorescent light replaced the flux of day and night, sunshine and shadow. After what felt like an eternity, she was transferred from the Emergency Department to a single room, where she was left alone with Rebecca. Mercifully,

Rebecca didn't talk, but instead just stroked her head till Carla finally drifted into a murky sleep.

'Mrs Reid?'

Carla sat up robotically. Her tongue was thick, her mind furry with sleep.

A tiny grey-haired woman with an impish haircut had slipped into the room. 'Mrs Reid, my name is Kathryn Pepper.' She set down a large black bag. 'I'm a doctor with DSAC. Doctors for Sexual Abuse Care,' she said gently.

She had very blue eyes, pinched-pink cheeks, and a Scottish accent that softened the angles of her words.

'I understand that you endured a terrible experience last night. Nobody should have to go through what you have. I am so very sorry.'

Carla felt the sting of tears. Sparse and thin they trickled down her cheeks.

'I'm here to gather as much evidence as I can against those who've done this to you. I know it must be the last thing you feel like, but it really is very important.'

Carla nodded.

'Would you like your friend to stay?'

Carla grabbed Rebecca's hand in affirmation.

Doctor Pepper carefully explained each step of the procedure, and then Carla submitted to the examination, her inelastic and bruised tissues once more assailed.

'That's everything I need,' the doctor finally said, meticulously sealing and labelling the last of several plastic bags. 'You have tranquillisers, antibiotics and painkillers charted. We can give you a sedative now.'

Tranquillisers? Sedatives? Carla had scarcely swallowed a tablet in her life. 'My husband,' she said. 'Nobody can tell me. Is he all right? The nurse, I think she was a nurse, promised to find out ages ago.'

'I'll go and see,' Rebecca proffered, quickly escaping from the room.

Chapter Six

BEN

Ghetto-star rollin, high on ice and shine; put a bullet in your back you cross my nigga line.

The words jettisoned out of the ghetto blaster and slammed into the walls of the bridge before escaping into the night to blend with the drone of traffic overhead.

The six of them sat huddled around the radio. The smell of rotting rubbish mingled with the sweet, marijuana air.

'Fuck off, Ben, if you can't hack it,' Tate said, spraying spittle over him. 'You just a wannabe or what?'

Ben wiped his cheek with his sleeve. He hated that word 'wannabe'. It drove straight through him like the shame he felt after the hidings Ryan, his mum's partner, dished out, bruising Ben's body, but mostly his mind. Ben *was* staunch. He *had* cred.

'TT, I'm just telling you what's going down, man. My auntie says—'

'I don't give a shit what your auntie says. Fuckin' motherfucker.'

That's why Tate was leader. He'd been born with metal running through his veins like the wires in a fuse box.

'The shit's swarming all over the hood. I saw a cop car this morning in our street, bro.' Ben couldn't help himself. Words just kept spilling out of his mouth, his bravado leaking like water through a sieve. He hated himself for his weakness.

Pumped and on point, and glock-shit-real; might roll in a grave, won't never be your slave.

Tate straightened, his body thrusting forward in rhythm to the mantra. 'If we go down, it's cool, man. Cool. My badge of glory,' he said, baring his teeth and picking at a piece of food stuck there. 'Now pass the joint and shut up about the pigs. You been broken-arse ever since the one-eight-seven. It's gettin' on my wick.'

The others were looking at Ben with contempt in their eyes. It was okay for them to be cocky. The police weren't hunting them. This wasn't how it was meant to be. Ben had done the farmhouse job to gain respect, move up the ranks. But things had spun out of control. He hadn't reckoned on them wasting anyone. The initial buzz of being part of something real was evaporating as fast as weed. 'Whatever.'

Suddenly Tate lunged forward and flicked off the stereo and torchlight, extinguishing the graffitied hideout.

'What the—?'

'Shut it,' Tate said, making a slicing motion across his neck.

Ben tossed off his hoodie and tilted his head, tuning in to the noises of the night. Lewis sniffed; his nose was always dripping. Simi rubbed his fingers together, the dull chafe of skin on skin. Then they heard it, the beat of bass intermingled with voices. Clods of air moved down Ben's throat.

'It's the GDBs,' someone hissed.

A bottle whistled through the blackness and exploded on a

concrete pipe behind them. Guffaws and high-pitched shrieks, then another random missile.

Ben felt the glass spray over his back like a passing shower. He didn't budge. None of them did, their eyes fixed on Tate, waiting for the command. Waiting.

None came.

No action.

The voices crossed over the bridge and faded. Ben breathed out.

Simi jumped up. 'Let's show them what's bloody what!' he said, wielding a razor blade, his voice caught between man and kid. 'Time to dust them up'

'Yo, Simi. Cool it,' Tate cautioned, flicking on his torch and shining it into each of their faces like a searchlight seeking out the enemy. 'We'll tag the highway when the time is right. That's gonna be our turf. We gonna own those motherfuckers.'

As Tate pumped the air with his torch, the light bounced around their lair, lighting up snapshots of concrete, mob messages, and a large cave weta clinging upside down to the dank roof. Tate gave a throaty laugh. Then they were punching the darkness with their fists, the echo of laughter swelling their numbers.

'Hey cuz, where'd you get ya mean shiner?'

Ben patched his eye with his hand. 'A hidin' from Ryan,' he said after a long pause, his voice robbed of power. 'Got in the way when the dude was dealing to my mother, didn't I?'

'Cunt probably deserved it,' Simi goaded.

Ben leapt up and grabbed the kid by the throat. 'Don't ever diss my mother. You hear me, or I'll waste you, man. I swear I'll waste you.'

Simi pushed him back into the wall. 'Whoa! Cool it. Just joking, bro. You're all wound up after your big night out with TT.'

'I'm warning you—'

'See what I scored today,' Tate said, cutting into the aggro. He was holding up a white plastic packet. 'Matte fuckin' silver,' he gloated, pulling out the spray can and shaking it like some barman mixing cocktails.

When it was Ben's turn, he sprayed the stuff into the bag, bunched it round his mouth and nose, and inhaled deeply. Then the chemicals were working their magic, wiping away the white boy crumpling under the shovel, the woman screaming as TT dealt to her, the old man writhing on the floor like an insect on its back.

It was soothing, numbing, cooling. Ben was cruising, wasted, joining his mates with their sticky silver lipstick – aliens high on matte silver.

Beyond

I watch and I weep. You have diminished the mana gifted by your ancestors of the great river, by your forefathers on that first 'great fleet' of canoes. You have brought shame on te tangata whenua, *on your* hapu, *your* whānau, *your* iwi.

But what do you even know of such words – of kinship, clan, family ties and tribe? You cannot speak te reo Māori, *the language that guards your history, that recorded your past. Your roots have long since been severed. Like tumbleweed tossed at the whim of every passing breeze, you roll free of tie and connection, free of community.*

I am not far from you, yet you cannot hear my lamentations, nor my karakia. *So should I cease my praying and turn my back on you? You are not the first to bring dishonour to our people. You will not be the last.*

No, I stay. For now. You see, this story, your story, goes back further than you.

Chapter Seven

CARLA

It was hot and stuffy in the packed church. Two circles of perspiration were spreading out under the organist's arms. She shifted on her seat and stretched out her legs to reach the pedals, puffy red flesh spilling out over her sandals like proving bread dough. The congregation stood.

Carla stared at the order of service. The pixelated image of her son looked back at her: languid brown eyes, disobedient hair, the thread of scar gently hoisting his upper lip.

A hymn filled the space outside her head, but Carla couldn't sing. Instead, she allowed herself to be distracted by the children in the pews across the aisle. Rangi and Rebecca's little girl was sliding her hands in and out of her dungaree pockets in an exercise of speed. Beside her stood a fidgety, flaxen-haired child with thin ponytails and transparent skin. She kept looking back, perhaps to see if Carla would break into sobs like she was supposed to. Then there were Bev's boys, jostling and shoving as they tried to stand on each other's toes.

Anxious to avoid eye contact with anyone, Carla tilted her head back and studied the dark beams of wood arching above her. She knew their pattern well, as she did the rest of the building – the liturgical-purple carpet, threadbare in patches; the wrought-iron candelabra; the simple wooden cross. She hadn't missed a service in years.

The music tapered off and Allan, the chaplain, cleared his throat. 'One of Jack's less well-known interests was his love of poetry. A passion he shared with his father.'

Allan had come round to Geoff and Mildred's place on the Monday to discuss funeral arrangements. Carla had been staying with her brother-in-law and his wife since being discharged from hospital. Geoff, a wiry, hollow-cheeked man, was Kevin's younger sibling. He owned several electronic retail outlets across Auckland. Over the years Carla had remained civil for Kevin's sake.

Allan smiled down from the pulpit. 'And many a wintry Sunday night at the Reids was spent around the fire reciting verse.'

Carla found herself smiling as she thought back to those Sunday suppers. Tangy gouda and pickled onions. The words of Fiona Farrell and Kevin Ireland. Jack's friends sometimes joining in on saxophone or guitar to transform the evening into a soirée of sorts.

Allan continued. 'I remember one particular evening enjoying this lovely family's hospitality. Jack gave a great Sam Hunt impersonation.' The pastor chuckled, then paused as if revisiting the occasion.

'And Carla has asked me to read a poem, *this* poem, by Sam Hunt today.' He looked down over his half-moon spectacles at the paper in his hand. 'It is entitled "Winter Solstice Song".'

> *We can believe in miracles*
> *Easy a day like this.*

> *For five minutes at sunrise the sun*
> *Broke through, first time in weeks,*
> *A kiss*
> *I took to mean arrival*
> *And five minutes up*
> *F— d off.*

The pastor's voice faltered over the swear word, which he'd chosen to abbreviate. Mildred frowned. Geoff cleared his throat. Carla felt a fleeting freedom.

> *But it is*
> *The year's shortest day*
> *When anything can happen,*
> *Miracles 'not a problem'*
> *The sun five minutes with us*
> *Came and left with a kiss.*
> *We believe in miracles. That, love,*
> *is all we have.*[2]

The ensuing silence was broken by a baby's cry, then the blowing of noses and a stifled cough.

Kevin was still in a coma. He needed a miracle.

The organist started up again.

'Carla, it's time,' Geoff said, a guiding hand on her elbow.

It all felt so wrong. So unreal. Kevin at least should have been there beside her. Instead she was alone at the funeral of their only son, surrounded by *other* people. The Reid unit had been disassembled and the individual parts now much less than the sum of them. She felt like a lone piece of Lego.

Carla turned and followed Geoff robotically to the coffin. Blake, her pimply nephew, stood next to the casket with a bunch of irises in the crook of his arm. Jack and Blake had never got on, so why was he standing right beside Jack's coffin, handing out the flowers? This was the funeral of *her* child. Blake was alive; Jack was dead. It should have been the other—She stopped herself mid thought. That she could think such a thing.

Carla took a single stem and laid it on the simple blonde box. Geoff had suggested a more ornate coffin; Carla had remained firm on this at least.

'Jack,' she mouthed, her throat too tight to release any more than a soft distortion of his name. Then, flanked by Allan and Geoff, she stepped to one side, and friends and family filed forwards to pay their final respects. Soon iris stems were scattered over the coffin in purple chaos.

Russell, Jack's best friend, lingered at the coffin, his eyes red and his face puffy. He had his hand around the waist of a young woman with long auburn hair and eyes that were a catch-your-breath blue. She looked down quickly to avoid Carla's gaze. Russell broke away and came over to Carla, crushing her in a clumsy embrace. 'Mrs R, I'm . . .'

As the last of the mourners filed out of the church, Geoff's family and Carla were left alone for the final blessing. Then she was being ushered out into the startling white light of day.

Two sallow undertakers dressed in death-black suits stood like sentries beside the hearse. They nodded solemnly, then made their way past Carla into the church. She felt a flash of panic. She couldn't leave Jack alone with them. She wanted to shout, 'Stop!' She wanted to cradle her boy for one last time, feel his warm skin against hers, smooth his wild eyebrows and ruffle his hair. She wanted to cry and sob and scream. She wanted Kevin. Needed him to hold her close and chase away these horrible people. She hated them all.

She looked back into the church. The casket stood beneath the stained-glass window, bathed in ecclesiastical sunlight.

Her mind drifted to familiar scenes on television of women in war-torn lands weeping over disfigured corpses – faceless foreigners wailing and cursing and giving vent to their pain. How she longed for that freedom, to anonymously abandon herself in the full embrace of grief. But as Geoff helped her into the Jaguar and the door closed with an expensive thud, her pain was tidily contained.

You realise you've just dashed your father's dreams. Her last words to Jack had been in anger. Now regret was tattooed onto her heart.

They gave her a sedative before the wake at Geoff and Mildred's house, the two tiny white pills drying up any residue of emotion and cloaking everything in an even fog. At the house, she escaped to the bathroom and hid there for a while until someone outside pretended to cough, making their presence known.

As she made her way back to the living room, Carla bumped into a couple who'd just arrived. She didn't recognise them, but directed them towards the refreshments. Five minutes later, the couple realised, much to their embarrassment, that they were at the wrong function; they were meant to be at a birthday luncheon two doors down. For Carla, this bizarre incident was entirely in synchrony with the day. Nothing made sense. The funeral of her son was some crazy mistake.

She floated through an afternoon of hushed voices and strained

60

expressions, while people from some other life sipped lukewarm tea, scoffed club sandwiches, and spoke in carefully modulated tones as they complimented Geoff and Mildred on their spectacular view.

Later, she persuaded Geoff to drop her at the hospital. 'I'll be fine. Really. I just need some time alone with Kevin. I hope you understand.'

Since that awful night, her every moment had been filled, her every emotion moved on before it had had time to develop depth or meaning. Left to catch mere glimpses of her new reality, Carla now craved the solitude that would permit the particles to separate out and settle. She needed to take an inventory of her life, identify and more fully comprehend what had been taken from her and what left behind.

Kevin lay similarly robbed of self by drugs that conspired to blanket his consciousness. His chest rose and fell with punctuated regularity as air was forced into his lungs and then squeezed out, each beep willing the next to follow. His wounds were healing, already mellowing the brutality and closing over the horror. Dried blood was less frightening than the glistening red stuff. The skin on Kevin's temple had knitted together and his black bruises were dissipating to a lemony hue.

Carla propped up a photograph on the monitor at the head of his bed – a picture of Kevin taken a few months earlier at a friend's barbecue. His wry grin. His sturdiness. His glow. She wanted those tending to him to see the man, not simply the broken body. How could they possibly visualise his stature and command, his intellect and kindness, from just those skin-draped hollows? He looked so small and feeble lying there, connected to a power point.

She drew the curtain around him, shutting out the misery of his Intensive Care bedfellows. His lips were dry and cracked, his mouth fetid. She leant down and kissed his forehead. He smelt of stale sweat. Then her tears were running down *his* cheeks, and it looked like he was the one crying.

Lifting the cool white sheet covering him, she saw that he was still naked, his grey skin punctured and patched and interrupted by plastic. Even his limp penis was a shrivelled conduit for a tube. She grasped his left hand – the only part of him apparently spared in the beating – and held it up to her nose. But it no longer smelt of him, just of hospital.

The doctors had encouraged her to speak to him. Read to him. But he couldn't hear her, could he? And what would she say? She'd not tell him about Jack; it would finish him off. She couldn't. Not yet, anyway. Perhaps she'd never even get the chance. She bit her lip.

'Mrs Reid.' It was the young, already balding, registrar. 'How are you?'

She wiped her face on her sleeve.

'Nice photo,' he said, looking at the picture propped above the bed. 'Gosh, he's got different coloured eyes.' Kevin's eyes had been closed all week.

The doctor turned to her. 'So how are things?'

She shot a glance back at her husband, at his small face stuck onto the front of his bandaged head. 'We had the –' then she mouthed, '– funeral today.'

'That would have been hard.'

Carla looked away. She didn't want compassion. Couldn't cope with it. It pulled up feelings that owned themselves. Anarchy lay in wait if she succumbed.

'It was time,' she said briskly. 'The delays were the hardest. Waiting for the post-mortem and all.'

He nodded.

'How is he?' she asked quickly.

They both turned to Kevin. It was easier focusing on him.

'He's made some real progress these past twenty-four hours,' the young man said, resting a hand on her arm.

She stepped away.

'We removed his chest drain this morning, as the tear in his lung appears to have sealed itself. Also,' he said, picking up one of the charts hanging at the foot of the bed, 'his kidney function is improving. The next couple of days will be critical. If he continues along this trend,' his finger traced the upward turn on the graph, 'we'll attempt to remove his breathing tube and wake him up. Hopefully he'll then start to breathe on his own. Of course, the biggest uncertainty remains his level of brain functioning. But one step at a time, right?'

She nodded.

A bit later they came to do a portable chest X-ray. Carla was in the way, so she slipped out unnoticed. There were still forty minutes left before Geoff was due to pick her up.

Once on the ground floor, she headed for the main entrance. As she stepped out into the weak afternoon sunlight, she tripped over the drip stand of a woman in a hot-pink dressing gown, sucking on a cigarette.

'Jesus, lady! Watch where you goin',' the woman yelled, her lips curling back to reveal a mouthful of stained, yellow teeth. 'You nearly fuckin' ripped this out of my arm!'

'Oh, go to hell, why don't you!' Carla said, regaining her balance and heading down the ramp, the residue of the expletive strange and foreign in her mouth.

Chapter Eight

BEN

It was three in the morning when Ben looked at his watch. His mind swam through the half-realities nurtured by paint and several joints. It had been a good night. They'd tagged the GDBs' turf. The next day promised war. His gang, the DOAs, was ready.

He leapt over a knee-high wall and wove through the carcasses of cars, derelict couches, and empty bottles that littered the front lawn. The lights were on and the door ajar. Music pounded.

'Hi, Ben.' His sister Brooke, her nappy sliding down her chubby legs and snot sliding down her chin, stood in the hallway smiling.

'Hey, Brookie. What you doing up? It's fuckin' late.'

Ben scooped up his sister. 'You stink, man,' he said, peering into the wet folds of her nappy. 'Let's get this shit off you.'

He carried her down the corridor to the bathroom and sat her on the floor while he filled a basin with water. As he tugged at the nappy it broke up in his hands and bits of jellied padding crumbled to the floor. He plonked her into the water and pieces of poo floated off around her. She started to cry.

'C-c-cold,' she stuttered.

'Shut it. You're not meant to crap in your pull-ups. Ryan'll be wild if he finds out.'

She stopped crying instantly.

Lifting her out with one hand, Ben grabbed a damp, grimy towel off the floor with the other, patted her dry, folded it around her into a makeshift nappy and carried her down the corridor.

As he eased open a door with his foot, the musty stench of human living greeted him. One of his siblings, he couldn't tell which, coughed. He pulled back the blanket and dropped his sister into the closest bed.

'Ben.'

'Shhh or you'll wake the others. Now go to fuckin' sleep.'

'Ben?'

'What?' Then he realised it wasn't Brooke speaking. It was Lily.

'Did you score tonight?' Lily asked, sitting up and rubbing her eyes.

'Nah. Go back to sleep.' He closed the door and made his way down the corridor.

The kitchen was empty. Everyone was outside in the yard. He opened the fridge and stared vacantly into the fluorescent box. He was after a feed, not a beer. He slammed the door shut, the loose bottles clanging against each other, and looked around. On the sideboard lay a defrosting packet of sliced bread. He fished out five pieces and began stacking them into a tower, spreading peanut butter between the cold white layers.

The music pounded. He could see Ryan, passed out on a couch in the backyard, some woman – not Ben's mum – draped over him.

'Slack-arse,' Ben muttered, pulling up a chair and sitting down to eat.

Soon the bread had comforted the angry hollowness inside. He could feel the noose of sleep tighten around him and he headed back to the bedroom. Brooke was already making loud, grunting snores. He flicked off his sneakers and crashed.

When he surfaced from thick, drooling nothingness, someone was calling his name.

'Go'way,' he growled, and turned over, pulling a mound of blanket with him. 'It's the middle of the fuckin' night!'

His eyes were still closed, but suddenly it felt as if a blackout blind had been peeled off his eyelids. Someone had opened the curtains and the room was all glare.

It must have been about seven o'clock, the only time the room got any sunshine. But it would be all tease; the weak warmth never hung around for long enough to dry up the dampness that trickled down the windows and crept up the walls. The shadows from the house next door would be lying in wait to bully the sunshine away.

'I'll fuckin' kill you,' he cussed to no one in particular.

'Watch your mouth, Benjamin!'

His eyes flicked open. Only his mother called him Benjamin.

The morning light seared his eyeballs and he quickly shut them again.

'Sorry, Ma. Thought it was one of the kids.'

He could smell her – gleaming glass, disinfected toilet bowls, polished elevators. He tried again, opening one eye and squinting at his watch. 'What's up?'

Before she could answer, a reminder of the other night landed with a thud in the pit of his stomach, jump-starting his day. He sat up and leant against the cold wall, his eyes darting past his mother to the door, the windows, the door.

His mother came into focus, the bruised shadow of night shift still hanging under her eyes, her long black hair scraped back into a ponytail to keep it from dipping into dustbins and buckets of bleach.

'It's Lily's birthday. We gonna sing to her.'

The relief of her words washed over him, followed immediately by the annoyance at being woken up for nothing. It wasn't that he'd had only four hours sleep; a Red Bull could sort that. It was that sleep was the only place he could hide from the other stuff – the screaming scrape of the shovel, the sweet stench of blood. It was taking over his mind like some rampant weed, tangling his thoughts and choking his freedom, every day worse than the one before. Unexpected noises made him jump. A knock at the door was always the police. People were looking at him strangely – watching him. That whining siren, it was always coming his way.

He'd washed his jeans, scrubbing them with dishwashing liquid till the water coloured brown and a thick rim of scum clung to the basin. Police could get clues off clothes. Clothes held onto invisible secrets.

'Jesus, Ma. Couldn't you have let me sleep?'

His legs were itchy under the denim. He scratched his thigh and adjusted himself. His mother threaded her fingers through his knotted hair.

'Poor you.' Her hand slid over his head, warm and soft. As a kid he'd been fascinated by her long fingers. How they moved through the air, gripped a spoon, handled a paintbrush. It was as if they danced to a beat different from the rest of her body – swift, magical, measured. He used to imagine her playing the saxophone or keyboard, something like that, where fingers were everything.

Now her touch, the weight and warmth of her palm on his head, her closeness, nearly tricked him into telling her . . . He ducked away.

'So you gonna wake him too?' he asked, his lip curling around the thought of Ryan lying passed out on the sofa, sweat, old booze, and some random woman seeping from his pores.

His mother gave him one of her stares, which hollowed him out like an apple corer. He felt bad for even reminding her of the loser she lived with. She had that effect on him. She could tick him off without saying a single word.

He got up, took a long piss, then sloped down the corridor after her.

It sounded like there were fifty people in the kitchen, every giggle and scream cracking his head open wider. But it was just the usual crazies – Anika, Lily, Brooke, and Cody.

Cody leapt up and ran over to tackle him at the knees. 'It's Lily's birthday! Lily's birthday!' he cried, panting with excitement, his lips pulled back in a silly Cody grin, showing off his puffy pink folds of gum. Poor Cody. It looked like pink batting had been packed around his tiny grey teeth.

Lily was sitting upright at the table, her Kim Basinger eyes taking in all the fuss. Ben didn't know how old his sister was, but she had two small spuds sprouting under her T-shirt. George in the gang had been the first to point them out.

'Happy birthday, Sis,' he said, slumping down at the table and massaging the pain from his temples.

'Whatever,' Lily said with a half-smile.

Their mother put down a plate in front of her. On it was a square of white bread with the crusts ripped off and hundreds and thousands sprinkled on top. A candle had been poked in the middle of it, but the bread wasn't thick enough to hold the thing upright and the candle kept listing to one side.

'You light it,' his mother said to Ben, passing over the match she'd just used to light a cigarette.

Ben cupped his hand around the dying flame and leant over the candle. The match died. His mother threw him the box and he tried again.

'Candle must be wet or the string is too short,' he said, giving up.

Lily's face fell.

Their mother rested her cigarette across the top of her coffee cup and tried again. No luck.

She was just about to pull out another match when she turned, grabbed Cody by his shirt, and slapped him across the backs of his legs. 'Put that down!' she shrieked, snatching her cigarette off him.

Cody, caught between a cough from inhaling the smoke, and crying, made a weird barking howl.

'Smokes are not for kids,' she yelled. 'I've told you a hundred times! They'll turn your lungs into black jelly.'

'And your dick'll fall off,' Anika whispered.

'But . . . but . . . you . . .' Cody said, sobbing.

Their mother turned back to Lily. 'Just pretend it's lit.'

Lily sat back and folded her arms. 'I'm not gonna pretend to blow out some candle when it's not lit. That's just stupid.'

Their mother gave one of her I'm-too-tired-to-fight sighs. 'Suit yourself. Let's sing, then.' She started them off and everyone, except Cody, joined in. Lily tried to keep her sulky expression firm, but soon it was cracking at the edges, and by the end of the song, she was grinning.

'Make a wish! Make a wish!' Cody cried, forgetting about the hiding.

Lily carefully folded in the corners of her slice of bread, as if sealing an envelope. But when she picked it up, the balls of sugar started falling onto the Formica table like coloured hail. Their mother hadn't used enough margarine to stick them down.

She took a slow, deliberate bite of her now almost naked bread and pondered her wish.

'I want some,' Brooke whined, pointing to the disappearing Fairy Bread.

Their mother put a plate with three triangles in front of them. 'Here we go.'

'How come we only get half each?' Anika complained.

'Yeah, how come?' Cody said, copying his sister.

''Cos someone ate most of the bread last night, didn't they?' their mum said, giving Ben an accusing glance.

Ben dropped his head forward, letting his long black fringe fall over his eyes. Everyone was talking too loudly. It was doing his head in. He pulled at a piece of jagged thumbnail and ripped it off with his teeth. The exposed bulge of skin stung as it connected with the cold morning air.

'What's lungs?' Cody asked, spraying Anika with crumbs.

'Close your mouth when you eat!' Anika growled, wiping her face with a dishcloth.

'Lungs are like balloons of air in your chest,' Lily piped up.

Cody frowned. 'I thought they was boobies.'

A baby started to cry. Ben looked round. He hadn't even realised that his newest sister, baby Dina, was in the room, propped up in her car seat beside the stove. His mother started rocking the seat with her foot.

'Fuckin' hell. Can I go back to bed?' Ben said, pushing out his chair.

'Cut your swearing, kid, and no, you cannot!' His mother grabbed hold of his sleeve. 'I'm the one been up working all night. I need you to look after the baby, and Brooke and Cody. The others are going to school.'

'But it's my birthday,' Lily said, tears brewing.

'And it's a school day,' their mother said, her eyes flashing. 'I'm not having another run-in with the bloody truant officer!'

'Since when does Cody need looking after?' Ben complained, yanking his arm away. Cody had been retarded forever. It was nothing new. The doctors at the hospital had told his mum it was because she'd been on the booze when she was pregnant with him. Poor Cody. He had tiny piggy eyes and a flat face, like he'd run into a wall or something. He was clumsy too, always getting the bash for knocking things over and dropping stuff.

Brooke and Baby weren't a problem. Ben would be able to escape after giving Baby a bottle; she always slept after a feed. And Brooke could come with him to the gang pad. But not Cody. Cody would blab about everything.

'Since I said so.'

'Why do you bother going to work anyway?' Ben snapped. 'You'd get the same on the benefit.'

He stumbled backwards as he felt the full force of his mother's hand on the side of his head.

'Cut your cheek,' she said, coming up close so that he could smell her empty-stomach breath.

He nearly hit her back, a reflex, but caught himself just in time.

She glared at him. 'I don't know what's got into you lately, but I've had my fill of it.'

71

She moved behind Lily and gently swept up Lily's long hair in her hands. Lily pulled away. Lily was different from the rest of them. She had their same caramel-coloured skin, but her head was a pop-up of fair curls, and she had turquoise eyes the colour of the ocean on a clear day. When she was born, Lil's dad didn't believe she was his kid.

'You skank! You fuckin' ho!' he'd screamed as Ben's mum had lain in the hospital bed, fending off his blows.

He got nine months for assault. That was the last they saw of him. The unfair thing was that Lily probably *was* his kid. Her fairness didn't come from some random *Pākehā* hook-up. Ben had once seen a picture of their grandparents; Lily was the spitting image of her grandmother.

Ben's mates were all desperate to get a piece of Lily, but she wasn't interested in boys. She was weird that way. While the rest of the girls in the hood hung out at the skateboard pit after school, Lil was in her room doing crafty stuff or foraging in rubbish bins outside shops, looking for scraps of material, cork, string, sequins – anything she could turn into something beautiful. Her best creations so far were a pencil case in the shape of a sausage dog, and a purple felt Barney-cum-cute-weird-monster thing, which she slept with every night.

'Maybe Debs can give us a lift to Spotlight after school and you can choose a piece of fabric from the discount bin.'

'Really, Ma?' Lily said, leaping up, her face beaming for the first time that morning.

Ben kept picking at his fingernails. He knew he'd get home later to find Lil sobbing in her room. His mum never managed to keep her promises, even though she meant to. She tried to be a good mum.

Debs lived down the road. She was their mother's best friend and Ben's godmother. He didn't understand the whole godmother thing, especially since no one in his family believed in God. His mother's take on it was that God had been made up by the government to get people to think there was more to this shitty life than there really was. Anyhow, his mother said Debs was like family. Ben wondered why his mother had to make up family when she didn't even bother with her own.

Debs was good value, though. She could make his mum laugh, and Ben liked it when his mother laughed. It thawed the cold, anxious bits inside of him. The only time he didn't like her laughing was when she was pissed.

A long day stretched ahead. The crew would think he was hiding out if he didn't pitch. And he couldn't miss the build-up to their clash with the GDBs. But he wouldn't risk taking Cody along.

There was a loud knocking on the kitchen window. Ben's whole body jerked.

'It's Debs!' cried Lily, running to the back door.

Ben breathed out. His mother looked at him questioningly. He looked away, avoiding her all-seeing eyes. She could read minds if you gave her half a chance.

Debs stepped into the room dressed in leopard-skin leggings and a mango-orange T-shirt that hugged the floppy folds of flesh around her midriff. Her morning hair had not yet been tamed and her lime-green fingernails needed a touch-up.

'Well, well, well. So what's the occasion?'

'It's Lily's birthday,' Cody blurted.

'Lily's birthday, eh?' Debs said, wrapping Lily in a tight squeeze. 'Just as well I popped round for a cup of sugar then, or I'd have missed the party.'

Ben knocked over his chair and headed for the hallway.

Debs raised her eyebrows. 'What's up with him?'

His mother whispered something. He turned just in time to catch her rolling her eyes.

Beyond

You never met your tīpuna, *Benjamin – your beautiful, gracious grandmother. You never experienced the weight of her presence and the wisdom of her words. Auē! For you were not raised within your culture's* kete, *and have not known the comfort and constraint of its robust walls, walls that would have protected and held you, restrained and shaped you. You should have been . . .*

In the beginning, in the time of moa, that giant flightless bird, there was an order, a belonging. This land was marked out by the ridges of mountains and the belly of valleys into rohe *– each region inhabited by those who shared a common ancestral tie – a tie which could be traced right back to one of the founding canoes that landed on these shores some eight hundred years ago. This ancestral strand has been woven through generations to form a giant basket holding all in its embrace – those from then and those of now. Months and years are arbitrary, the physical and the spiritual simply part of the same, for all of time is held within its clutch. And all of Māori. Connectedness is everything. Connection to our soil, our people, our past.*

Chapter Nine

BEN

'Got a problem?' Tate shouted across the street.

'Yeah, I got a problem. You tagged our turf, you motherfuckers.'

'So what you gonna do about it?' Tate said, his head tilted, his eyebrows nonchalantly raised. He looked so relaxed he could have been buying smokes at the corner store.

Ben never felt calm when his gang was about to rumble. He was so pumped up his hands were trembling and his nostrils flaring like a horse waiting in the starting stalls.

They were standing across the street from the GDBs, the potholed tarmac dividing the night into two. Blue versus red. Ben worshipped his blue bandanna. He could lose his name behind it and be just eyes. When he tied on the cotton kerchief and his hot breath blew back on him, he knew he was for real, part of something bigger. The clutch of cloth was better than any school certificate. It was a lifetime membership to everything that mattered.

Tools. Face. Gangsta-ready.

'Gonna kick some arse,' Simi said not even moving his lips,

like some ventriloquist. Then he stepped off the pavement and pimp-rolled into the middle of the road. Halfway across he stopped, pulled the finger at the GDBs, then turned and swung back to his crew.

'Chancer,' Ben said with a snigger.

Even though Simi was the youngest in the gang – a 'noob' – he had attitude. He came from a family of eleven, the youngest by five years, so he'd had to be a loudmouth to survive. But he was a rock in a bag of pebbles. All his brothers and sisters had done well at school – one was a sales manager at The Warehouse. Another, some celebrity chef in Australia. Then there was Simi. He'd been playing truant for as long as Ben could remember, hanging out at the dairy and earning his grades in dope smoking and tagging. People quickly forgot he was short and baby-faced, because his character filled any space, like the Michelin man.

Tate cranked up the rap pounding at his feet.

Don't bring your bitches, just needles and riches; my place, not yours . . .

A dog barked. Ben looked over his shoulder, his eyes fixing on a wrinkly old woman sitting outside on her porch. When she saw him eyeball her, she got out of her chair and scuttled inside like a little cockroach, dead-bolting her front door with a rattle and clunk.

Ben sniggered. He wasn't planning on hurting the old duck, but it felt good to have his power respected. Her house was a state house special: peeling, sherbet-green weatherboard box, two windows, one door. Next one along was identical, except mallow-pink. The one after that, Pineapple-Lump yellow.

'This joint is messing with my brain,' Ben said to no one in particular.

'We gonna put you in the dirt, you cunts,' Tate shouted across the road, hooking his forefingers into the waist of his jeans.

'Totally,' Simi said, shaking his short legs like a wrestler readying for a match.

'Oh yeah?' from across the street. 'Big words for a pussy army. Go home, it's past your bedtime.'

An empty vodka bottle rocketed through the air and shattered, the taunt exploding at Tate's feet. He didn't budge. A bubble of blood sprang up on his shin. Slowly and deliberately, he bent down and wiped it off with his forefinger, then stuck the bloodied finger in his mouth and sucked.

'Hey, bros,' he said turning to the rest of the gang. 'I taste blood. I say, red is straight dead.'

'All words, no action,' came the reply from the GDBs' woolly-haired leader. 'Trick and treating like some ho. Go to church if you scared of the bash.'

Ben didn't see Tate throw the piece of concrete. He just saw it strike the guy in the belly, dropping him instantly. One down. Tate was a smooth operator.

While the enemy army gathered around their fallen man, the DOAs savoured the satisfaction of their first hit. Then like a pack of wild dogs, the GDBs slunk forward.

Ben fingered the cold metal in his pocket.

The flick of knives. The rush of rubber. Fence paling on skull. Wood on bone. War! Sneakers skidding on bitumen. Machetes carving up the night. Dogs barking. Voices roaring. Flesh exploding. Frightened eyes in lolly-coloured boxes peeping out from behind threadbare curtains while the bros ruled.

Out of the corner of his eye, Ben spotted someone hoofing Danny. Rage exploded inside his head. Danny was family.

No one messed with someone in his gang. Danny, Tate, Simi, Matt, George – they were his love and hate, his every day, his personality and purpose. They were his answer. Without them, he was nothing.

'Cunt!' he screamed, moving in on the guy with the evil smirk. Ben's fist connected with his pockmarked face. It felt good. His anger, tonight at least, had found a home.

His enemy stumbled and fell, before managing to scramble away. Ben picked up a broken bottle and gave chase, dodging and diving through the disorder until he'd caught up with his prey. Then he was bottling the guy, again and again and again. Suddenly a fishing knife came out of nowhere and sliced through Ben's hoodie, his T-shirt, his skin. He didn't feel anything at first – just saw his sleeve gaping. Black spots started dancing in front of his eyes, and he realised that the blood dripping into the pool of red was also his – blue mixing with red.

Grit pressed into his cheek and his ear felt as if it was folded in two. He tried to lift his head to relieve the pain, but it was as heavy as a wheelbarrow full of rocks. The tarmac tilted. He opened his eyes wider, trying to stop the halo of blackness from seeping in.

'It's the pigs!' someone shouted above the din. Instantly, the tangle of bodies and roar of hate evaporated, hazy shapes melting into the night, to leave only Ben and the bottled boy behind.

Ben's mind cleared as stills from the farmhouse night flashed in front of him. He had to get away.

He hauled himself up. Spots crowded his vision.

For a moment, he teetered there in the bubble of red and blue light; then his legs began to bend like plasticine softening in the sun, and he crumpled again to the kerb.

It was a relief to give over to being caught. It had been hell the past six weeks, lurching between sweet oblivion and cold, sober fear. His nails were ragged stumps and his eyes racooned with tiredness. His abs were now so flat they were hollow, the meat sucked right up against his bones like heated plastic wrap, and his nerves were all frayed and worn. He thought about the time he and George had been out in the Manukau Harbour in George's dinghy when a storm blew up. Being finally flung into the water had come as a relief after hours of trying to keep the boat afloat.

'Look straight at the camera.'

Ben stood against the whitewashed wall, his jaw locked, his eyes staring down the lens.

A flash of silver-white light.

'This way.'

Another flash.

Ben stared at his ink-printed fingertips poking out from under the sling. He couldn't feel three of his fingers.

'I've booked 'em, Ray. All under age. Two from the Glenfield GDBs and one from the DOAs.'

'DOAs?' the old cop repeated, looking to Ben for more information.

Ben sucked his teeth.

'Dead On Arrival,' the other cop translated, filling Ben's silence. 'New North Shore feeder gang.'

'Bloody lucky he *wasn't* dead on arrival.'

They both snorted.

'One's gone on to Middlemore Hospital with facial injuries and a punctured lung. This one had a laceration to his forearm. It's already been stitched.'

The doctor had said the scar on Ben's arm would be a significant one. Ben was pleased. He'd have something to show for it.

The older cop sighed. 'Take him down to the cells. He can sober up on the concrete.'

Chapter Ten

CARLA

Carla went rigid as the cold metal slid into her vagina, the speculum forcing her open.

'Just breathe deeply and try to relax.'

Relax. Carla grimaced at the absurdity of this directive.

'Hopefully this will be the last of these for a while,' her GP, Naomi, said, peering down the beam of light into her.

Carla stared at the perforated ceiling, following the pattern of dots to different dead ends.

'The good news is that I can't see any blisters,' Naomi added, feeding the swab into a long plastic tube and sealing it. 'But keep taking the Zovirax. It'll reduce the frequency of further outbreaks.'

Carla nodded and started to sit up.

'Just a sec, Carla, while I have a quick feel of your abdomen.' Naomi rubbed her hands to warm them. Carla gave an involuntary shiver.

'Is the pelvic pain settling?'

'Uh-huh.'

After pulling on her slacks, Carla sat down in the chair

beside the desk while Naomi typed up the consultation notes.

Carla looked around. *My husband wears the pants, but I choose which one's he wears* – the slogan on her doctor's forgotten mug of cold tea. Naomi's twin boys smiled down at Carla from a solid pine shelf, their faces positioned between *An Atlas of Common Skin Conditions* and *Counselling the Grieving Patient*. On the wall above these was a crayon drawing of a stick figure with a big speech bubble: *Thank yoo docta abil for mayking me beta*.

Carla had been with Naomi for five years, ever since Linda Metcalf had retired. Naomi was refreshingly young and exceedingly competent. Even Jack had been happy to join her books; not that it was ever for much – a strained calf muscle, tennis elbow, a bout of glandular fever.

The printer began to whirr. Naomi looked up and stretched out a hand to Carla. 'How are things, Carla? Honestly?'

Carla lowered her hands onto her lap. 'Alright, I suppose. I haven't been sleeping that well, though. Not since Kevin's discharge. He wakes most nights with nightmares.'

Naomi nodded.

'We're in a motel now, too. I couldn't stand it at Geoff and Mildred's any longer. The doctors at the head injury unit are letting Kevin attend rehab clinic as an outpatient, much to Geoff's disapproval, of course. But I needed Kevin home with me. The motel is on a main road. It's very noisy.'

Naomi didn't say anything. Carla liked that. Her GP was a good listener, unlike some doctors who talked more than they listened.

'It'll be better when we can get back to the farm,' she added quickly, feeling suddenly guilty for complaining. The waiting room outside was packed full of sick people.

'We could up his medication,' Naomi suggested, checking Kevin's discharge summary, then searching through the chaos on her desk for a prescription pad. 'Perhaps we should also reconsider starting *you* on an antidepressant.'

Carla clenched her teeth.

'Your brain is in a state of chemical imbalance, Carla, after all the stress. Poor sleep, loss of appetite, feelings of hopelessness – these are symptoms that your body is not coping.'

'We have to sell the farm,' Carla blurted out. 'I won't be able to manage it with Kevin the way he is.'

Naomi looked up. 'It's early days. I don't think you should make any big decisions for at least six months. Let me try to arrange more assistance for Kevin in the meantime. Is the district nurse still visiting?'

Carla nodded.

'So how about it? Shall we try you on a low-dose antidepressant?'

'No!' Carla said, abruptly lifting her handbag onto her lap.

'It's nothing to be ashamed of,' her doctor said evenly. 'You've been through so much. You're not going to become addicted, if that's what's worrying you.'

A tablet for this, a tablet for that! What about just getting on with the hand life dealt? Anyhow, what did they all know? Nothing anyone could glean from medical school or *Counselling the Grieving Patient*. Some small pill was not going to miraculously bridge the divide and re-enrol her in living.

Carla stood up. Naomi was typing up the remainder of the consultation and as she scrolled down the screen, Carla saw Jack's name flash up, heading a February consultation. She froze.

Naomi quickly closed the file. 'Silly computer. It has a mind of its own.'

Carla hesitated. 'You saw Jack recently?'

'Yes,' Naomi said, her face colouring. 'I did.' Then she stood up and gently steered Carla towards the door. 'I'll see you in a week. Try to get some rest.'

'Uh, yes . . . Thank you, Naomi.'

'No charge as usual, love. Direct to ACC,' said Marge at reception.

Carla turned, preoccupied with what she'd just seen, and collided with Vera Wilkinson, secretary of the tennis club, all cloying perfume and green polyester.

'How are you?' Vera cried, dousing Carla in a cloud of stale cigarette breath. 'The police confident of an arrest, I hear.' Her bosom heaved with excitement. 'Saw it in the *Herald*,' she added quickly, obviously anxious to distance herself from the salacious rumour mill.

A hush settled over the stuffy waiting room.

'That's what they tell me,' Carla managed, a sense of panic rising within her. She tried to edge past, but a child was playing with a Buzzy Bee on the floor, blocking her escape.

'Just a matter of time, then, before they catch the bloody animals. Excuse my French, but really, not worth the air they breathe.'

Carla contemplated climbing over the child.

'Such a lovely lad, your Jack. What a tragedy, love.'

Carla's chin began to tremble.

'And who's going to foot the bill when they do finally catch them? Who's going to keep them fed and watered? I'll tell you who. You and me, honey! Our taxes. I hear the new prison they're planning to build will have central heating! Central heating, mind you!'

Carla's cell phone started to ring deep within her handbag. She sucked in a stuttering breath and excused herself.

Outside, she steadied herself against a parked car and fumbled with her phone.

'Hello?'

It was Marge, the medical centre's receptionist. She'd witnessed the Vera encounter from behind her desk and had rung Carla to facilitate a getaway.

Back at the motel, the stiff maroon curtains were still drawn and Kevin was still in his pyjamas, dozing in an armchair. It was almost midday. She'd left him there at nine. The only difference was that now a pallid banana smoothie stain was weeping down his front, and the sour stench of urine hung in the air. A children's programme was screening on the television, all glitter and pink music.

Carla screwed up her eyes, trying to squeeze away the pain of seeing Kevin like this. She put her parcels down.

'Sorry I'm late, love,' she said, mustering an artificially upbeat tone. 'Naomi was running late. I had to wait for over an hour before she saw me. I'm gasping for a cuppa. Will you join me?'

Kev shook his head.

'Sure? There's some of Bev's shortbread left.'

'I said no!'

The doctors said his recovery would be slow. It could take up to two years and the endpoint remained uncertain. Could this be the Kevin she'd be left with? He never used to be abrupt or rude. Never . . .

She sat down on the arm of his chair and ran her fingers through his thinning hair, tracing the crease of puckered purple skin zigzagging across his scalp.

'They said we can go back to the farm next week. Lorraine – you know, from Victim Support – called. It will be good to get out of this place. Back home, eh?'

He shrugged.

'Ke—'

'Not that way, stupid!' he blurted as a cartoon rabbit scampered across the screen.

Carla closed her eyes. Then her cell phone was ringing again.

'Carla, Steve Herbert here.'

'Yes, Steve.'

'I've got some news.'

Carla's heart vaulted in an internal gasp of apprehension. 'Would you and Kevin be able to come down to the station? It's not something we can really discuss over the phone.'

Chapter Eleven

CARLA

Carla turned off the highway and slowed for a changing traffic light. The car behind honked, willing her through the amber. She glanced in the rear-view mirror. A woman towering above them in her SUV was shaking her head and gesticulating irately. Carla looked ahead.

Kevin was in the passenger seat, sucking on an unpeeled mandarin, the juice trickling down his chin onto his clean white shirt. At least he was out of his pyjamas.

Excitement coursed through her body. Excitement? She felt ashamed. There was nothing to be excited about. Nothing Steve Herbert had to say would reverse the course their lives had taken. Yet, it was too hard to live in a constant state of pure truth. Sometimes she had to let herself surface to a world of superficialities, where the state of the weather and what was for dinner mattered, where catching the thugs who had ruined her life *was* something to get excited about.

The light turned green and she depressed the accelerator.

What lay ahead? They were moving towards a destination. Surely anything would be better than the past forty-five days in hell's anteroom, stuck in time like a horror movie paused on a violent scene.

She found a parking space right outside the new police headquarters. Not yet softened by planting, the monolith rose starkly against its suburban surrounds. Stippled concrete and tinted glass towered over the other buildings, intimidating them into submission.

Kevin climbed out of the passenger side, left his door open and started across the parking lot into the path of a reversing car. The driver screeched to a halt.

Carla grabbed Kevin's hand and yanked him backwards. 'Careful, Kevin!'

Visibly shaken, he lifted her hand to his mouth and started to kiss it. 'Sorry, Carly. Sorry. Sorry.'

Carla pulled him in to her and hugged his melting frame. He was all angles and bone. 'It's OK, my love. It's—'

Kevin shoved her back at arm's length and stared at her intently. 'Why are you crying, Carly? Don't cry. Please don't cry.'

'I'm okay, darling,' she said, fishing out a tissue from her bra. 'Mummy's fine . . . Oh God, I mean . . . I mean, *I'm* fine. Here, hold onto me.'

Obediently, he clasped her arm, and they crossed the car park together.

The vast reception area was familiar by now – sparse, save for an empty water dispenser in the corner and a row of grey airport-lounge chairs lining the back wall. A strong dose of disinfectant had successfully erased the Saturday night just gone.

Carla sat Kevin under a poster warning of the dangers of letting children swim unattended, then approached the counter. A generic blonde policewoman greeted her.

'I'm here to see Detective Inspector Steve Herbert.'

'And you are?'

'Carla Reid. He's expecting us.'

Carla watched as the young woman's face softened, just as everybody's did when they learnt who she was.

'DI Herbert will be right with you. Please take a seat.'

As Carla sat down, Kevin released a deep sigh. He did this up to a hundred times a day. It was as if he would suddenly remember to exhale. The doctors were unsure of the reason for this, but thought it would probably settle down with time. Carla took them at their word. Kevin had to get better.

The glass doors at the entrance slid open and a stocky woman in a floral sundress and strappy leather sandals hurried in, her face flushed, her manner agitated. Her bottom wobbled as she walked.

'I am must to report a thief,' she said in a Dutch, or perhaps German, accent. 'Somebody did smash the window of my campervan and they steal my bag. Passport too.' Her voice wavered.

The policewoman opened a drawer and pulled out a yellow form. 'You'll need to fill out one of these.' Her pleasant yet matter-of-fact manner reminded Carla how commonplace trauma and disaster were at the station, and how promptly they were stripped of all hyperbole and fuss.

A door to the left opened and Steve Herbert appeared, his shoulders filling the narrow doorway. He stepped into the room.

Carla shook Kevin awake; he'd already dozed off.

'Kevin. Carla. Sorry to keep you waiting,' Herbert said, shaking Carla's hand. His firm, warm grip hinted at everything she yearned for; she didn't want to let go.

'Can I get either of you a drink? Tea perhaps? Or a coffee?' he asked as he swiped his security card and led them through a warren of offices to an elevator.

'A milkshake,' Kevin mumbled. 'A lime milkshake.'

Carla shrugged apologetically.

'Sorry, Kevin, no can do,' Herbert smiled. 'Just cheap instant coffee and no-name-brand tea bags, I'm afraid. You'll have to have a word with your local MP.'

'I bloody well will,' Kevin said, shaking his head too many times.

They got out on the fifth floor. Carla knew Steve's office.

'Come in. Sit down.' He closed the door, locking in the view over Albany, the grey carpet, the truth.

The inspector looked exhausted. He'd worked non-stop since that night, heading a fifty-strong team from CIB, and keeping Carla informed every step of the way. His daily call had become her raison d'être. Even when there was nothing to report, he still rang or dropped in to see how she and Kevin were doing. To untangle him from her life now would be to let it completely disintegrate.

Was this it, she wondered? The end. The motion of the enquiry had soothed her. The questions, the talking, the rehashing, had all worked to keep Jack somehow alive, sweeping her along with the promise of something better. Perhaps she didn't want closure after all. The investigation had ordered her minutes and structured her days. It had kept the terrifying emptiness at bay.

Herbert seated himself on the edge of his desk. 'Carla. Kevin.' His tone was measured and deliberate. She nodded, willing him on.

'We arrested two youths on Saturday night in connection with a gang incident on the Shore.'

Carla's mouth went dry. She put her hand out, searching for Kevin's. *Arrested two youths . . . Arrested two youths . . . Arrested two—*

A ringing telephone punctured the moment.

'Sorry!' Herbert leant back to pick up the receiver. 'Steve Herbert, Homicide.'

Carla waited, teetering on a high wire.

'When's the hearing? Yup. I'll get one of the boys onto it right away. No problem. Thanks for letting me know, Derek. Cheers.'

Herbert scribbled something down on a piece of paper before getting up and putting his head out the door. 'Jen, hold all further calls, please.'

Carla's shoulders were aching and she could feel the dull creep of a headache tightening across the back of her head.

Herbert took up his perch on the desk again. 'As I was saying, we picked up some youths involved in a gang incident over the weekend, and we have reason to believe that one of them was involved in the incident on your farm last month.'

Last month. March. Fine, crisp days hinting at an approaching change in season. Kevin's birthday. Their wedding anniversary. The first feijoas. Persimmons hanging like orange orbs in the orchard . . .

Now the grey skies of approaching winter were more comforting in their distance from *that* block of days on the calendar. March would always be stained with horror.

'Fingerprints place one of the youths at the farm on the night of the twentieth. We're still awaiting DNA confirmation from body fluid samples.'

Carla blushed and slumped back into the chair, her brain struggling under this fresh load. So the perpetual motion was finite after all. The madness was about to settle. She was scared.

'I mean what's so blimmin' hard about making a lime milkshake?' Kevin blurted out, kick-starting time again.

Carla burst out laughing – embarrassingly raw, uncontrollable guffaws that quickly turned to tears.

Chapter Twelve

CARLA

A sixteen-year-old boy from Glenfield has been charged in connection with a violent home invasion in March of this year. The suspect was arrested following an unrelated gang incident in Birkdale. The charge currently stands at aggravated robbery. However, Senior Detective Inspector Steven Herbert, who is heading the investigation, says further charges are likely to follow. Police are still searching for a second person in relation to the incident.

The accused has interim name suppression and has been remanded in custody following a brief appearance in the North Shore Youth Court. He has been referred to the High Court for trial and sentencing.

Angry protesters gathered outside the courthouse today demanding tougher sentencing and calling on the government to address the alarming increase in youth-gang-related violence.

Carla sat under the canopy of a large magnolia. An icy wind gusted across the empty park, stealing a newspaper she'd found folded on the bench. She jumped up to retrieve it, but the wind toyed with her, swooping the pages of print just out of reach. Eventually, the bare branches of a tree snagged the rehashed news of her life.

In the past she used to read the newspaper every morning. Without this ritual, her day had felt incomplete. Kevin, by contrast, had never been very curious about the world beyond the farm gate, *The Willows* seeming to sate his needs and shelter his shyness.

But she had grown up in the city and relished the pulse and politics of it. As a child, she'd travelled extensively with her parents, both of whom believed that a true education lay beyond the classroom walls. By the age of eleven, Carla had protested outside a bullfight in Spain. By fifteen, she'd hiked through Tibet. And by sixteen, had witnessed first-hand the atrocities of apartheid. Her father, a political science lecturer, had been a learned and deeply principled man who'd fought tirelessly for the underdog, rallied support for unions, and was always challenging bureaucratic limits. She had been raised, not on *Peter Pan* or *Alice in Wonderland*, but on tales of the 1951 Waterfront Strike and the 1970 All Blacks tour of South Africa, when Māori players had been made 'honorary whites'. And so it came as no surprise when her father had expressed disappointment in her decision to marry Kevin, 'the stolid, cardigan-wearing farmer'. He had clearly harboured greater ambitions for her. To him, a life working the land was so entirely bland and insular.

Now the machinations of the real world no longer interested her either. She hadn't read a paper in weeks. She was in print and tired of her own story, no longer able to distinguish which bits really belonged to her and which were simply the fiction of an overzealous reporter.

Ten o'clock. Another day yawned in front of her. She'd been up since five and already attended an appointment at the Rape Crisis Centre, preferring an early session so that she could leave it behind and not allow it to monopolise her day. But it was too early to return to the motel. The district nurse and occupational therapist would have both been and gone, and Kevin would be settled in his chair in front of the television. Nothing would have changed. He needed her. She'd always needed him. Yet now it was time alone she was chasing. Kevin had come to epitomise the cruel riddle she was living, his almost normal appearance tricking the eye and supporting the pretence that nothing had changed, when everything had. Everything. His greying hair, different-coloured eyes, and weathered skin were parts of a familiar shell. But her soulmate, lover, and best friend had all died on that awful night, along with their only child. At least when she was away from Kevin she could pretend. To be around him was to be constantly reminded of her loss.

'Josh. Josh, careful! You're going too fast.'

A small boy on a shiny red bike flashed past. In slow motion, Carla saw the speed-wobble, the pitch, the somersault, then the bent metal and grazed limbs. A howl brought her to her senses and she leapt up, reaching the injured lad just ahead of his mother.

'Oh dear, you poor poppet. Here, let me help you.' She lifted the bike off the child. 'There we go,' she said, putting a hand on the child's leg. It was warm and covered in fine downy hair.

'There's blood. There's blood! MUM!' the youngster squalled.

'I know, but it'll be—' Carla began. Then the mother was upon them, and the boy's twisted face softened.

'Oh, Joshy. Oh dear.' She hoisted him up.

'Here, let me help,' Carla offered, righting the skewed bike. 'Are you parked nearby?'

'No. Uh, we live just around the corner.' The woman was distracted and Carla felt like an intrusion. 'We'll walk home, thank you. I'll send my daughter to collect it shortly.'

'I can, really . . .'

But the woman had already turned and was heading down the pathway, the boy sobbing quietly into her shoulder. Carla held her hands up to her nose and inhaled. The warm smell of child.

The incident took her back to the first time Jack had come off his bike just after his eighth birthday. Kevin had bought him a brand-new ten-speed model. Ten-speed! Jack had been beside himself with excitement, and the envy of all his mates. That is, until the afternoon Russell came tearing into the kitchen. Carla was making gnocchi and up to her elbows in flour and mashed potato.

'Come quick, Mrs R! It's Jack. He's had an awful accident.' She remembered as if it were yesterday, running and running and not knowing what she would find.

At first count, a gaping lip, a split knee and a raw-red tummy.

'Ma, I've broken my teeth,' Jack had cried, two skew pegs poking out of his gums where his brand-new adult teeth had gleamed that morning.

'Just be grateful it's only his teeth,' Dr Johnson had said as he'd stitched Jack's torn lip. 'Teeth you can replace. It's not as easy to mend an eye or a brain.'

They'd all been shaken up for some weeks after. It was Jack's first serious accident and left the small family feeling vulnerable and cautious, as if they'd skimmed too close to the edge. Jack had been a belated and much-wanted gift, his arrival incredible after so much heartache and waiting. Always in the back of Carla's mind was the fear that he could so easily be taken from them.

'There are no guarantees in life,' was Kevin's well-worn line. 'We can't wrap the kid in cotton wool. He's going to have many more tumbles in life, Carla, I'm sure of that.'

Chapter Thirteen

BEN

The air in the van was a foul brew of disinfectant, traffic fumes, and old urine. Ben slid along the cold metal seat as they lurched round a corner. He locked his fingers into the grill to steady himself. He felt strangely excited. Being arrested wasn't so bad after all. It was definitely better than the endless empty days of no action. The fear that had held him in a headlock for six weeks, now seemed almost silly. Another court appearance was guaranteed credibility with his crew. And when he got out, he'd be able to command some serious respect.

The van slowed in the morning traffic. A silver Honda Odyssey pulled up behind them. The driver started applying her lipstick in the rear-view mirror. A boy and girl wearing school blazers and striped ties were sitting in the back seat. Ben could see them craning their necks to get a look inside the van. He leant close to the small square of window and pulled a face, but the kids didn't register. One-way glass.

Ben had never owned a blazer, nor proper school shoes for that matter, and his mum had never driven him to school. She didn't own a car – not one that worked – though she did walk him to the end of the road on his first day of school. He grinned now when he thought of her shouting her mouth off at the truant officer as she chased the small, jittery man off their property. Mind you, she still gave Ben a hiding for wagging.

'You'll never get out of this shithole if you don't go to school,' she'd yelled. Yet sometimes she was the one keeping him home when she needed him to look after the younger ones.

Then there was the day Mr Roberts, his science teacher, made fun of him in front of the whole class. Ben walked out of the room, through the school gates, and never went back.

He stared at the cars snailing behind them in the traffic. Sometimes, when sober, Ryan would tinker with the car wrecks that lived on the front lawn, promising to fix one for Ben's mum. It never happened. She preferred Holdens, anyway – the new, brightly coloured ones. Ben used to dream of winning the Lotto and walking into one of those flash car yards to choose his mother the biggest and shiniest vehicle on the sales floor. He sneered now at his foolishness.

As the van slowed and turned into the courthouse driveway, something hit the back window. Orange yolk slid down the glass. Then a camera lens was pushed up against the window and there was a burst of ice-white light. Had name suppression been lifted?

Ben blinked and quickly rearranged his expression: teeth clenched, eyes steeled.

'Hope you rot in hell, you piece of shit,' a woman screamed, her eyes bulging, her mouth twisted. 'Scum of the earth!'

Scum of the earth. That was a good line. He'd use it. He began to tap his sneakers on the floor of the van and click his fingers to an imaginary beat.

To you we might be
scum of the earth,
but we're loyal to our brothers,
won't never spill the truth.

. . .

Poor little rich boys

. . .

driven to school,
you ain't lived life
till you killed a few.

He was kept in a holding cell for about an hour with a guy who reeked of garlic and couldn't speak any English. Then it was his cellmate's turn in court and Ben was left alone. He preferred being with the other dude, even if he did smell bad.

When it was his turn, Ben was handcuffed to a screw and led upstairs to the courtroom. He'd tied the upper half of his prison overall around his waist so that his FCUK T-shirt could be easily seen, especially if there were going to be TV cameras. He rolled into the dock.

The room was long and narrow and smelt of recently vacuumed carpet. At the front, ruling the space, was a long desk on a platform. Facing it were four rows of tables and chairs. At the very back of the room were benches filled with people.

When Ben entered the dock, the hum of voices went quiet. Blood was crashing through his head like water down the Huka Falls. He scanned the faces in the room with the same anxious nonchalance of a traveller entering an airport arrivals lounge. He was hoping to spot some of his crew.

'Benjamin. Hey, Benjamin! Over here!'

It wasn't hard to spot his mum's brown face among the pale ones, but seeing her really threw him. He hadn't given her much thought since his arrest.

Water started to leak from his eyes. He looked away and dug his chewed nails into the palm of his hand to distract himself from being so weak.

Ryan wasn't anywhere to be seen – no surprises there – but his mates? He'd have expected them to show. It was a public hearing. He checked again. Not a single member of the DOAs there to support him. He really wanted them to see him now, a senior pro, not some juvie. But maybe they were scared. He just wanted to tell them he was airtight and would never grass on them.

'All rise.'

The judge, a thin, white-haired Pākehā woman, walked in and sat down behind the desk at the front of the room. A large purple stain spilt from her forehead onto the side of her face. Where it stretched over her head, no hair grew. Her glasses, small circles of naked glass, kept sliding down her nose. Each time she pushed them back up with her middle finger, it looked like she was flipping off the courtroom.

Everyone sat down. Ben too. The guard yanked him back up. Then a man in a dark suit stood up and addressed the court with a crazy salad of words. Ben couldn't understand anything. Next was a woman in crazy-high shoes and a tight yellow skirt. After her, another woman. The judge swivelled this way and that, like she was watching a tennis match.

Ben felt weird, as if he was in some gaming alley watching somebody else's game. Courtroom characters on a PlayStation screen deciding some bad dude's fate.

When it came time for him to enter a plea, the guard had to nudge him.

'How do you plead?' repeated the judge.

'Guilty.'

'In a voice the court can hear.'

'Guilty.' But it was not how Ben had planned it to sound. It should have come out proudly, a guilty that screamed, 'Screw you!'

The judge set a date for sentencing, closed the folder in front of her, blew her nose with a loud, wet sound, and said, 'You may stand down.' Then Ben was being led away. At the courtroom door he turned and gave the DOA finger sign, hoping to claw back some mana after that pathetic plea. He didn't look at his mum, though. He felt really stink about that later.

Beyond

You admit you are guilty and now must pay. I cannot argue with that. Your ancestors lived by such a code. It was called 'utu' – a rule respected by all, which restored the balance and made right the wrong. The cornerstone of collaboration between our people. Were one hapū to infringe on the boundaries of another, violate their women or diminish their mana, then men would go to war to reclaim that which had been taken.

But see, I am getting distracted again. I must continue with the story I had begun to tell. I pick up with a giant floating island spotted by Māori at Poverty Bay in the July of 1769.

What relevance has this to you, you say? 1769. You were not alive. Nor your father or grandfather. And so?

Remember what I said before – connectedness is everything. With this giant floating island the trajectory of your history would change.

The sighting was in fact no odd-shaped island, but a vessel with rig and sail, a barque captained by one Lieutenant James Cook. Such a sight. Can you imagine the fear and wonder of your ancestors? A fair-skinned man towing behind him a whole new civilisation – new tools and technology, religion and recreation, new food and plant life too.

Such a tide of change. So much good and so much bad yoked together for the journey forward. A future of wheat and flour and warm baked bread. Of literacy and learning and innovation. A future of fevers, boils, and unexplained death. Of greed. The musket too. And the white man's way. Auē!

Chapter Fourteen

CARLA

Lorraine from Victim Support drove them back to the farm, Carla in front, Kevin in the back.

The radio crackled, The Warehouse promising everyone a bargain.

Carla worried at a piece of dry skin on her elbow.

They passed the Christmas tree farm, its conifers halfway to Christmas height. The tennis courts, where gorse clawed at the roadside fence. The school, its prefab buildings turning their back on the busy highway.

She felt as if they'd been away for a very long time, the familiar now strangely foreign.

It started to drizzle and the windscreen wipers screeched across the glass, a dead leaf trapped in their clutches.

Lorraine put out a hand. 'You okay?'

Carla nodded.

Then Lorraine was indicating to turn. The car slowed to a standstill. As they waited in the middle of the road for a gap in the traffic, a truck transporting animals to the abattoir overtook them, buffeting the small car and filling it with the stench of ammonia.

They swung into the driveway. The pukeko postbox was still headless. A couple of months back there'd been a spate of incidents with postbox vandals in the area. Kevin hadn't got around to fixing theirs. Now he probably never would.

The car rattled over the gravel driveway lined with bare-limbed willows. The day lilies were also spent, their dry, brown stems standing to attention above the limp, yellowed foliage. Only the flaxes still looked robust, their taupe leaves untouched by the change of season.

As the car emerged from the stark tunnel of trees, the garden opened up.

'Oh, what a lovely place!' Lorraine exclaimed. But autumn had already passed its prime and the garden was turning in on itself, reds and greens making way for dry leaves and fallen splendour.

Carla struggled with the car door.

'Hang on a minute, Carla. It's the central locking.'

Carla continued to rattle impatiently at the handle and finally the door swung open. She leant out of the car just in time to vomit on the lawn.

Lorraine came round to help, holding Carla's hair out of the way with one hand and supporting her forehead with the other. 'It's going to be hard at first,' she said softly.

Carla wiped her mouth with the back of her hand. 'Sorry.' Her palate and nostrils burnt. 'I'm sorry.'

Lorraine led the way into the house, reintroducing them to their home of twenty-seven years. Carla stopped on the threshold. A vase of yellow carnations stood on the console table surrounded by a collection of sympathy cards. Jack's pottery lion had been shifted.

She reached for Kevin's hand and they stepped inside together, the pungent smell of cleaning agents promising bleached memories and sanitised surfaces.

'Your brother Geoffrey tells me the freezer is full,' Lorraine said. 'People have been dropping in meals all week.'

Carla put down her handbag and moved slowly down the corridor. Each room had been faithfully restored, though small clues told that it was strangers who had reordered her life. On the bookshelf, poetry and fiction were mixed up, and the mauve hand towel in the guest bathroom did not match the larger green towels. Dustbins stood naked, minus plastic liners, and the set of pewter frogs on her dressing table had been laid out in a straight line, the new arrangement spelling out a violation.

'Hold on, Kevin. Just a minute,' she heard Lorraine say as the toilet door was pushed open and the toilet seat flung back. Carla pretended she hadn't heard. Kev often couldn't make it to the toilet on time now.

Pulled by some morbid magnet, she continued toward the garage.

She opened the door and scanned the room, her eyes hungry for detail. The air was concrete cold and devoid of any recognisable smell, and the floor stippled with pale patches where chemicals had stripped away dark stains.

Carla knelt down and ran her hand over the concrete.

'Carla? Carla, where have you got to?'

She stood up quickly. 'Coming!' Then she saw it, beside the door handle, midway up the wall – a black dot, no bigger than a five-cent coin, raised like a blob of paint on a canvas. She peered closer and touched it. The scab on the wall came away on her finger, exposing a bright red blotch on the wall beneath.

'There you are,' Lorraine said, bursting into the space.

Quickly Carla slid her hand into her pocket, protecting this last little piece of Jack.

Chapter Fifteen

THE JOURNALIST

Mike Adams picked his way across the overgrown lawn, stepping cautiously over a rusted barbecue grid, warped bicycle wheel, and the deflated crescent of a punctured soccer ball. Two abandoned car wrecks dominated the derelict yard. Inside one of them – a doorless yellow Toyota – sat three children, two in the back, one at the wheel. As Adams approached, they stopped playing and eyed him with a mixture of suspicion and interest.

'Hiya,' he said, lifting his hand in tentative greeting, his shirtsleeve riding high to expose his chunky divers watch.

Dark eyes peered and heads tilted.

'Who're you?' demanded the lean boy in the driver's seat. He looked of school-going age. Dark curls fell to his shoulders. Each rib of his bare chest was delineated by a ripple of skin.

'Who you?' mimicked a little girl in a luminous green T-shirt, snot streaming into her words.

'My name's Mike,' he said, squatting down on his haunches to put him at eye level with the smallest of his audience.

The little girl was now right beside him, quizzically eyeing his white Converse trainers.

'Is your mum home?'

'You mean Miriama?' the older boy said, taking hold of the little girl's hand and yanking her backwards. Adams nodded, standing up again and sliding his hands into his jean pockets.

'Yeah, she's here.' He tossed his head towards the house.

The third kid, who had remained in the car, seized the opportunity to usurp the driver's vacated seat and speedily ensconced himself behind the wheel. But his success was short-lived. As soon as the older boy discovered the insurrection, a squabble ensued and Adams was left to make his own way to the house.

A supermarket trolley overflowing with empty beer bottles guarded the paint-peeled door, the excess scattered across the porch.

A dog growled, startling Adams. The culprit – a suckling mongrel bitch – stood at the end of the veranda, long teats drooping from her mangy frame. Four runts niggled at her, chasing the piggy-pink pendulums of skin.

Adams breathed out. The creature clearly only had energy for a token snarl.

He rapped on the square of frosted glass. A washing machine on spin-cycle whined loudly inside. He knocked again, louder this time, and through the glass saw the silhouette of a woman approaching.

The door opened partway. A barefooted woman in faded jeans and a once-white tee leant out.

'Yup?'

'Mrs Toroa?'

'Who's asking?'

'I'm Mike Adams. *Kia ora.*'

'*Kia ora,*' she replied sardonically, her economical gaze translating into, *And who the fuck might you be?*

'I'm a reporter for the *Herald*. I was wondering if—'

The woman's face tightened and her dark eyes narrowed. 'Not another bloody reporter! Listen up, 'cos I'm only gonna say this once. Get lost!'

Adams intercepted the door as it slammed shut, wincing as his arm broke the force.

'Look, uh. Look, ma'am, I know you must be fed up with the media scrutiny and all,' he said, struggling to hold open the door, 'but I'm writing an article about your son. I want to tell *your* side of the story.'

'You're all the same, you bloody reporters!' she raved, leaning more heavily on the door.

Adams flinched. With his free hand, he fumbled in his back pocket, dropping his wallet onto the ground. 'I'll pay for the inconvenience,' he said, quickly securing the wallet with his foot. The pressure on his arm eased.

Minutes later, and twenty dollars poorer, he found himself inside the sitting room. The place reeked of cigarette smoke and dank mould. He looked around. A naked light bulb hung from the ceiling. Two fist-sized holes decorated the otherwise bare back wall. A stack of empty KFC tubs cluttered one corner. On the table stood a paintbrush in a jar of cloudy purple water, and beside it, an open box of watercolours and an oblong piece of painted card.

Adams removed his sunglasses and sank onto the sofa. Stuffing oozed from the cushion like shaving foam. He picked up the painted piece of card and held it up. His hand was shaking. The painting was unfinished, one corner still the untouched grey of a dismantled cereal box, but advanced enough to be coherent – a marketplace with sagging awnings, crates of overripe fruit, baskets of mottled vegetables. Flies, dogs, a jostle of people. Well-placed dabs of colour for a head, a dress, a gesticulating arm.

'This is good,' Adams said. 'Really good. Who's the artist?'

'Get on with it,' she said, ignoring him. 'If my partner finds you here, you're dead meat.'

Adams licked his lips and pulled himself out of the dip in the couch. He opened his notebook and produced a pen.

'Mrs Toroa—'

'The name is bloody Kāpehu. Never married Ben's father.'

'Oh sorry. I mean, not that you didn't marry, just that I got your name wrong.' Her mouth twitched, barely camouflaging a smile. Adams felt stupid. It wasn't as if he was new to this sort of work. The story had been his initiative, his editor running with the idea. It was a well-worn issue, juvenile crime, but he was good at finding the angle, teasing out different truths. He'd wanted to be a lawyer, but his grades weren't good enough.

'How do you feel having a boy up for murder?'

'Jesus, man! How do you think I feel? Fuckin' over the moon?' She sucked her teeth loudly. 'You fellas are something else.'

Already he'd been lumped with 'you fellas'. . . The first minutes of an interview were everything. He'd already blown it. He was behaving like some junior intern, his apprehension out of all proportion to the task.

'Could you see it coming?' he persisted. 'I mean did you ever get an inkling when he was growing up that—?'

'He's a good boy, my Ben!' she said, her vehemence and passion taking Adams by surprise. 'He just got in with the wrong crowd.'

'I didn't mean to . . .' He averted his eyes, not brave enough to let them accompany his words. 'Murder . . . That's a serious charge.'

She didn't reply.

He looked up. Her taut face had slackened and the hardness had loosened. A shine of water tracked across her eyes.

Adams swallowed.

She must have been pretty once, he thought. She had a high, rounded forehead and full lips. But her hair fell away from a middle parting to drape limply down the sides of her sallow face. She was thirty-three – he knew that from the research he'd done – yet the years had weathered her body and added at least a tatty decade to her.

A baby started to cry.

She didn't move.

'Ben been in much trouble before this?'

She sniggered, exposing discoloured teeth. 'You could say.'

'So did you get help?' he asked abruptly. 'I mean, what did you do to try and stop him?'

She looked momentarily taken aback at Adam's change in tone, then shrugged. 'What could I do? I got other kids to worry about. I clean offices at night. I can't keep them locked up, can I?'

He refused to give her the satisfaction of shaking his head.

'Look,' she said, staring directly into his eyes. 'I'm real sorry for what he's done. For that . . . for that family.' She stopped, chewed the inside of her cheek.

'And your partner. So he's not Ben's father—'

The baby's crying grew louder and more desperate.

'He's a member of a motorcycle gang, isn't he?'

She looked up slowly, her lids lagging. Then she stood up and left the room.

Adams shifted on the couch. Was this his cue to leave? He pulled out his business card and put it on the table.

He was just about to get up when she reappeared, a baby on her hip. The sour smell of a soiled nappy filled the room. She sat down, stuck a hand into her T-shirt and pulled out a drooping breast topped with a large maroon nipple. The baby's mouth hit the bullseye first time and began to suck furiously.

'How old?' Adams asked, trying not to focus on her breast. His wife was expecting. Eight months. Their first.

Kāpehu looked up to the ceiling, as if doing a calculation in her head. ''Bout five months.'

Adams couldn't tell whether it was a boy or girl. 'Very cute,' he said.

She looked down at the baby in a strangely detached way, as though he'd just pointed out something she hadn't noticed before.

'The kids in the yard yours too?'

'Two of 'em,' she said, craning her neck to look out the window. 'Six altogether. Another in the oven.' She tapped her board-flat stomach, then let out a chesty laugh. 'So much for breastfeeding being a contraceptive, eh! You gotta smoke?'

Adams shook his head. He felt a rush of anger at the thought of her smoking while pregnant and breastfeeding. His wife had been so careful to avoid any risk to their unborn child.

She arched her back, fumbled in her jeans pocket, and retrieved a crumpled box of cigarettes. So she had her own!

She pointed to a box of matches on the table, and leaning forward, got him to light one for her.

As she inhaled, the baby came off her nipple and started to cry. Deftly she swung it under her other arm and lined it up with her left breast. Adams wondered where the milk came from; her frame was so spare, her body all chipped and used.

'Any chance Ben could be innocent?'

'Oh for fuck's sake, the boy's 'fessed, hasn't he?' Adams felt the heat spreading through his hair. Another pointless question he'd not even planned to ask. This was a disaster. There was no rapport – a journalist's most important tool. Too much other stuff seemed to be getting in the way.

He stumbled on. 'Have you or Ben's father spoken to him since he's been in custody?'

A car door slammed. 'Sure I have,' she said, pulling the baby off her breast and laying it down on the couch beside her, before emptying the glass of dirty paint water out the window and hurriedly sliding the painted card, paintbrush, and box of paints, under the sofa.

'But it's real difficult 'cos I haven't got no transport, have I?' she said, sitting back down again and picking up her squalling charge. There was a thud and then the sound of footsteps. Adams' eyes met Kāpehu's. His limbs felt suddenly heavy.

A huge man strode into the room.

Adams' eyes widened. Tattooed biceps bulged from under a black sleeveless jacket, and black leather trousers hugged a pair of tree-trunk thighs. Adams took it all in – the steel-capped boots, slit of sunglasses, the tail of greasy hair, and in an instant he was a boy again, cowering in the corner.

'Yo,' the guy said with a grimace, his legs locked astride. 'Visitors, have we?' He removed his sunglasses and his black eyes swung from Adams to Kāpehu, to Adams. 'And who the fuck might you be?' Adams was already on his feet, his notebook squirrelled away, perspiration sucking his blue Polo shirt to his skin in dark wet patches.

116

'Just another bloody Jehovah's Witness,' Kāpehu said, tossing her head with feigned casualness. Adams looked down. His business card was lying on the table. Perspiration trickled down his sideburns onto his cheeks. He stepped forward, trying to obscure it from view. 'Just on my way.'

'Too bloody right, you are.' Adams stumbled as he moved toward the door. Glancing back, he saw the card was gone. He tipped his head at Kāpehu, then turned and hurried out.

As he passed the car with the kids playing inside, the mongrel deserted her litter to snap more seriously at his heels.

He swung a foot at her, leapt over the low wall, and flicked his car remote. Inside, he hit the central locking button, fumbled with the keys, and pulled off; the car lurching in fits and starts down the avenue.

Ten minutes later, and out of state-house territory, he pulled up under a tree, switched off the engine, and remained there until his legs had stopped shaking.

Chapter Sixteen

CARLA

'I hear he's entered a guilty plea, thank God,' Vera said, dabbing at the cake crumbs on her plate with her forefinger. She'd dropped in unannounced, bearing a home-made banana loaf.

They were sitting out on the deck overlooking the garden. It was a grey day, but at least not raining. Although freshly mown, the lawn looked untidy; it had been churned into long ridges of mud where Rangi had got stuck on the ride-on mower. The roses were straggly, their leaves peppered with black spot, and the lavender was dry and woody. Geese had soiled the deck with droppings, and the outdoor cushions had grown fine webs of mould. The roof had sprung a leak in the laundry, the gutters needed clearing, and the swimming pool was a slimy shade of green.

Kevin stuffed a whole slice of banana loaf into his mouth and slurped his tea, spilling clumps of wet cake down his front.

Carla daubed his mouth with a dishtowel. He swiped it away.

'At least there won't be a long trial,' Vera persisted. 'Just the sentencing in the High Court, then.'

Carla nodded. Steve Herbert had advised her against speaking

118

to too many people. 'It'll suffocate you, Carla,' he'd warned. But Vera had a knack of worrying at a loose thread until it eventually unravelled.

'I'm meeting with a real estate agent later,' Carla said, changing the subject. 'It's time to put the farm on the market.'

'Best,' Vera concurred, pouring herself another cup of tea.

Carla regretted refilling the pot.

Later that night, after she and Kevin had finished watching a programme about orangutans in Borneo, Carla readied Kevin for bed. They no longer slept in the same room; Kevin was too fractious and sometimes soiled himself.

'Do you alarm the house at night?' Vera had pried earlier. Carla knew that Vera was really asking whether she was scared of sleeping alone. In truth, nothing frightened her any more. While some victims apparently became paralysed with fear, Carla felt a strange sense of numb detachment. Sometimes it bothered her that her emotions had become so blunted, that she was skimming across the surface of life. She felt like an astronaut adrift in space, unsure of how to get back to the craft, and not even certain she wanted to.

'What did you make of the estate agent?' she asked Kevin, as she unbuttoned his shirt. 'Do you think he's right that the farm won't sell easily because of people's superstitions?' She was still in the habit of running things by Kevin. After a lifetime together, it was a hard habit to break.

'Didn't like his shoes,' Kevin said.

She couldn't decide if this was her old Kev's sense of humour breaking through, or simply the meaningless observation of a brain-damaged fool. She wanted to give him the benefit of the doubt, or at least pretend.

119

She laughed. 'Me neither.'

His quick wit and dry sense of humour had been one of the first things that attracted her to him.

Kevin's shirt dropped to the floor. She hoisted him to his feet to remove his trousers. As he rose, she closed her eyes and kissed him on the mouth, a deep, hungry kiss. His lips were dry and peeling. She leant into him, his bare chest grazing her blouse.

The first time they'd made love was on their wedding night. She'd been both excited and apprehensive. Despite her parents' worldliness, sex was never a topic discussed, her mother in particular keeping a Catholic silence on the matter.

But Kev, the burly farmer with thickset hands and no-nonsense demeanour, had surprised her with his tenderness, and shown her the way. It was to be the start of an incredible love affair, so it felt quite absurd when they couldn't conceive a child; their bodies fitting so perfectly together. Eight years later, when she did eventually fall pregnant, Carla quickly forgave the heartache of those barren years, safe in the knowledge that the child she was carrying had been conceived out of absolute love.

Now Kevin pulled back and pushed her away. She tripped and fell backwards onto the bed. Then he was wiping his mouth with his hand, his big pink tongue slathering over his arm as he tried to rid himself of her kiss. 'You taste bad.'

BEN

It stank inside the Chubb security van, the sharp sweetness of ganja-poking fingers through the rancid stench. Ben scratched his nose with his left hand, his right cuffed to Diamond – a pro lagger who'd been in and out of the boob pretty much all of his life.

Ben watched as Diamond drew on the joint he was smoking. After a while, he couldn't stand it any longer.

'Hey, brotha, give us a toke. I haven't been wasted in forever, man.'

Diamond cocked his head to one side as if he hadn't heard correctly. Then slowly he lifted their conjoined arms, and before Ben could react, brought Ben's arm down like a bullet on the edge of the metal seat.

Pain fired through Ben's arm. He cried out and tried to drag his wrist away, but Diamond held firm. Water pushed out of Ben's eyes and tracked down his pain-hot cheeks. He rocked back and forth, murmuring to himself as he tried to soothe the agony. The thrill of this adventure was fading fast.

Finally the van jolted to a stop.

'We're home, darling,' Ben's companion purred, a loud fart accompanying his words.

A bell. Voices. An intercom. Then the scraping of metal and the van jerked forwards.

Ben peered out of the small windowed cube of light. A tall blue gate was grinding closed. He needed fresh air. He hadn't eaten since breakfast and his wrist was throbbing. A soft bubble of skin had ballooned at the base of his hand, causing him to yelp every time the handcuff rode over it.

The van door swung open and white afternoon light rushed in, stunning him.

'Okay, guys, out!' a guard bellowed.

Ben's travelling companion yanked him forwards and they jumped in unison to the ground.

It was a hot afternoon, yet Ben couldn't stop spasms of shivering from highjacking his body. He was standing in the middle of a long yard. At one end towered an ominous building, its black scoria walls rising up against the sky. The slab of darkness was interrupted only by chalky bird droppings, which tracked down the wall like white tears. At the opposite end of the yard stood the arch they'd just driven through. Topped with silvered hoops of barbed wire and a sun-bleached flag, it straddled the gated entrance to Mount Eden Remand Prison.

A pigeon swooped low. Ben felt the wind from it wings. It circled once, then landed on a ledge of the black building, between the vertical bars of a window.

The sun ducked behind a cloud, importing a gloom more in keeping with the grim surrounds. The gate screeched again. Ben turned. Another van was pulling in to the yard. With any luck Tate would be in this one.

The two had been apart since Tate's arrest, catching only corridor glimpses of each other at Auckland Central. The police had told Ben his accomplice had 'spilt the beans and bleated like a baby'. After that, there'd seemed little point in denying the charges. Only later did he learn he'd been duped. Tate hadn't cooperated at all, and Ben had dropped them both in it.

A squalling noise like the sound of cats fighting came from above. Ben looked up. An arm covered in tattoos was reaching out between the bars and throwing signs. 'Come here, sweetie! Come, come, come.' A coldness thudded up his throat.

'Welcome to Mount Eden Prison.' A female officer dressed in an olive-coloured uniform with a coffee-brown tie stood in front of them, her legs apart, her arms packed neatly behind her. Three diamond studs ran up her right earlobe. An enormous bunch of keys more suited to a dungeon hung from a chain on her belt. Another guard, this one the size of a nightclub bouncer, stood behind her, like some grotesque shadow.

'The first thing you need to know is that Mount Eden is a transit prison,' she said briskly. 'Which means you will only be kept here while on remand. You will *not* be staying once you have been sentenced, so don't get too comfortable. You *will* be moved on.'

At the receiving office, Ben was assigned a number. He was told to remove any 'instruments of suicide' – his belt and the laces from his trainers. After that, his jeans kept riding down over his butt and his trainers slopped on and off when he walked. His few possessions were packed into a large brown paper bag, and an officer wearing a pair of latex gloves handed Ben his bedding, a grey tracksuit, and a copy of the prison rules. 'Stick to them rules and your stay with us will be a happy one.'

Ben held up the piece of paper and squinted at the meaningless squiggles.

At the medical station, he got undressed behind a curtain, keeping on his trainers. The nurse, a red-faced woman with enormous breasts, weighed him, listened to his chest, examined his hair for lice, then made him piss in a pot.

She eyed his Nike trainers. They were new, bought with money from the farmhouse haul.

'I'm not leaving my trainers in some paper bag,' Ben said, pre-empting any request to remove them.

'First time in prison?' she said with a knowing smile.

He stared at her.

'You can keep those shoes, son, for as long as you can hold onto them.'

He relaxed his jaw. 'I think my hand's broke, miss.'

She lifted his wrist with her gloved hands and examined the blue-black bulge. 'How did it happen?'

He shrugged.

She eyeballed him sideways, before carefully moving his hand up and down.

'Jesus!'

'Don't think it's broken,' she said, releasing it. 'Just bruised. Now tell me, is your family mad at you for what you've done? Are they still speaking to you?'

He nodded. She ticked a box on a clipboard. He didn't know whether the tick was for *mad at you* or the *still speaking to you* question. He didn't care.

'Ever thought of harming yourself?'

She must have taken his silence for a yes, because he spent the first night in a Special Needs unit in a stitch gown.

'Can't be ripped, so don't try.'

The green lino walls had no corners, one curving smoothly into another. It felt as if he was locked inside some giant ball, just how he imagined it would be inside the ZORB at Rotorua. Simi's brother lived in the sulphur-smelling city, and once he'd shouted Simi a ride in the giant, tumbling ball. It had sounded intense – 'the most awesome ride ever'– rolling down a hillside, the outside world spinning away until there was just bellyaching laughter left.

But this green room was no fun ride. Ben looked around. A steel bed stood against the curve of wall. Under it was a disposable cardboard potty. On the ceiling was a bonnet of black glass with a flashing red light that winked at him every twenty-six seconds. And every fifteen minutes a guard pressed his face up to the small window in the door. The light was left on all night. Ben was glad for this though, even if it did shine into his sleep and wind itself around his dreams. Darkness was scarier.

Next morning he was permitted one free phone call. He called his mum.

'You okay, boy?'

'Yeah . . . Hey, Ma, don't forget to visit. You gotta call 0800VISITS. Tell them to get me to make an appointment or they won't let you in. You hear me?'

'Sure thing, baby.'

'Also money for food, a TV, and a radio.'

'Who do you think I am? Fuckin' Santa Claus?'

He could hear the other kids screaming in the background; the loudest squeal was probably Cody.

'I gotta go,' she said after a long pause.

'Yeah.'

'Look after yourself, Benjamin, boy. You hear me?'

'Sure.'

Then the phone went dead.

Beyond

The law. You must be chewing on that now, boy. Or perhaps your own small world is still wrapped too tightly around you, like an unfurled koru, *and you cannot see beyond it.*

I was talking about the law when last I left off. I keep on, even though you do not yet hear me. What I hope for is that my words reach you on a dream, words that find and mend the severed cord, which catapulted you into this darkness.

New people arrived on this land – white settlers and those men left here for months at a time to catch our seals and harpoon our whales. And with them came an unruliness we had not experienced before – a disorder fuelled by alcohol, greed, and a lust for women.

Even some of our own, usually those living along the coastline of this beautiful land and so the first to come into contact with this new pale tribe, were sucked into the downward spiral, trading their wives and daughters, and land they did not individually own, for the musket. The musket – a weapon which surpassed all others. A weapon that promised power.

The British Crown held some concerns for the 'indigenous' people, as they were wont to call us. However, of greater alarm to them was the competition amongst crooked land agents and nations hungry for this 'new' and valuable country. The Crown had to have control. So in haste a treaty was drawn up which would give the Queen the right to impose her law on this far-flung place and the singular right to buy our land.

And somewhere, woven in amongst the words, was also the intent to safeguard our interests . . .

Chapter Seventeen

CARLA

Carla looked out of the window at the chain of identical townhouses reaching down the slope of freshly turned earth. With echoes of British council housing, another row rose up behind these in a paler hue. And behind these, another, and then another, the cancer finally curtailed by a main road, which carved a thoroughfare through them.

The farm had not sold easily, as the agent had predicted. The market was flagging, and trying to sell a farm that had once been the scene of a murder *was* a big ask. Carla felt as if she was selling off some stained, second-hand garment.

A developer finally bought it, haggling her down to well below the government valuation. 'Love to offer you more, Mrs Reid. I really would. But my hands are tied. I'll barely recover costs. People are superstitious creatures, you know, and the farm is very run-down.'

Her agent advised her to accept. It was the only offer they'd received and he was right, the place was run-down. The garden had reverted to weeds and the charm of the homestead had long since expired. Then again, a farm in the fastest-growing district in the country should not have needed charm to sell. But Carla was tired. And she needed the money; the farm's finances had been in a worse state than Kevin had ever let on. Learning of his secrecy had come as yet another blow, further eroding the certainty of the past. She offered Rangi and Rebecca most of the stock in lieu of money owed them, and accepted the developer's bid. Later, she learnt that he'd got council approval to subdivide the land into ten lots, selling on each for more than he'd paid her for the entire farm. But she didn't curse or despair, instead, simply mused at the parallels it reflected in her life – the whole butchered, the remainder a corpse of disconnected fragments.

She decided on Unit 32C in a morning, putting in an offer at midday and by four o'clock, owning the unit. It was all she could afford, and the position meant she'd be close to The Bays and therefore to Kevin.

His specialists, concerned that the additional stress would be detrimental to his precarious state of mind, had advised her to put Kevin in respite care before packing up. It would also give Carla a much-needed break. She hadn't been able to afford a night nurse, and by the time the move had come round, was exhausted. At first she'd baulked at the idea of putting him in care. It meant she was opting out, dispensing with her marriage vows – *for better or for worse, in sickness and in health*. Yet The Bays offered something better than anything she could ever muster.

Kevin didn't even look up when she left him there that first day, the institutional aroma of cabbage and mince already vying for his limited attention.

She phoned later to check on him. The nurse reported that he'd been asking for Carla all afternoon, but advised against speaking with him, warning it would only upset Kevin further.

Carla replaced the receiver and stood alone in her new lounge, cardboard packing boxes piled high around her. She'd managed to reduce the moving costs by opting to unpack herself. Vera and Bev did offer to help, but she'd declined. Anything and everything once precious to her had been fingered and handled, inspected and analysed. She needed to stop the relentless scrutiny, the vulgar dissection of her life. No one other than she would unpack her belongings. There wasn't much anyway. She'd been ruthless about getting rid of stuff, with the exception of Jack's things.

After locating the kettle in the 'smoko' box, Carla made herself a cup of tea, then sank down onto the new cappuccino-coloured carpet and picked at one of Bev's salmon and cucumber sandwiches. Already she yearned for the heady cocktail of the family home – polished parquet floors, woodsmoke, cow manure, and old-fashioned roses. Her new apartment with its thin walls, budget kitchen, and Pacifica wool-mix carpet, was devoid of soul. She could have been posing inside some generic housing catalogue.

She tried to force out tears, but none came, only a silly barking noise. How she longed to cry, yet even that release was denied her. She lay back on the floor and stared up at the low ceiling, eventually drifting off to sleep.

She awoke with a jolt, her chin wet with drool and one arm thick with pins and needles. The smell of fish was strong in her nostrils – a half-eaten salmon sandwich lay beside her on the carpet, the dry bread curling up at the corners.

Carla sat up and took a swig of cold tea, flushing the scum of sleep off her tongue. Outside, it was already dark. Through the walls, she could hear the muffled tones of the evening news. She rubbed her eyes and squinted at her watch – 6:12 p.m. Slowly she got up, her body holding onto the awkward position in which she had fallen asleep, and she shuffled through the small apartment. 'Compact' was the word the agent had used. She felt the loss of her history acutely – the holes in the walls where she'd impatiently guessed at stud positions when hanging a picture; the golden stains blooming over her oven window; the layer of ash in the fireplace grate; the picture window which led the eye into a garden of birthday parties. The history of a home.

Her solitariness was unsettling. She'd lived alone before, but of her own choice as a rebellious and determined young student. Now the solitude had been thrust upon her and she longed for the very connection, company, and oversight she had once shunned.

She wandered into the kitchen. Fingers of white light from her neighbour's kitchen just metres away poked into the room. The proximity to strangers felt uncomfortable.

Carla switched on her own light, the neon strip stuttering to attention, and fiddled with the venetian blind. It dropped a few centimetres, then jammed. While adjusting the cord, she peered out of the window. A small hand was wiping clear a porthole on the steamed-up window opposite, in which an Asian woman's smiling face appeared. Carla successfully dropped the blind.

The next month passed in a haze of broken sleep and mercurial moods. Nights seeped into mornings, and mornings into afternoons. When asleep, Carla was plagued by disturbing dreams, and when awake, by questions. What if she'd secured the garage door that night? What if she hadn't invited Jack over for their anniversary dinner? What if they'd gone to a restaurant instead? Why had she uttered those final cruel words to him? What did it matter if he wanted to live in the city? What if . . . ? Why . . . ? If only . . .

Food and hygiene became incidental, Carla's body gradually losing the plumpness and turgor of well-being. She went outdoors only when she had to, and used the answering machine to bounce unexpected callers. Unable to concentrate for any length of time, she gave up on reading and turned to television, often watching mindlessly for hours at a time.

One night she awoke from a feverish dream, her body wet with perspiration and her bedclothes in disarray. The red numbers of the bedside clock fluoresced in the blackness. It was just after three. Her bladder was full.

The bathroom light was unforgiving, her gaunt reflection made even more unattractive by the craters of rust already pitting the cheap cabinet mirror like acne scars. Wide-awake, she shuffled down the hall to make a warm drink, and was startled to discover her kitchen again illuminated by her neighbour's intrusive light. It was three in the morning!

She peered through the glass. There was the woman again; her back turned this time, and rocking an infant on her hip. Carla had bumped into her neighbour once when she'd been putting out the rubbish. They'd introduced themselves and exchanged simple niceties, but when 'Mingyu' had invited her over for tea, Carla had quickly made an excuse. After that, she was careful to venture outdoors only when she knew she was unlikely to meet the petite Asian lady.

The scene now before her transported Carla back to the night-time vigils she and Kevin endured after Jack's birth. It had taken a full three years before they'd managed to get an uninterrupted night's sleep. Exhausted and robbed of her sanity and good humour, Carla had found herself resenting the colicky bundle she'd waited so long for. In the end, it was her faith, and Kevin's quiet support, which got her through.

Carla had always kept a strong faith. It did not really fit into the prescribed Catholic mould of her Italian upbringing, but was rather a distillation of many religions, a code of living, a reassurance that the force of good would ultimately win out.

Kevin, on the other hand, was a self-proclaimed atheist when she met him. Stonehearted nuns had marred his childhood in a Catholic boarding school. Being locked in cupboards, beaten for minor misdemeanours, and worse, had served to permanently taint the notion of religion for him. As far as he was concerned, God, if there was indeed a deity, had failed him.

Over the course of their marriage, however, Kevin mellowed. Perhaps it was Carla's quiet conviction that finally enlisted him. And while he never openly admitted it, she suspected that in recent years he'd come to even share some of her beliefs.

Carla slammed down the mug in her hand and turned off the kettle. The irony. Kevin had been right all along. Religion was a nonsense. A fiction to make the pain of a random existence seem purposeful.

She opened the bread bin and put a hand into its cool cavity. Then her fingers were wrapping around her secret. The absurdity of hiding the bottle was apparent to her. There was no one to hide it from, only 'the other Carla', the one she pretended she still was.

Impatiently, she fumbled with the cap before filling her mug with the clear colourless liquor.

The first mouthful shocked, the second numbed, and by the third, the angles and edges of her life were being sanded and smoothed.

Chapter Eighteen

THE JOURNALIST

Mike Adams sat at his PC, trying to fulfil the three-thousand-word brief. He wanted the piece out of the way and done with. His wife was at a baby shower, so the evening was all his; he had no excuse. Yet the story refused to flow, every phrase vetoed en route to the screen.

Word count: 207.

He stood up and rammed his chair back under the desk. The computer screen flickered, threatening to shut down. The Word document reappeared. Adams quickly pressed *Save*.

Out of the apartment window the black cone of Rangitoto Island was silhouetted against a bleeding sky. Very apt, he thought. That's what Rangitoto meant in Māori – 'bloody sky'. So he hadn't forgotten everything he'd been taught.

He loved their tiny apartment for the view alone. Rangitoto was as haunting as the *Mona Lisa*, revealing the same silhouette irrespective of the viewer's vantage. He always felt a calm come over him when gazing upon the dormant volcano. It never failed to take him outside of himself and make him feel part of something bigger.

The smell of lamb vindaloo wafted up from the takeaway below. He was hungry. He grabbed his wallet and headed for the door.

'Fifteen minutes,' said the little Indian man with Dr Spock ears. So Adams decided to take a stroll along the waterfront instead of paging through out-of-date magazines.

It was high tide and waves pounded against the sea wall, spraying a cool, briny mist over him. It felt surprising, the wetness, in contrast to the stale air of the apartment. It felt real.

The sound of a bicycle bell jolted him out of his reverie; he'd crossed into the cycle lane.

'Keep your hair on!' he shouted after the orange Lycra apparition, even though he knew he'd been in the wrong. But he was unsettled and angry. The interview with Toroa's mother had been a disaster. His worst. And he'd nearly got thumped in the process. More than that, though, it felt as if the very ground under him had shifted. His journalistic aspirations seemed suddenly artificial and academic. It had been a strange past few weeks as it was, with the pending arrival of their first child ushering in a raft of powerful emotions and a period of self-scrutiny.

What had he hoped to achieve interviewing her? Give the underdog a voice? Identify the reason criminals were becoming younger and younger? Instigate some social reform?

Had he really believed he could write something of depth that would inspire people to stop, think, and even change? He'd once aspired to becoming a lawyer – been in love with the notion of helping his fellow man. Who was he fooling? A career in law had all the allure of *Pākehā* prestige and offered a safe distance from his past. When he didn't get into Law School, he opted for journalism, espousing the same idealistic motivations. Perhaps his intentions had once been pure, however they'd long since been buried beneath a much stronger drive – to sell the story, impress with the manipulation of words, win awards. Those were the real sirens leading him on and gradually eroding his integrity.

Today's interview had been different. It had unexpectedly pierced his carefully cultivated mantle.

Adams thought back to the afternoon. He felt confused and conflicted about it. He was angry with the woman for smoking when she had a baby on the way. For even having another child when she'd already had six, one of whom was a murderer.

Yet the purple bruises encircling her arms, they troubled him. And her tired, pregnant body. The vehemence in her voice too, when she spoke about her son. It reminded him of . . .

And she painted! He shook his head and laughed out loud. An elderly couple out walking their dog turned and stared.

Miriama Kāpehu painted. Beautifully. Despite all the crap in her life, she still painted.

He was frustrated with himself for losing his objectivity, for letting emotions cloud the journalistic process. He was also angry at his own dishonesty.

His mum.

He hadn't thought about her in the longest time.

The waves sucked his thoughts out to sea, then brought them crashing back.

It was too hard – the confusing debate in his head. Had he been fooling himself all this time?

Suddenly he felt unanchored and lost. He had a child on the way. He owed it authenticity. Owed it a code of living he subscribed to, not merely paid lip service to. But who was he? What was he? He'd turned his back on his heritage. That surely spoke louder than three thousand words.

He stopped and stood in the shadow of a giant pohutakawa tree. Three night-kayakers were carving lines through the moon-silvered water. A girl jogged past, her blonde ponytail swinging from side to side, then a couple passed pushing a pram. This was the sedate Mission Bay landscape he and his wife had bought into. He'd thought he belonged. He'd worked hard enough to lose any trace of his upbringing, to lose the shame. He sniggered. Even his Māori greeting with Kāpehu had clunked awkwardly.

Adams turned and wandered back along the water, catching glimpses of *Pākehā* lives through warmly lit windows. At the restaurant, he collected his order and headed back to his apartment, but the turmeric-stained container never got opened. He had lost his appetite.

Chapter Nineteen

CARLA

'Miss Carla. Miss Carla. You inside?'

The thumping woke Carla. She groaned and rolled over.

'Miss Carla?' the high-pitched voice persisted.

Carla pulled herself upright, a crack spreading through her head like expanding concrete. 'One minute!'

She lurched towards the door, one foot sinking lower than expected, the other rising too high in compensation. She fiddled with the deadlock and finally succeeded in opening the door.

Her neighbour, Mingyu, stood in the hallway, her perfectly oval face creased with concern. There followed an uncomfortable pause.

'Hau, Miss Carla, you fine? You not look so good.'

'Yes I'm fine,' Carla said irritably. 'Thank you.'

Mingyu stepped back out of the reach of Carla's breath.

'What is it?' Carla asked.

'Is two o'clock in the pm. I'm worry because your garbage is not outside. The truck, already he come. I think maybe you are sick, no? You up very late last night. I see your light.'

'No, I'm not sick. I just slept in.'

The petite woman craned her neck to see past Carla, her eyes narrowing on the empty vodka bottle on the floor.

Irked by her neighbour's nosiness, Carla made to close the door when Mingyu smiled and quickly said, 'You like cup of tea?'

Carla hesitated. Her first impulse was to decline. Something stopped her. Perhaps it was the thought of the door to her duplex closing once again to leave her alone with just her damaged thoughts for company. Perhaps it was the fear that she would reach for another bottle.

'That sounds nice,' she managed, careful to enunciate each word.

Her neighbour grabbed her hand excitedly. She had very delicate, cool hands.

'I'll just put on shoes.'

There was a neat row of footwear outside Mingyu's door, so Carla removed the sandals she'd just put on.

Her neighbour's apartment had the same layout as hers, however being a corner unit, got more sunlight. The chrome light fittings and black-leather furnishings were not to Carla's taste, yet were strangely comforting in their difference.

It smelt different too – of people, and apples, and real living. And the windows were open, so the air felt new. There were three large red apples in a wire fruit bowl on the bench top, a cloud of fruit flies proof that they were not ornamental. A radio played softly and a dishwasher sloshed and gurgled in the background. In the middle of the living room stood an ironing board, and beside it, a plastic basket piled high with crumpled washing. Carla took it all in.

A pressure cooker started to whistle, startling her. The steam released was sweet and meaty.

'Mmh, smells good,' she said, feeling almost hungry. 'What are you cooking?'

'I make leek and pork soup,' Mingyu said, beaming. 'My baby, she start to eat solid and like very much.'

As if on cue, they heard a little grunt coming from behind the laundry basket. Carla peered over to see an infant laid out on a sheepskin rug. It was a baby girl, her features as delicate as an orchid in first bloom, her hair a wispy black mohawk. She was sucking her toes and pulling on a mint-green bra, which was hanging over the side of the washing basket.

'Hello, little one,' Carla said, bending down to tickle its feet. The baby's skin was the colour of toffee. 'How old are you?'

The infant's face puckered, her bottom lip quivered, and then she let out an almighty wail.

'Six month on Friday,' Mingyu said, hoisting her up and smothering the child in kisses.

Carla drank in the scene before her – the splodgy sound of lips on skin, the smell of baby shampoo and talcum powder, the little feet and dumpling toes. Then her heart was racing and panic was climbing up her throat. She needed air. Needed to get out of this place. It was too confronting. She had to get back to the security of her own apartment. Back to where her emotions could be kept in check.

Her eyes swept around the room and out of the window to her own kitchen. It was strange to see it from this vantage point. She half-expected to see herself standing there beside the bench, sipping a mug of tea.

But the room was dark and empty.

She didn't want to go back.

Not yet.

'Green tea or English Breakfast?' Mingyu asked, touching Carla lightly on the elbow. 'I'm not good at make coffee, sorry.'

'Green,' Carla said without thinking. She hated the taste of green tea, but she'd been distracted by the fingers on her elbow, the brush of another's skin, the imprint of warmth.

Mingyu covered the dining table with a white lace cloth and poured tea into willow-patterned bone china cups.

The tea was unexpectedly bland at first, each sip amounting to nothing, yet the amalgamation surprisingly satisfying. Carla had two cups and three almond tuiles. Everything was so delicate and genteel; she felt quite grotesque in comparison.

'You not happy.'

She was caught off guard by her neighbour's directness. She hadn't been prepared for anything more than light, courteous chatter.

Carla pretended to misunderstand. 'No, the tea is lovely. So, how long have you been in New Zealand?'

Mingyu fixed her with a no-nonsense stare. 'You are pretty lady. Too thin, but pretty. Why you live alone? Why no one visit?'

Something in Mingyu's childlike, uncomplicated concern cracked Carla wide open, and before she could stop it, the flotsam and jetsam of her life gushed out.

For a long while she huddled in the crook of her neighbour's arm, crying quietly, while Mingyu rubbed her back and murmured foreign words that soothed and calmed.

Chapter Twenty

BEN

Jocko was about forty-five. He had a red face, brassy-yellow hair, and a belly that hung over his belt distorting the tattoo of a serpent. He didn't talk much and sucked his teeth continuously. When he did talk, it was with a fast rise-and-fall Scouse accent. He was also in the habit of keeping the television on full volume till lights out. On the plus side, at least Ben had scored a cellmate with a TV.

Jocko, however, was not as content with the match. He cussed and complained for days before finally settling into a sulky resignation. The first thing he did was draw up a list of rules, which Ben was warned to abide by if he didn't want to cop a hiding. Rule One dictated that Ben face the wall whenever Jocko was using the toilet, this ordeal sometimes lasting for up to an hour. Ben was also forbidden from climbing off his top bunk after lights out, which meant he had to relieve himself in an L&P bottle if the need arose.

The cell, with its pitted concrete floor and metal bunks, was pretty sparse, except for Jocko's few posters of semi-naked women. One small basin, discoloured by a yellow stain where a non-stop drip had left its name, hung off the back wall beside the toilet with its broken black seat. High in the wall was a small window that sometimes let in cold stripes of sunlight – the warmth long since sucked out of them.

Ben barely slept his first night on East Block. For one, he couldn't get warm. A guard told him he could put in a special request for an extra blanket if he wanted, or get his family to bring in warmer clothes. But it wasn't just the cold keeping Ben awake. He was scared . . . of the next day . . . of the bash . . . Being a member of the DOAs didn't feel quite so cool any more. Those long empty days at home had never looked so appealing.

He'd been awake forever when the morning buzzer finally sounded and a wave of clanging metal moved down the corridor as the guards conducted their first muster of the day. Inmates spilt noisily out of their cells into the passageway.

Ben decided against a shower, unsure whether the rumours about what happened in boob bathrooms were true. Instead, he swung over to the trestle table where breakfast was being served. The porridge smelt good. He collected his bowl and plastic spoon and looked around for somewhere to sit.

'Back to your cell. Lockdown again till eight,' barked a huge Samoan guy sporting a tall chef's hat.

So Ben settled himself back on his bunk with his breakfast. The porridge slipped easily into his stomach. Five spoonfuls and it was finished.

'Seconds?' Jocko burst out laughing, his mouth wet and red, his swollen belly stiffening as if about to burst. 'This ain't no holiday camp!'

At eight their cell was unlocked again and Ben joined the queue of East Block boys as they were led through a run of gates into an exercise yard.

The sunlight was a rude shock after a day inside. Ben rubbed his eyes and looked around. An almost invisible ceiling of fine wire mesh covered the yard. It was so fine that if he closed an eye the roof of the coop disappeared into the cloudless blue. Contraband thrown from Grafton Road met a wasted fate here. Fifteen-metre-high walls topped with rounds of barbed wire bordered the space. Snagged T-shirts and punctured balls hung like trapped insects in the web of wire.

The inmates broke off into small groups.

Ben headed for the benches at the far end, trying his best to look nonchalant. The morning heat helped, soon melting his tight innards. But he still kept a skittish eye out for what was going on around him.

'Yo. Nice trainers.'

Ben squinted into the sun. Then the light was eclipsed.

'Roach sends his compliments.'

Ben turned to walk away.

A hand hauled him back. 'He don't much like being ignored.'

Ben shook off the heavy's grip.

'He'd like you to join him behind the privacy wall.'

His first thought was to run, but where? He was locked in to this space till eleven. He shot an eye up to the bridge where the screws kept lookout. The windows of the tower were made of one-way glass, so he couldn't even see if anyone up there was actually looking his way. He figured if he just stayed in full view, nothing too bad could happen.

From nowhere, a huddle of bodies materialised and quickly surrounded him. They were so close he could smell their sweat. They chatted and fooled among themselves – an innocent gathering to the onlooker's eye – as they jostled Ben toward the prefab privacy wall.

Behind the wall were two toilets. Sitting on the lid of one was a scrawny guy covered in ink. His most striking tattoo was on his forehead – a dagger dripping blue blood onto his right eyelid.

'The noob with the trainers,' was Ben's introduction.

'Just get the fuckin' shoes.'

Ben turned to gap it, but his breath was stolen by a king hit, and by the time the guards saw his body poking out from under the privacy wall, the pack had long since scattered.

'Code One, remand yard! Code One, remand yard!'

He spent eight days in the sickbay with a broken nose and a cracked jaw, sipping meals through a bendy pink straw. When an enquiry into the incident was lodged, he said he'd tripped and hit his head. He didn't need any survival guide to know this was the correct answer. And the Nikes fitted Roach perfectly.

Beyond

The inmates took something of yours, Benjamin. They stole your shoes, just as you stole a life not yours to take, and just as your ancestors were robbed of their land by white men with muskets. You tried to fight back. Your fellow inmates were stronger and you succumbed. Life throws up such patterns all the time.

Why do I continue to watch over you and feel the pain of your lowly life when matters of the flesh are no longer mine? I am at one with this universe, with the silent coves of the Marlborough Sounds, the golden grasslands of the Aoraki, the shimmering waters of Kaikoura's coast. I am the call of the weka and the cry of a morepork. I am the shudder and boom of thunder. The sound and the silence of this earth and sky. I am complete.

My answer is simple, boy. I watch over you because you are a part of me and me of you. The same thread binds us, earth to earthling, sky to soul. We are different phases of the same. And though you have been cut loose of this connection, I stay, for a reason that goes beyond you, into the future. You see, if you remain cut loose from your culture, so will your descendants, and so will theirs.

Back then to my story. 1840. Beside the River of Waitangi where the Treaty I was telling you about was so hastily drawn up. A pact between the English and your ancestors, and signed by many Māori chiefs in the belief it promised cooperation and respect. But . . . Yes, there is a 'but'. There were two versions of this seminal document — two translations, two understandings. Two misunderstandings.

Chapter Twenty-One

CARLA

Kevin had his back to the door when Carla walked in. He was finishing his lunch and the smell of fish pie clung to the walls of his cubicle.

'My darling,' she whispered, kissing the top of his head. His hair hadn't grown back over the scar – the purple fleshy ridge rising up like a railway track between his sparse greying bristles.

He looked up, bemused. 'I've had enough. Take it away.' As Carla lifted the tray, her elbow accidentally toppled his pink plastic mug, flooding the leftover mash with redcurrant cordial.

'Now look what you've done, you silly woman!' he burst out. 'You've got no business working here if you can't do the job properly. What's more, I know you've been fornicating with Mr Meady in Room Twelve. He told me. You're just a whore.'

'Stop it, Kevin! Stop! It's me, Carla.' She fought to keep her voice steady. 'Me! Remember the farm? *The Willows*? Rangi and Rebecca? Do you remember our son, Jack?'

Some days he was lucid, other days so confused. And lately, it seemed that he was having more bad days than good. He had so little reserve, that any ailment – a simple urinary tract infection or even just a head cold – could tip him into delirium.

'Pah!' he exclaimed, fiddling furiously with his dressing-gown cord.

'They've put the thugs away,' she said slowly, sitting down next to him. 'The ones who did this to you, my darling. Fourteen years for one. Nineteen for the other.'

It was the first day of the rest of their lives, she told him. They had to grasp what had been given them, accept it, and move on.

Kevin rubbed his nose roughly and stared ahead.

'Look what I've brought,' she said after a time, delving into an old Farmers plastic bag to retrieve two scrunched balls of tissue paper.

Kevin looked on with eye-protruding fascination. Carefully she unwrapped them, smoothing out the creases in the paper with meticulous attention. Then she placed first one, and then another crystal glass on the side table.

'I thought we could share a drink together, just like old times. Toast the future. Look at maybe getting you back home with me. What about it?'

Without waiting for a reply, she lifted out a bottle of sherry and poured two generous glasses. 'I love you, Kevin. I love you, for ever,' she said, handing him a glass.

He eyed it quizzically before tipping his head back and swallowing the liquor in one wet gulp. Surprise splashed across his face as the alcohol gushed unhindered down his windpipe, and before Carla had time to take a sip herself, Kevin's swig had been rerouted and sprayed all over her clothes with a vigorous cough.

'Oh, Kevin!' she cried, dabbing at the sticky maroon liquid.

Kevin coughed again, and again, and again, his face turning

puce, then dusky. He hauled himself up and stumbled around the room.

Carla chased after him, trying to slap him on the back as his coughing turned strangulated and feeble.

Panicking, she leant on the emergency button, before running out into the corridor. 'Help! Somebody, quick! My husband. He's choking!' Kevin was prostrate on the floor by the time the two nurse-aides burst into the room, one carrying a large cylinder of oxygen. They knelt down beside him and tilted his chin upwards, forcing his mouth open to check for an obstruction.

'It was ju-ju-just the drink,' Carla stuttered, pointing to the bottle of sherry.

'He didn't choke on his food?'

Carla shook her head.

The nurse slammed an oxygen mask over Kevin's blue lips and rolled him onto his side.

'I must reiterate, Mrs Reid, that this sort of behaviour is totally unacceptable.'

Carla was sitting in Tracy Lomax's office. The manager, a parrot of a woman with a tight blonde bun, was lodged behind her vast mahogany desk. She peered at Carla from around an oversized arrangement of fake magnolias.

'The rules we have here are in place for a purpose. Our responsibility is first and foremost to our patients, all of whom, as you well know, have suffered from some sort of head injury. With temperaments labile and reflexes impaired, alcohol is forbidden. Absolutely forbidden!'

'I'm so sorry, Tracy. It's just that I wanted to . . .' Carla stopped.

Tracy arranged a conciliatory smile. 'Fortunately, this has not had a dire outcome, but I'd leave Kevin to sleep right now; he's had more than enough excitement for one day. The doctor will check him over a little later.'

'Do you think—?' Carla leant forward in her seat. 'Tracy, do you think Kevin will ever be able to come back home to live with me?'

The hospital manager took off her glasses and fixed Carla with a sobering stare. 'Mrs Reid . . . Carla,' she said slowly, 'I do not believe you would be able to cope with Kevin on your own. Not unless a huge amount of additional support was put in place, which would be incredibly expensive to sustain on a long-term basis. ACC wouldn't cover a half of it.'

She paused. 'Kevin is not doing as well as we'd hoped, especially following the second brain bleed.'

Carla scanned the woman's words for hope.

'Look, we are having a team meeting later this month with the doctors, physios and OTs. I'll put it out there. My feeling is that you won't manage on your own. He really has deteriorated. I personally don't believe Kevin will be able to live independently again.' Carla nodded robotically and stood up, muttering another apology as she backed out of the office.

'I am obliged to file an incident report,' Tracy called after her.

'I understand.'

Carla wandered down the corridors, passing the open doors of other residents' rooms – peep shows on broken lives.

She drove home not seeing the road, instead navigating the troubled highways of her mind, and it was only when she turned into the driveway of *Willowlands Residential Park* that she realised she had driven back to the farm and not her apartment.

Reluctant to reverse onto the busy highway, she motored on

through the new subdivision with its schist pillars, landscaped driveway, and imported date palms. She came to a roundabout where the old barn had once stood. Distracted, she let the car veer towards the grassy bank, before suddenly overcorrecting. The wheels spun on the loose gravel and the car glided across the road, mounted the opposite verge and came to an abrupt halt.

Carla was shaking as she climbed out and steadied herself against the hot, dusty car. Her surrounds came into focus. She was disorientated. Her breathing picked up. The pieces of a familiar jigsaw were all jumbled up.

Surfaced roads. Missing trees. Absent fences. New homes sprawling over freshly turned earth. The dam now bordered by sandstone pavers. An ornamental boulder rising out of the water like the artificial whale at Kelly Tarlton's aquarium. DOC-green benches dotted around the brackish water, lending the place a park-like feel. A large red sign warning off children unaccompanied by an adult – a far cry from Jack's carefree afternoons spent catching eels and guppies, no adult in sight.

She wandered down the road towards one of the new houses – a Spanish monolith, all turrets and arches and terracotta tiles. She could just imagine the real estate jargon: *Hear the castanets as you sip sangria on the deck and watch the sun set behind majestic hills!*

A token willow tree had been left standing. The rest were now stumps poking through the land like amputated fingers. The house was obviously empty, save for a lone tradesman working on the guttering.

Carla lifted her skirt and hoisted herself over the fence, the freshly painted creosote blackening her thighs. She made her way around the perimeter of the newly demarcated property to the foot of the hill on the other side. Overgrown gorse and wild

153

blackberries left angry welts on her ankles as she scrambled up the rise, her city-idle legs tiring quickly.

She'd forgotten about the summer screech of cicadas, the din now competing with the growl and whine of a distant digger, and the *tap tap tap* of a solitary hammer.

Her heart started hammering in her throat and not just because she was unfit; she knew she should turn back and preserve the picture she held in her mind. But her legs kept moving, carrying her up to the top of the knoll. She had to see for herself. She had to.

Even though Carla had prepared herself for the inevitable, it still came as a shock, and when she saw it, she crumpled to the ground.

'I hate you!' she screamed, curling up on the dry, prickly grass. 'I hate you!'

The farmhouse was gone. She knew it would be. In its place was a rectangle of rubble bordered by a band of fluorescent orange plastic, from which hung the sign *Trespassers Will Be Prosecuted*.

It was the only place in the apartment suitable; new homes weren't built with the high studs of older buildings. The rail ran across the bathroom from the pockmarked mirror to the opposite wall. It was a structural support, but also handy for hanging wet washing. It would do.

Carla removed her shoes and pulled herself up onto the slippery white rim, so that she was straddling the bathtub.

The rope she'd found in her allotted cubicle of storage space in the basement of the building. It was one of the few things she had brought from the farm. Kevin used to always go on about how indispensable a good rope was. 'Useful for myriad things from towing vehicles, to retrieving dead cows from ditches.'

The knot slid smoothly along the rope, reducing the slack until the hairy fibres were prickling her neck. Being a former Scout mistress had paid off; the knot would hold.

From her position she could see out of the sliver of open bathroom window. The evening light was a gentle mauve on teal. Beautiful. But just another trap. God was putting on one final show of splendour in a last-ditch effort to woo her back to this world. Well, it was too late.

A spider hunkered in the crook of the window frame – two almond beads of body, a splash of white on brown, long legs splayed like the rays of sunshine in a child's drawing. The outline of the creature was so distinct that Carla felt as if a net curtain had just been lifted on the world and she could see in focus for the very first time. The whisky might have had something to do with that, though she'd been careful to not overdo it, throwing back just enough to quash the voices inside her head. She still needed to be in control.

The noose was now uncomfortably tight. She swallowed against its resistance, then closed her eyes and let her toes slip inward over the bath rim, her feet losing the firm reply of cold enamel.

Chapter Twenty-Two

BEN

'Lio Va'a to visits. Lio Va'a to visits,' the PA system boomed across the exercise yard.

They were playing Crash, a cross between rugby and bullrush. Lio wiped the sweat off his forehead, spat onto the ground, and headed for the gate.

'Lucky. The bitch must be gagging for it,' some guy cooed.

'That's the third fuckin' visit this week,' bleated another.

Since Ben had been at 'The Rock', he'd had that command only twice – once for a lawyer's visit, the other time when Simi and George had come to see him.

They'd told him the DOAs had disintegrated, what with both him and Tate being inside. Matt was prospecting for another gang, and the rest were just cruising. They said Ben had earned props and had real cred in the hood. Said he would easily get into another crew when he got out.

It was good seeing his mates, but also weird. Strangely, Ben felt more alone with them around. Even though the three kept up the act that their lives were still intertwined, he knew that at the end of the hour they would walk through the sliding metal gate and he'd be the one left behind. They also seemed quite immature – like kindergarten kids, when he'd graduated to big school.

One good thing about their visit was that they'd brought him cigarettes and a phone card. He used it to give his mum a call. She promised to come visit, just as she'd promised a hundred times before. Said she was just waiting for Debs to get down from up north, then she'd catch a ride in with her. So Ben kept booking four visits a week, the maximum permitted, just in case. Visits had to be booked from the inside. If an upcoming visit wasn't written in the book, it didn't happen.

When his mum did finally get her act together, she arrived at some random time and they wouldn't allow her to see him. 'No booking, no visit.'

That's when Ben levelled one of the screws and got five days in Secure. It was five days of hell – in a freezing cell with just a thin foam mattress on the floor and a putrid-smelling bucket in the corner. One hour a day to exercise alone in the yard; the other twenty-three in lockdown. And because of his assault on the guard, he was reclassified IDU-1, which meant any visitations for the next three months were permitted only from behind a wall of glass. Ben wasn't overly concerned; it wasn't as if he had visitors lining up to see him.

Getting back to East Block was sweeter than a tinnie, and doubly sweet because Jocko had been moved on to Paremoremo, the maximum-security prison just outside of Albany. So Ben now had the whole cell to himself.

The only bad thing about his cellmate moving out was that his TV went with him. Jocko had kept it switched on day and night, even when coverage was down and there was just static. But Ben had got used to the intrusion, the incessant din plugging the dark ditches in his mind. The new long hours of nothing nearly did his head in. Crazy thoughts kept sprouting like seedlings in a dark cupboard, till his head was a tangle of them. Often the thoughts came without proper words attached – Ben didn't own many words. Thoughts that left him anxious and angry.

'Toroa to visits. Toroa to visits.'

Was he dreaming? Ben looked up at the bridge. It was Shirley.

'You fooling with me, miss?'

She smiled down at him. 'Name's in the book, Ben.'

'Yeah, but I made them bookings just in case someone turned up, random-like.'

'Cut your fussing and get your arse to the gate.'

Ben's pulse picked up. He didn't know what it was about, but it was definitely better than another faded day of slow boredom.

Shirley came down off the bridge and escorted him. He liked her, the only cool screw in the joint. She even knew his name, and whenever she saw him, she stopped to talk. 'So how you doing, Ben? Keeping on the straight road?' or 'Your day going OK, Ben?'

At Visits he stripped off in front of the guard and handed over his clothes. The guy shoved them into a numbered locker and handed him an orange overall, which he put on back to front. Ben knew the drill from the few visits he'd had. He slipped on the overall and turned around for it to be zipped up from behind. The zip was then secured with a plastic tie. It was the same procedure around his wrists, to ensure that no contraband could be stashed up his sleeves or inside the overall. Not that this was likely to happen, since he'd be separated from any visitor by an inch of glass.

He sat down and waited, watching the second hand creep around the cracked white clock face. He could read digital, but he couldn't tell the time off this ancient instrument. In fact, the whole building was practically prehistoric; the date it had been built, eighteen something-or-other, was inscribed on the arch over the entrance. Rumour had it the place even hosted a few hangings before executions were finally outlawed.

'Is this visit going ahead or what?' he asked, the suspense getting to him.

The screw didn't look up from his paperwork.

After what felt like forever, the guy's radio crackled, giving the go-ahead. He got up unhurriedly and scanned his clipboard. 'You're IDU-1,' he said, stating the obvious.

Ben was used to the overkill. In prison, protocol was everything. Words, rules, procedures, guidelines – they were uttered, repeated, ticked, checked, rechecked, confirmed, and reconfirmed. It could drive a dude crazy. But oddly, it was also reassuring. A shield against the unpredictability of what could go down inside.

The guard led him down a narrow corridor into a shoebox of a room with a viewing window at one end. There was the shape of a person on the other side, but he couldn't see who it was – the light was coming from behind his visitor, and the glass was smudged with greasy fingerprints.

He stepped forward and the silhouette was at once familiar.

Ben's heart whooped and then crashed. 'Fuck!'

'Sit down and speak into the receiver,' the screw ordered from behind him.

Ben felt for the chair and sank down slowly, unable to take his eyes off the face peering back at him. The left side of her face was swollen like a fermented breadfruit. A purple-black cloud swung over her one eye. Her lip had been split in two, each half jutting out awkwardly to move independently of the other. Her long limp hair had been brushed over the top of her head in an attempt to hide the fresh clearing of bare scalp. And when she tried to smile, Ben saw that his mother's front teeth were missing.

He put his hand to the glass, almost glad for the barrier. She looked too fragile to touch, like she'd crumble on contact.

She lifted her hand to meet his. Her knuckles were grazed and two fingers had been strapped together with grubby pink Elastoplast.

They stayed like that for a while, mother and son, hands touching . . . glass. It reminded Ben of when, as a child, he'd measure his palm against hers, and she would laugh, telling him he was getting so big he'd soon be a man.

He picked up the receiver with the same sense of helplessness he used to feel when one or other of his mother's partners started knocking her about. This time, though, it was a pane of glass, not fear that kept him from her.

'*He* do this to you, Ma?' he finally managed, his anger climbing up over the horror in front of him. Ryan had outdone himself.

Tears swam across her yellowed eyes. 'Didn't bring takeaways home quick enough,' she said grimly. She pulled down the corner of her lower lip down and winced. 'Fast food not fast enough.'

She laughed hoarsely, then began to cough. 'But nothing a bit of sticking plaster can't fix, boy. So don't you go worrying over your old ma, you hear me? I'm made of strong stuff.' She shifted on her chair like an old person. 'That's not why I'm here. I wanted to tell you what I'm about to do.'

Ben closed his eyes.

'But first, tell me, how you doing, kiddo?'

He shook his head.

'You lookin' kinda scrawny. They feeding you enough?' She rummaged through her bag. 'I brought you some toffees.'

Ben jumped up and thumped his fists down on the counter. 'Fuck, I'll kill him, Ma. I'll fuckin' kill him!'

'No point getting all worked up, Benjamin. I got a plan. Sit down. Listen. I want you to be better than him. You can't go around beating up the screws. They said that's why you behind this glass.'

Ben couldn't hear her any more; he'd dropped the receiver. His head was all fire and anger and pain. He turned to the prefab wall divider and dropped a hole through it, right into the next booth.

Two screws burst in. 'That's it, Toroa.'

'I'll fuckin' kill the bastard!' he shouted, dodging one screw and winding the other.

'Ben, don't!' his mother shouted through the abandoned receiver.

Two more guards rushed in. Ben thumped and kicked and bit and scratched. Then he was in a headlock and his mother's frantic screams were part of a silent movie he never got to see.

Days later, he learnt that when they found her body, a Women's Refuge card was still hidden in the side of her shoe, and the money she'd squirrelled away for months in the toilet cistern, in her purse. They told him she never made it to the refuge. Ryan had tracked her down soon after she left the prison in Deb's car with the kids all squashed in the back seat. He'd taken her out in front of them, in front of Lily and Cody and Anika. In front of Brooke and Dina.

Cole, one of the laggers on East Block, read Ben the newspaper

161

article, filling in the gaps left by the sparser version relayed to Ben by the authorities. Cole said she'd been stabbed over ten times and that Ryan had cut Debs too when she'd tried to intervene, landing her in hospital with a collapsed lung.

Ben never got to go to his mother's *tangi*. The authorities refused him permission. He was too much of a risk to the community.

Beyond

Your mother's tangihanga *lasted five days, Benjamin. Even though she had turned her back on her* whakapapa, *it did not turn its back on her. Her family came to collect her and took her body home. On the marae her aged mother and her aunties and sisters washed down her bruised and battered body and prepared her for her final journey. Miriama looked beautiful lying there wrapped in a cloak of fine feathers, in the soft embrace of her* whakapapa.

Many came to pay their respects. They came to speak about her, and honour her and her ancestors, pressing noses with your mother for one last time. If you had been there, the aroha *that swirled would have found its way into your heart, of that I am certain. You would have glimpsed something you have not known, boy — the ritual, the rites, the connection.*

On that day your mother was farewelled and welcomed. Such is death — an ending and a beginning. Ka kite ano. Haere mai, *Miriama.*

Your mother's body lies in the earth, son, but her soul soars. She is at one with the universe.

Chapter Twenty-Three

CARLA

Voices.

'Has a referral gone off?'

'Yes.'

'Next of kin notified?'

'Not yet. Husband is mentally impaired following an attack earlier this year. Do you remember the home invasion on a farm out Albany way?'

'The son was murdered, wasn't he?'

'That's the one.'

'Jeez, no wonder. Poor woman.'

'The ward clerk is trying to get hold of the husband's brother.'

'Are drug and alcohol levels back yet?'

Carla lifted her eyelids. Fuzzy black ripples spread out against a sea of light. She closed them again. Woolly white circles, a memory of the light, swirled and bled into the black.

'She's waking.'

'Continue on with the round. I'll catch up in a minute. Don't forget to check Mr Levy's digoxin levels.'

Flattened vowels and rolling Rs. A foreign accent. The sound of hooks tracking along a runner. Curtains being drawn.

Then she remembered. The rope. The bath . . . She was still alive.

Carla opened one eye just enough to let in a slice of light, light now muted within a cocoon of green. Green curtains. A bed.

She opened the eye wider. There was a man in a white coat at the foot of the bed.

A smile. 'I'm afraid you didn't make it.'

'What?' Her voice sounded alien. Not hers. As if planted inside of her.

'St Peter wasn't quite ready for you.'

Tears trickled down her cheeks, yet there was no emotion to accompany them. She felt nothing.

A hand offered in greeting. 'I am Nikola Jovovich.'

Carla did not move. The hand touched her. It was warm.

'Medical registrar, North Shore Hospital.'

Of course! Hospital green.

'You came in last night after being resuscitated by ambulance staff.'

The tears kept coming, emotion now catching up.

'The psychiatry ward upstairs is full, so you've been given a bed on the medical ward.'

Carla opened both eyes. The man stood up and closed a small gap in the curtains, sealing them in to the surreal green space. 'How are you feeling?'

If she spoke again, she would surely be registering her membership to life.

'May I listen to your chest?' he asked, pulling a rainbow-coloured stethoscope from his pocket. 'Excuse this,' he added with a smile. 'I've just finished a run in Paediatrics.'

He had dark skin and dark eyes. A fine line threaded over his upper lip and disappeared into his left nostril, flattening the vermillion cupid of his lip. A repaired harelip. His nose was sphinx-like, standing acutely away from his face. Under his white coat he wore a blue shirt and a navy tie with silver diagonals. Curly dark hair burst up under his collar where pinpoint black dots took over, demarcating where he'd shaved.

Carla sat up and leant forward so that he could slide the cold disc down her back. He smelt of eucalyptus and hospital.

'Take a deep breath in through your mouth . . . and out. Good. In . . . and . . . out.'

Was he reminding her how to breathe?

'The bruising around your neck is quite marked, and you have some superficial bleeding into the whites of your eyes,' he said, flicking a torch across her face. 'Don't get a fright when you see yourself in the mirror. It can take some time before the blood is resorbed. It looks worse than it is.'

There was a buzzing noise and the red light on his locator flashed. He read the message.

'Sorry. They need me upstairs. I'll pop back later.' He straightened the crumpled cover over her feet. 'The psychiatry team should visit sometime this morning. Get some more sleep if you can. Unfortunately, it can be very noisy in here.'

He was about to pull back the curtain, when it was wrenched open by a small round man with a helmet of grey hair. 'Not a queue again. I need to pee!' the man said in a very proper English accent as he fumbled with the drawstring of his pyjama pants.

'Hang on, Mr Parker. Not here! This is *not* the toilet,' Jovovich said, spinning the man around. But it was too late. A fountain of yellow sprayed over the registrar's shoes and the side of Carla's bed.

Jovovich pushed the button on the wall behind Carla. 'Did I say this was not a psychiatric ward?' he said, with a chuckle. 'Welcome to the madness of North Shore Hospital.'

A male nurse appeared and pulled up Mr Parker's pants. 'Archie, this isn't the toilet. Come with me. I'll show you where it is. Remember to ring the bell the next time you need to take a leak.'

'Yes, but that's not the point,' protested the old man. 'What about the brazil nuts?'

The nurse rolled his eyes and Carla couldn't help but laugh.

'All right for you to laugh,' joked the registrar, throwing a white towel onto the puddle beside Carla's bed and mopping his shoes with a clump of paper towels.

'I'm sorry. I shouldn't . . .'

'What we don't do to get our patients to smile!' he said. 'Actually, the poor chap isn't crazy, just confused. His electrolytes have gone haywire. Normally, he's pretty sharp.' The registrar turned to leave, then looked back. 'By the way, there is a Chinese lady waiting outside. Your neighbour, I think? She found you last night. Dialled one-one-one. You up to a visit?'

Carla's grin faded, the real world again intruding. She shook her head. It hurt.

Through the morning, she drifted in and out of sleep, the activity on the ward precluding her from venturing beyond a light doze. But she was grateful for the distraction. It prevented her thoughts from settling. She was floating above her own body like a helium balloon, her connection with the world as tenuous as a piece of string.

After lunch, a big woman sloped in to the ward. 'I am Mona, the psychiatrist on call,' she said, introducing herself in a voice as heavy as her thick-soled lace-ups.

She had dyed-red hair fashioned into a blunt bob, and each of her fingers sported a chunky silver ring, one even wedged into the creased angle of her thumb.

After a brief preamble, Mona moved through a mental health questionnaire, leaving long pauses between each of Carla's responses, as if willing Carla to elaborate.

So this was psychoanalysis, thought Carla.

'We use medicine to balance the brain,' Mona explained, as she charted Carla a course of antidepressants. 'Later, will come counselling.'

Carla felt exhausted by the thought of more talking and reflection and exploration.

'I will arrange for the Crisis Team to visit you at home. We will send notice of the outpatient appointment in addition.'

Finally Mona left, her sensible shoes squeaking down the length of the polished lino corridor.

Later that afternoon, Geoffrey and Mildred visited, with a bunch of white carnations and a box of scorched almonds. Carla hated carnations.

It was an awkward visit. Mildred spent ten minutes trying to find a vase for the flowers, while her brother-in-law skirted the fact that Carla was lying in a hospital bed with dark-blue ring around her neck and bloodshot eyes. He kept clearing his throat and saying, 'Yes, well,' and 'So there you have it,' and 'Good, good,' while Mildred kept the conversation as light as if they were taking tea in Cornwall Park.

'Geoff, we must be going,' she said after a time, her eyes protruding in a theatrical show of checking her watch.

'Yes, yes, must be off. Prior arrangement,' Geoff said apologetically, leaning forward to brush his cheek past Carla's.

'Onward and upward, eh, old girl? You must be strong, dear. Come stay with us over the bridge for a while. Give yourself a break.'

Mrs Doering, the ninety-three-year-old lady in the adjacent bed, was delighted with the carnations. She had emphysema. Her son had forbidden her another cigarette. She winked at Carla as she shuffled off 'to the toilet' for the sixth time that day.

Dinner was served at five, announcing itself with the metallic fanfare of institution food. The *Soft Diet* sign above Carla's bed translated into pureed apple and yogurt, instead of the steak-and-mushroom pie.

'Darn! Too late for dinner,' Dr Jovovich said, striding into the ward.

'I can offer you some boysenberry yogurt?' Carla said, holding up her half-eaten pottle. She surprised herself with this tease; it wasn't twenty-four hours since she'd tried to kill herself, yet here she was slipping back into the superficial banter of living.

'What you could do with is some of my grandma's chicken soup,' Jojovich said, inspecting the contents of her tray. 'Food for the soul, I tell you.'

She smiled.

'So,' he said, sitting down on the edge of her bed, 'we can fix the body, but can we fix the mind?'

There was something very likeable about this man, something very good about him.

'Mrs Reid, I have visited the place you are at now,' he said, his cheekiness all of a sudden evaporating.

She looked at him, at his flattened upper lip, which must have marked him as different from birth.

'Six years ago, my wife and daughter were killed in Kosovo

while I was working. They brought them by ambulance to the hospital where I was on duty. I could not save them. One day I was part of a family, the next day I was an island in the middle of a wild ocean, an island no one could reach. I think you know that feeling.'

Carla looked at him, lost in his brown eyes.

He continued, 'Where every minute is empty and drags its feet toward nothingness.' Her face prickled. 'How do you recover from that? From the sudden pointlessness of life? From the pain that cuts into you so deeply no words in any language can speak accurately of it? Poets try, authors, artists too – even doctors. But they don't come close, do they?'

She shook her head. This man had let himself in.

'What I can tell you is this. One morning, you will wake up and the sun will be a bit brighter than the day before. You will hear again those forgotten sounds of birds in a tree and bees around a hive. You will smell baking bread and feel hungry. You will laugh at silliness and the laughter will come from here.' He put a hand over his heart. 'Not here,' he said, touching his mouth. 'One day the pictures you have in your mind of broken bodies will make way for pink complexions and happy eyes, and you will find there is still living to be done.'

Chapter Twenty-Four

BEN

'What you done this time?' someone shouted.

'Maybe they got it wrong, Toroa. You're innocent, right?'

Ben gave them the finger and rolled over to the gate. Shirley was waiting for him. He put his hands through the grill to be cuffed, then pulled them back so she could unlock the gate.

The only sound as they walked came from his shoes and hers on the concrete – bass and percussion. Since he'd lost his mum he didn't care much about anything any more, just the next joint, or the juice that messed with his brain and iced the pain, the stuff that promised peace.

They passed the corridor that led to Visits. Where were they going?

Shirley answered his thoughts. He could have sworn she was psychic; she always seemed to know what was going on in his head.

'Mr Ngata's summoned you. Don't know what it's about. You'll find out soon enough.'

They passed through the dome. It was only the second time Ben had been out of these gates and into the admin block. The first time was when Mr Ngata had told him about his mother's death.

The rope twisting Ben's insides pulled tighter. Perhaps Ryan had topped himself. Now that would be good news. As far as he knew, he was still being held at Auckland Remand, just down the road. If they ever brought him to The Rock, Ben would waste him himself.

In admin, the air was warm, the place bright, and the light white. He could smell coffee. Coffee! And the sound of no noise. Just the low, smooth rumble of voices from behind closed doors, as smooth as a Holden's engine. It was as if he'd stepped out of an ancient black-and-white photograph, all angles and edges, into the calm modern world of colour.

Shirley knocked on the superintendent's varnished wooden door.

'Come in,' came a deep voice.

Mr Ngata was sitting at his desk. Behind him was the painting Ben remembered from last time – a prisoner's canvas of spinifex and beach, sea and sky. That same cerulean sea that last time crashed over him with Ngata's words, 'Sorry, Ben. It's your mother. She's dead.'

This time Ben didn't wait for Ngata to speak; instead he swam straight into the blue, letting the colour wash over him before any words could.

He is helping his mother paint the wall out front of their house – the knee-high barrier with crumbling pillars and honeycombed bricks. He and Lily used to hold serious balancing competitions on that wall. His mum had always wanted a white fence out front. Painting the pathetic wall was a compromise. *'What you painting the dumb wall for?' some guy (not Ryan, maybe Ben's dad) raves. 'Housing New Zealand isn't going to thank you!'*

Ben is wearing the stripy yellow scarf his mum has taken a whole

winter to knit. He wears it only as far as the end of the road before
taking it off and hiding it behind a tree. After school it's not there any
more. At home he gets a hiding with the kettle cord. His mother swears
it's the last thing she'll ever make him, and it is.

They get to the public swimming baths and climb over the back
fence because his mum doesn't have enough money for the entrance fee.
She tries to teach him and Lily how to swim in the shallow baby pool,
but a lifeguard comes over and throws them out because someone has
reported seeing them scale the fence. On the way home, his mum does
a funny impersonation of the lifeguard to cheer them up.

'How are you doing, Ben?' Ngata's voice burst into the
memories. It was neither super loud, nor suspiciously soft, yet a
voice impossible to ignore.

'OK.'

'Good. That's good,' the manager said, pulling his mouth to
one side in an involuntary tic. There was a long pause. 'Look, Ben,
I'll get straight to the point.' Ngata twirled a pencil in his hands.
'I've had a request come down from the top. It's a bit irregular
but—' He gave a small cough. 'Mrs Reid has requested permission
to visit you.'

Through the open window, Ben could hear the drone of
traffic on the Grafton overbridge. The window was taunting him,
pretending everything was normal. An open window without bars.

'Mrs Reid would like to meet with you, Ben.'

'Say who?'

'You know, man,' Ngata said impatiently. 'The victim of the
crime that landed you inside.'

The warmth leaked out of Ben's body. The room tilted. His
tongue felt fat in his mouth. 'What about Tate?' he blurted out.
'Tate should do it. He's the one th—'

Ngata shook his head. 'Been transferred to Christchurch.'

'Nah. I'm not meeting with no ho. I want my legal.'

Ngata got up and came out from behind his desk. 'You are not obliged to,' he said calmly, perching right in front of Ben. Ben focused on the bridge of black freckles on Ngata's nose. 'But a doctor has written to the Head of Corrections.' The manager picked up Ben's file and flicked through it. 'Said it would help the lady move on, get her life back on track. We call it restorative justice.'

Ben shook his head.

'I think you at least owe her that.'

'I'm doin' the time,' he mumbled, head down.

'It's the kind of thing the parole board would look kindly on,' Shirley piped up from behind.

Ngata tipped his head in acknowledgement of her suggestion. 'I think this is something that would benefit you in other ways too, Ben,' he said getting up and switching on a fan that was positioned on a metal cabinet in the corner. A breeze blew over the room. The rush of cool air felt like freedom.

Ben turned to Shirley. 'It's not like I got parole anytime soon. I'm just beginning my lag.' He turned back to Ngata. 'Nah, not interested.'

'You don't have to give me an answer right now. Why don't you sleep on it?' he persisted. 'I think this is a chance for you to make right some of the wrong. See it as an opportunity to do some good, eh?'

Shirley escorted him back to the yard. They walked in silence. Only when she was unlocking the last gate did she speak.

'Look around you, Ben. You've reached a dead end. Nobody but you can turn your life around.' The gate clanged shut.

'Look who's back,' Afi cooed. 'So they've decided to keep you in here after all.'

Ben rammed a fist into Afi's face, cracking his right eye socket. Shirley saw it all, so Ben spent the next fourteen days in the Secure Unit.

Three days in the pit was easy. Seven was borderline. After ten, Ben's mind was sagging in the middle. Weird faces floated through the lemon-coloured walls, and nightmares hijacked his dreams. But what haunted him the most were Shirley's words. 'I'm disappointed in you. What would your mother have said?'

The whole fortnight he couldn't get those words out of his head. Shirley was nothing to him, just another screw, a nobody in his life! But her words nagged and niggled and wore him down.

'Hey! Hey, you!' he pushed his mirror – a stainless steel disc – through the cell's bars, angling it so that he could see the guard stationed at the end of the corridor.

'What's up?'

'Need to talk with Mr Ngata.'

'Sure. And what about an audience with the Queen?'

'Listen, you fuckwit. Shit. I mean, please, sir. You can even ask Shirley. Mr Ngata wants me to make a decision 'bout something real important. Well, I have.'

'We'll talk about it when you're finished your stint down here. Still six more days in the Shangri-La, and watch your mouth or it'll be another week.'

As Ben kicked the wall, his barefoot split open, a jagged line zigzagging across his toes. 'First aid! Fuckin' first aid. I'm bleeding!'

The guard cursed, slipped on a pair of disposable gloves, and ambled over.

'You're nothing but trouble, one-one-four-three.'

175

The doctor stitched him up in the sickbay, but before Ben was taken back to the pit, he asked the nurse to pass on a message to Ngata.

He didn't hear anything more for five days. Then on the sixth, the day he got back to East Block, the call came through.

Beyond

Nothing but trouble! That is true. I slip between your thoughts and find little to redeem you, boy, though I continue to search for a glimmer of light to lessen my load. You do not heed the call for utu, for a way to make right your wrong. It is not revenge or retribution your victim calls for, but more a measure of acknowledgement and reciprocation. An act, which could send ripples far further than you.

But you are not alone in your waywardness. Each day the wind brings news of another and another and another. I see an entire orphanage of the dispossessed, the youth who have lost their way. How did it come to this?

Again I come back to the story I was telling. Do you remember I spoke about Te Tiriti o Waitangi? The pact between two peoples. As a consequence of this important document, the English expected sovereignty in the purchase and governance of land. The Māori's expectation was of consultation and co-management instead.

Language can be a beautiful thing, Benjamin. Words carry the weight of meaning, directness of intention, the peculiarity of culture. Words define reality, and therein lies their power. But also their weakness! A poor translation is about loss – loss of meaning and intent. The poor translation of The Treaty of Waitangi heralded the loss of a whole people, in fact.

Differing expectations begat cycles of hostility, war, defeat, and confiscation; hostility, war, defeat, and confiscation. Of course, the musket was master, and so your ancestors soon found themselves stripped of most of their territories.

Do you know that when the British advanced on the peaceful Parihaka community situated in Mt Taranaki's embrace, children ran out to greet the soldiers with song and dance and gifts of food. Yet still the people were driven from their homes, their prophets imprisoned and their cultural kete squashed and trampled on.

The word Waitangi means 'the waters of lamentation'.[3] The irony of what lay ahead was perhaps not lost on nature.

Chapter Twenty-Five

CARLA

Carla had arranged to meet Lorraine from Victim Support in the Visitors' car park at Mount Eden jail. Though they were both coming from the North Shore, Carla wanted to drive herself; it obviated thirty minutes of courteous conversation.

Lorraine was very caring, her big bosom and deep voice comforting, her common sense sobering, but Carla had had enough kindness and sympathy to last a lifetime. She'd had her fill of being monitored and supported, observed and assisted. Her suicide bid hadn't helped either, the incident now escorting her wherever she went as if written in bold across her forehead: *I am a risk to myself. Watch me.*

In truth, she was feeling a lot better since the antidepressants had kicked in. They'd shaved off the rough edges of her days and diluted her indifference. Her sleep had improved too. So she was feeling strong when she turned into Normanby Road.

She knew this part of town well; her once favourite delicatessen was just a few blocks away. In her 'before' life, she'd not infrequently made the forty-minute journey across the bridge to stock up on pasta, salami, unpasteurised cheeses, and chocolate. A young Jack had enjoyed these culinary expeditions too, indulging in every free sample on offer and eagerly lapping up his Italian heritage. The cheerio-sausage-and-chicken-nugget meals fed to him at friends' houses paled when compared to the plates of finely sliced Parma ham, black figs, plump green olives, and creamy gorgonzola his mother served.

From Normanby Road, Carla swung into Lauder. Ahead of her, the stone towers of Mount Eden jail rose up like some Dickensian monolith. Her newfound steel bowed. She gripped the steering wheel. 'If this is what you need to begin to heal, then we will arrange it.' Nikola Jovovich's words played over in her mind. 'Confront the evil, acknowledge your anger, then set the debris free.'

It had been an extraordinary meeting when he had returned to her ward. They'd talked long into the night, standing side by side in the visitors' lounge, looking out over the silvered waters of Lake Pupuke. Nikola's awareness of the human condition was profound. Most importantly, though, he showed no pity in his dealings with her, just empathy. She felt as if she had always known him – the dark hair, sleepy brown eyes, his marked lip. How he reminded her of Jack.

When they finally parted, the night was melting into a charcoal dawn and Carla knew she could carry on living.

BEN

The lawyer shook Ben's hand, making him feel important. Lawyers always did. The guy smelt clean. Lawyers always did.

'Remember, Ben, you are not obliged to answer any questions if you do not wish to. Anytime you want to terminate the interview, just let me know.' He turned to Mr Ngata. 'I'll be within earshot, will I?'

Ngata nodded.

Then the guard unlocked the door and Ben was led into the visiting hall. The space was the same familiar space, except that it was now empty of people. The huge mural on the wall opposite dominated the room. A six-foot blue dolphin rising out of the sea. Neptune, half-naked with his golden crown and trident, standing beneath it. It must have been painted by the same prisoner who'd painted the spinifex picture in Mr Ngata's office. Parts of the mural were scarred where the paint had flaked off or someone had etched their name into the myth, exposing raw stone.

The repeating pattern of chairs – two blue chairs, one orange, two blue, one orange – was more obvious now that there were no kids scrambling over the seats, no orange overalls, giggling girlfriends, or weeping wives.

Ben bobbed to the rap in his head and scraped out the dirt from under his fingernails. A trapped pigeon in the room kept flying into the high windows. *Flap, flap, crash. Flap, flap, crash.*

At the front of the room, a circle of chairs had been positioned around a table. Ngata broke the ring, pulling out a chair for Ben. A guard looped a chain through Ben's cuffs and around a table leg.

'They gonna keep me lunch? 'Cos I'm gonna miss lunch,' Ben said, flicking his thumb to stop it shaking. But before anyone could answer, the door at the far end opened.

Ben stared down at his jandals.

'Thank you. That's fine.' The voice, a woman's, stung Ben like

181

a wasp. He bit the inside of his cheek. 'Just a bit of distance. Some measure of privacy would be good, thank you.'

'We do need to adhere to strict procedure, Mrs Reid. Your security is paramount.'

'I understand. Thank you.'

Ben didn't look up. He knew the voice as if it had been branded onto his brain. She'd hollered enough that night. He shot a glimpse toward the door. Two women. Neither recognisable.

The lawyer walked up and patted Ben on the shoulder. Ben wasn't sure if this meant, 'You're cool', or 'Watch your step'.

The women sat down opposite, followed by the same psychiatrist who'd put Ben in a stitch gown on his first night in the boob – a bony chap with transparent skin and a limp grey ponytail.

Ben knew one of them had to be the Reid woman. The voice he'd heard belonged to her. What confused him was the hair. He remembered long dark hair; it was forever tangling up his nightmares. He looked up under a tilted brow and his eyes met the same eyes that stared into his dreams most nights. His breathing picked up. Suddenly he was drowning in the ocean on the wall and there was no land in sight. He pushed his hands together, his palms wet with sweat. This had been a stupid idea.

'We will open with a *karakia*,' Mr Ngata began.

Māori words. Ben didn't understand them, but at least his hands stopped shaking.

The psychiatrist's whispery voice intruded. 'Ben, Mrs Reid is here today to get some resolution and express what impact your crime has had on her and her loved ones.' The guy kept dipping his head as if to avoid random missiles. 'This is to help her get closure. It is also to help you along your path to redemption. An important step for you both. We are grateful for your agreement.'

Ben could smell the psychiatrist's breath from where he was sitting – a skipped breakfast breath. Ben spread his legs and leant forward over the table. His hands were shaking again and he had to hold them away from each other to stop the cuffs from rattling against the metal table leg. Ngata said something to the woman that Ben couldn't make out. She nodded, pulling her shoulders back.

Suddenly she was talking, her words pushing their way through the emptiness of the hall.

'Ben. May I call you that?' She'd already claimed some sort of ownership of him by using his name. He stretched his lips tightly against his teeth. 'I needed to meet with you today . . .'

At first her voice was slow and deliberate, the words solid, but they quickly began to crack and splinter.

She began again. 'Thank you for agreeing to meet with me.'

Ngata sneezed. The lawyer said, 'Bless you.' The trapped pigeon swooped across the room. *Flap, flap, crash.*

'I have come here today to ask you a question. Just one question.'

The pigeon finally gave up and landed on a ledge, its plump chest heaving.

'Why?'

White pigeon poo trickled down the far wall.

'Why did you hurt my family when you could have just taken our things and gone? Can you answer me that?' Her words were now coming out faster. 'Why did you rob me of my son? My husband? Why us? Why did you have to hurt us?'

183

The 'whys' were hitting Ben like bullets from an assault rifle. Why, Ben? Why? Why? So much for just one question!

The psychiatrist leant across and whispered something in the Reid woman's ear. She stopped and stared straight at Ben, her eyes no longer hiding, but driving out of their sockets.

Ben shrugged. What was he meant to say?

'Do you know how much pain you have caused? Pain that is just so . . . so . . . It *never* goes away. Never! You stole my husband. My son. You took everything important to me and left me with nothing! For what? Some loose change. A television. Radio. The money will have been spent by now, and I'm sure the thrill of . . .' She dropped her voice, hesitated, then spat out the next words: 'The thrill of . . . of what you did to me, long faded.'

Ngata approached. He bent down and whispered something to the psychiatrist.

'Have you given us any thought? What it's like for me without them?' She was on a roll. She wasn't stopping any time soon. 'Have you thought—?'

'Mrs Reid,' the bad-breath psychiatrist interrupted, holding his hands together in a polite plea. 'Let's try to keep this a little less emotional, if we can. I know it's hard, but—'

'Less emotional?' she cried, spittle flying across the table. 'Less emotional!'

She laughed. 'How can I keep the murder of my son and the torture of my husband less emotional, you tell me, sir?' Her face was a furious red, her eyes like those of a crazed dog. It was as if someone had pressed the fast-forward button and her words were careening around the room, and Ben's brain. He wanted them to stop. He clenched his teeth, arranged his best bored expression, and tried to focus on the rap that had restarted in his head.

'Just imagine,' she butted in again, 'that there's this thing you want more than anything in the world. You never believe it will be yours. You want it so badly, you hurt.'

What Ben wanted right now was to be left alone to smoke some weed in the yard.

'Then one day, suddenly, unexpectedly it comes your way. You can't believe how that feels. You just can't imagine.'

To score some weed *would* be his lucky day.

'I never thought that I would be able to have a child.' She slid a hand into her pocket. The guard behind her stiffened. 'You're still sixteen, aren't you?'

Silence.

Ben could cope when she was just ranting, but not when she wanted something back.

'Jack was sixteen when this picture was taken.' Without warning, Ben was staring down the barrel of a photograph, a black-and-white snapshot of the guy he and Tate had wasted in the garage that night, the kid with black hair and scarred lip, the kid with surprised eyes.

They'd cased the joint for some time. The lights in the house had been on and the curtains open, which made it easy. They'd cracked open some beers in the bushes, warming up the chemicals already spinning in their blood, and waiting till the time was right. For Ben it was his first big job. For Tate it was important too; he was prospecting for a proper gang. The idea of leaving the juvies behind and running with a real crew appealed to Ben. But it wasn't just respect he was after; he wanted to show everyone . . . Ryan . . . that he was somebody.

When they finally made their move it was almost too easy; the garage door had been left wide open. They crept through the shadows of lawnmower and shovel, chainsaw and tractor, past the Peugeot – keys still in the ignition – past the tower of paint tins . . . Then, without any warning, a figure was there standing in the doorway.

The darkness kept them hidden, but their break was short-lived. A blue tide of light swept across the floor and stopped just in front of Ben's shoes; the guy had opened a fridge door and was taking out a beer. That was when Tate reached for the shovel . . .

Tate did the main bit. But it turned out that it wasn't so easy to take out the enemy. The guy just wouldn't stop groaning. That's when Ben had to help.

He looked away. He wouldn't give the Reid woman the satisfaction of studying the photograph. 'I'm out of here,' he said, pushing his chair back. The table came with him, metal screeching along the floor.

'My client is getting distressed,' the lawyer said, quickly moving in.

The woman, perhaps realising her moment was soon going to be over, jumped up and started shouting. 'How did you feel when your mother was killed? How did you feel?'

The words hit Ben in the gut, winding him.

'Fuck you, bitch! Fuck you!' His voice banged into the walls.

The circling sharks closed in, and through the chaos of bodies and voices, the woman was steered away.

As she reached the door, Ben shouted after her, 'I dunno what you want from me, lady!' Then she was gone.

* * *

Outside in the yard the sun was still shining, and after a while the cold darkness inside of Ben started to thaw. He'd missed lunch, but there were still two hours left to drift in the open before lockdown, before he was locked away with just his thoughts for company – thoughts that nailed him to a darker place.

Beyond

Every night I hear the Pākehā *woman weeping, her tears as soft and persistent as the rain that falls on the West Coast. I feel the weight of her sorrow and the emptiness of her existence. You laid this on her, Benjamin. You! I feel the shame of what you have done as if you were born from my womb. I feel this mother's pain. Differences do not divide us. To suckle an infant is to suckle an infant.*

Still I keep on with my story, but not to excuse. Never to excuse. For though each man hauls behind him the weight of his history, in the end what he does with his life is his to own. No, I keep on to explain where I think the road went crooked, and to hopefully catch you on my hook with words. If I can catch you, then perhaps I can raise you up again and bring you home.

The white man was hungry for Aotearoa and his appetite insatiable. Year after year Māori were divested of their land, till we found ourselves on mere slivers of soil, unable to feed our whānau. *The white man drained swamps from which we'd always fished eels, cut down forests in which we'd always hunted, and built roads and railways to support his newly acquired land, not ours. He was stingy with his wealth and* reluctant to loan his 'indigenous' fellows the capital needed to develop what little land we had left.

To survive, our men and women were forced to seek work away from home, shearing sheep, digging for gum, erecting fences – mostly temporary jobs that offered such meagre wages. And so it was that our once proud people slipped slowly into poverty.

Children were taken out of school, either to accompany their parents in search of work, or to help out in the home – every hand needed to survive. Farms fell into disrepair. Houses were unable to hold off harsh winters or a scorching summer. Crops died. Stock died. People died. Babies and children, young adults and old. And more of your heritage died too. For you see, Benjamin, poverty swallows everything. God, culture, community, hope.

Chapter Twenty-Six

CARLA

Jin, Mingyu's baby daughter, panted excitedly and waved her tiny hands in the air as she tried to grasp the parrot suspended above her. It took several failed attempts before her grunts of frustration turned to gurgles of delight and she pressed her pudgy fingers into the soft felt belly of the bird. However, her pleasure was short-lived, the cheeky toy springing again from her grasp.

'Is that wicked Lulu teasing you?' Carla said, setting down her book and scooping up the wailing infant.

Jin sucked in a stuttering breath, then the tears won over and her crying became more fractious.

'I think you're a hungry bunny,' Carla said, bobbing towards the kitchen. 'Goodness, look at the time! It's nearly eleven o'clock. No wonder you're grumpy. Naughty, naughty Carla!'

She took out a bottle of milk and a small Tupperware tub of pureed pumpkin from the fridge and placed them both in the microwave.

Jin wasn't at all interested in the pumpkin, but reached straight for the bottle. Carla squeezed out a drop of milk on her wrist to test the temperature, then gave it to her charge. Minutes later Jin lolled back against Carla in a satisfied creamy stupor.

An hour crept by with Carla on the couch, cradling her soft bundle. She'd been taken aback when Mingyu had first asked her to babysit. She and her neighbour had grown close, and Carla adored Jin, finding any excuse to pop in for a cuddle. But the responsibility of looking after the child, that was another thing altogether. Of course Mingyu, in true Mingyu fashion, persisted, dispelling Carla's fears with a wide smile and casual toss of her head, and so Carla cautiously agreed to help out. It wasn't long, though, before 'a couple of hours now and then' stretched to three mornings a week, freeing Mingyu up to return to part-time work as a florist. However, the benefits were not all Mingyu's. For Carla, the long road to healing had at last begun.

It was the touch she cherished most. She'd been starved of this most basic of needs for so long. At the age of forty-five she'd found herself sequestered under an invisible cloche, forced to survive on a handful of throwaway gestures – a casual pat on the back, a peck on the cheek, the careless brush of flesh against flesh on the bus. Minding Jin had afforded Carla with a tangible connection to life.

'You stay for some tea?' Mingyu enquired, as she always did on her return from work. 'Or coffee. I know you prefer. I try to make today. I'm even buy fresh-ground bones.'

Carla laughed. '*Beans*, Ming. Not bones! Coffee beans.'

It was part of the ritual, and Carla loved it, sitting round Mingyu's kitchen table with a warm drink in hand, chatting.

'See, these men get only three year,' Mingyu said, pointing to the newspaper headline: DAIRY THUGS GET THREE YEARS. COULD BE OUT IN ONE.

191

Carla shrugged. What difference would it make if they got three years or thirteen? It wouldn't change what they had done. And it wasn't as if they would come out of prison reformed. If anything, they'd probably be worse.

She was now able to think about these issues in a more detached manner. Nikola Jovovich had been right. Even though the meeting with Toroa had been unsatisfactory, she'd at least been given a voice and acknowledged. This had freed her from some of her demons and given her new strength, absorbing some of the hate and hopelessness that had been corroding her soul.

'Hau, Carla, in China they not keep these bad people,' Mingyu said, making a melodramatic gesture of beheading.

Carla laughed. She loved her friend's refreshing honesty.

Mingyu pushed the paper aside and looked through the mail Carla had left out for her on the bench. 'Oh ho!' she exclaimed, retrieving a blue aerogramme from the top of a pile of advertorials. 'Long last, a letter from my mother.'

Carla had noticed the unusual stamp when she'd collected the mail that morning. 'She must miss you a lot.'

Mingyu nodded, slicing open the letter along its seam and hungrily scanning the page. 'But in one year she have Jin for company.'

'What do you mean?' Carla asked, her chest tightening.

'In eight month we send Jin back to China for few year to learn Chinese way of life and language. It also give me chance to work full-time. Then she come back for New Zealand school.'

'But . . . You . . . How can you send her away? You're her mother!' Carla felt the loss already. 'Surely . . .' She'd been foolish to allow herself to start caring for someone again.

Mingyu looked up, clearly taken aback by Carla's tone. 'Carla, is the way we decide to do it.' Her voice was gentle but firm.

BEN

The buzzer chiselled through Ben's dreams. He'd overslept, thanks to the dope he'd scored off Storm. Daylight saving hadn't helped.

He rolled off the bunk and pulled on his trackpants, rubbing his eyes to sharpen the outline of the new day. He took a leak, his urine dark and strong smelling.

Metal grated on metal as the guards moved down the wing, unlocking the cells. The key turned in Ben's lock. He waited for the guard to pass before pushing open the door and presenting himself for the first muster of the morning. On his left slouched Storm. On his right . . . No one. The Pakistani was probably still asleep.

Storm noticed his absence too. 'Wakey wakey, Osama,' he taunted.

A gruesome snapshot popped into Ben's head. The marijuana had definitely worn off, because the image broke through in crisp detail of the skinny Indian kid lying on the shower floor the day before, his trackpants bunched around his ankles.

Ben squeezed his eyes shut, but the picture was still there.

'Prisoner one-seven-nine-seven . . . Prisoner one-seven-nine-seven.'

'He's not coming, miss,' Ben called out to Shirley.

'Go wake him then, Toroa. I had to present myself on time this morning; he can do me the same courtesy.'

Ben yanked open the unlocked cell door.

The nervous Indian was a first-timer. Still a 'clean skin', with not one single tattoo – not even a small skull or cupid's heart or clenched fist the size of a fingernail. Nothing. Rumour had it he was a bright kid all set to go to university, then got pissed up to his eyeballs after final school exams. First time he'd ever touched the hard stuff. Crashed his old man's car into a bus stop, putting two people in hospital. When the cops hauled the kid from the wreckage, his blood alcohol was three times the limit. Some judge decided to send a strong message and gave the kid three months in the slammer.

'It's gonna be a tough bid if you play different from the rest, praying to . . . to whoever the dude is you pray to, and only eating rabbit food, bro,' Ben had warned on the kid's first day inside. But after that, Ben made sure he ignored the noob. It was safest. And it wasn't long before Storm and his crew did the boy over.

Ben stood in his neighbour's doorway. The skinny brown kid was hanging by a strip of sheet from the window bars, his spindly legs crumpled under him like a dead insect.

'Jesus!'

'What's up, Toroa?'

Ben turned. Shirley was standing behind him. 'IRO, Code One, East Wing! IRO, Code One, East Wing!' she shouted into her radio.

Ben lifted the boy onto his shoulders while Shirley cut him down. He was so light, just skin and air. A soft sound bubbled out of the dead boy's mouth.

'Shit, bro,' Ben whispered. 'It would've been okay. You should've just stuck it out.'

After his sentencing, Ben had to be shipped out of Remand. He was destined for Paremoremo, or Pare as it was known on the ground – Auckland's maximum-security. It had a reputation for being the toughest joint in the whole of Aotearoa.

Diamond took sadistic pleasure in painting a terrifying picture of the place, but Ben knew his descriptions would be pretty accurate. After all, Diamond was a prison-made product. He'd grown up in borstals and done time in every lock-up in the country.

He told Ben to make sure he ate his meals with his back to a wall and not to go anywhere without looking over his shoulder at least twice. His advice didn't help. Already Ben hadn't been sleeping well, and his dreams just grew more weird and frightening. The Paki's dead eyes. The Reid woman's hair. Dolphins and naked kings. A sharp red sea. Red waves up to his neck and so thick he couldn't swim through them. If he woke and opened his eyes, the wet would be sweat and the thick waves his blanket, all twisted and tight. Then he'd lie awake till morning to keep the blood at bay.

His case officer, Eric, seemed to start taking more notice of him – especially after he found the booby trap Ben had erected around his own bunk. So he booked Ben in to see the mental health nurse. She had a downy blonde moustache and a tuft of black hair growing out of a mole on her chin. Ben sat in her windowless office while she pelted him with questions. How did he feel about his mother's death? And the Indian boy hanging himself? How did he feel about moving to Pare?

Ben didn't say much. He didn't know how to say what he was feeling. There was a disconnect between the words he owned and the feelings he felt.

The nurse decided his 'paranoia' was caused by depression, so got the prison psychiatrist to prescribe him some meds. Then she explained all the possible side effects in nauseating detail – tiredness, diarrhoea, delayed ejaculation . . . Ben laughed. It wasn't as if he was getting any inside, and when he was wanking, well he had all the time in the world. Fourteen years, in fact. Anyhow, he didn't swallow a single tablet, and not because of any side effects. He reckoned the screws were trying to poison him.

The pills were no use for trade either. At least cold-and-flu tablets had some buying power, but no one in prison was interested in trading ten cards of Cipramil.

Chapter Twenty-Seven

BEN

'Pare was built in the 1960s when you wasn't even around, kiddo,' Diamond said to Ben. 'You wasn't even a swimmer in your old man's balls.' He let out a throaty guffaw.

Sometimes Diamond could drone on about absolutely nothing. Today, however, he owned Ben's attention.

The Chubb van they were riding in swung around a corner, forcing Ben up against his fellow lagger.

'Was based on a U-S-of-A design,' Diamond continued, shouldering Ben off him. 'The quadrangle meant for ex-e-cut-ions.' He stretched out the word for maximum effect.

'And you will swing from the neck until you are dead,' he said, mimicking an American drawl. 'But,' he added, his mouth turning down in disappointment, 'never came to that. There's three cells next to the quad which spos'd to be the waiting cells for the condemned. Know what I mean, eh? Fuckin' death row, man!'

Diamond hadn't stopped talking about maxi since they'd left Mount Eden. It was just Ben's luck to get transferred with him. Mind you, he was hungry for any information about his new home.

He closed his eyes and climbed the scaffold in his mind. Saw the cloud of darkness fall behind his lids as a black bag was dropped over his head. Felt the rope tighten.

He opened his eyes wide, pulling his lids right back over his eyeballs.

'What you staring at?' Diamond barked.

'Nothin'.'

Diamond had his back against the square of window, blocking Ben's view; so when the van stopped, Ben was surprised to discover that they were already in the middle of the Paremoremo yard – another regulation enclosure with generic familiarity. But that's where the similarity ended. And it wasn't long before Ben found himself wishing for the long, cold corridors of The Rock. Paremoremo was different. Bigger. Blanker. More serious.

This is it, thought Ben. The final stop for the next thirteen years. The place where hope dies.

He and Diamond were locked into one of the holding cells until processing. The cell was bare, save for a brass plaque positioned above the door. Diamond read out the words, parading his literacy and mastery of Māori. '*Kotahi ano te kaupapa; kote oranga o te iwi*: *There is only one purpose to our work, the wellness and well-being of the people.*'[4]

Ben liked the sound of the words. They were full and round and had a sort of rhythm.

At the Receiving Office he learnt about his new crib: Ground floor. Cell 3. B Block. West Wing. Colour code blue. He couldn't believe it. Gang colours were forbidden in the boob, yet here he was being given a blue overall. One of the units at Pare was officially blue! The Crips and Black Power guys would surely be having the last laugh.

He lined up for the regulation strip-search of new inmates. He'd endured one in Receiving at Mount Eden too, and another the time the drug dogs picked up the scent of dope in his cell. But rumour had it, as per Diamond's info, that at Pare at least two strip-searches were done every day on random laggers.

Ben took off his T-shirt while two screws looked on. He lifted his arms slowly. Nothing. He put his shirt back on before dropping his pants and spreading his legs. He bent over. Nothing. He knew they couldn't do an orifice exam – only police permitted – so they never found the bundle in cling film he'd squirrelled away. It would keep him going for a time, a bit of crush and needle.

His crib was smaller than his last, and there was no sharing in maxi. He thought he'd never want to share again, but the long hours alone since Jocko had moved on had changed his mind.

He climbed onto his new bunk and peered out of the barred window. No green in sight. No grass, no trees, no moss, no leaves. Nothing but rounds of razor wire cutting up the sky. Razor wire moved when you touched it, sending ripples jangling down the line. According to Diamond, the bleed-out time was four minutes if you got trapped and sliced.

'No point going to the yard,' his case officer instructed. 'It's already after three. *Kai* is at four, then lockdown at five.'

Ben knew what would be for tea. Roast chicken. It was on the menu at Mount Eden too, and would be at every prison around the country. It was part of the national menu plan for prisoners, all eating the same thing on the same day at the same time.

He lay back on the grey blanket, which felt like a scouring pad and smelt like one too. That's when it hit him how much he missed smells. Normal smells. Prison laundered out all trace of the outside world. As a kid he'd loved his mother's smell – a sweet earthiness breaking through the cigarette smoke and cleaning agents.

Ben breathed in deeply, held onto the air, then let it out with a stuttering sob. Pressing his fingers into his eyes sent ripples of green and white light swelling into black. He blew his nose on his shirt and stared up at the ceiling. A trail of ants curved across the cell, making a perforated line down one wall and ending in a dark full stop.

He got up and went over to investigate. Where the line ended, the tiny creatures were swarming over a hardened blob of chewing gum. Ben pulled it off the wall, shook off the ants and stuck the knob into his mouth. It was hard and tasteless, but after he'd worked it a bit it grew softer and more elastic. He took it out of his mouth, divided it into four and used it to stick up his only poster – the one he'd found crumpled in the yard at Mount Eden. It featured *The Blues* just after they'd defeated *The Force* in Perth, so qualifying for the semi-finals against *The Sharks* in Durban. The poster was munted, but Ben liked the line-up of solid guys with their victorious grins. Sometimes he imagined he was one of them; he'd hear the fans scream as he caught the ball, outmanoeuvred his opponents and sprinted for the try line. And for a fleeting moment, when the crowd gasped and a Mexican wave rolled, he felt good about himself.

He'd played rugby in school a bit, but by intermediate his mates had all bulked out, while he'd stayed lean and wiry. He stopped making the team. By that time, he was no longer a regular at school anyway.

A shadow fell across his cell. He looked up. A huge guy, all shiny flesh, filled the doorway. His face was as flat as a dinner plate, and his right ear was missing a wide wedge of flesh.

The visitor put his nose into the air and sniffed. 'I smell dog. But hey, guess what, it's the runt of the pack.'

It hadn't taken them long. Ben had been in his new crib only half an hour and already Ryan's affiliations had caught up with him.

Diamond told him he would likely be in with a mix of the gangs. It wasn't like in Mount Eden where they kept you apart. Here it was divide and conquer.

'Just don't take the bait,' Cole had advised. 'And ignore the taunts.'

'Know what's for tea?' the big guy boomed. 'Roast chook. Roast fuckin' chook. My favourite.'

'Name's Toroa,' Ben managed, his insides wobbling as he prepared for the bash.

'But a skinny runt like you won't be needing a feed, now will you?'

Ben stared at him.

'My boss gets real hungry and he don't like to see good food wasted on trash like you. So, listen up, brother. Every night I'm gonna come and get your tea. Just the meat mind you; Rider ain't too partial to vegetables.'

'Lockdown in twenty,' a screw called out.

The guy in the doorway glanced casually over his shoulder.

'Leave the chicken on your plate covered by a piece of bog roll. When the plates get cleared, I'll collect it. I don't want to have to mess with your pretty face.'

Later, Ben stared at the drumstick. The skin had been roasted to a golden colour and the flesh was going be sweet, he could just see it. The guys in the kitchen had done a good job.

He dipped a finger into the pool of gravy. It was salty. He

swept his mashed potato through the sauce. In two scoops it was gone. Then he toyed with the chicken, pushing it this way and that around his plate. Finally, he covered it with a square of white toilet paper.

It would be many months before he got to eat meat again.

Beyond

Benjamin, I feel a blooming in my breast. You responded to te reo
Māori *– your people's language – even though you did not understand
the very words you heard. This is good. So good. The words, they belong
to you. Their pull is deeper than any conscious thought or tutored
knowledge. Your response springs from a deeper place, a place with
origins in the beginning of time.*

Time . . . I must move on with my story.

*So determined was the white man to assimilate all Māori that he
worked hard to dismantle our tribes and our whole Māori way of life.
Even our precious language was discarded. Our children were now
taught in English,* te reo *actively discouraged.*

*And we bought into this ideal. The English dream. The clothes,
discipline, the sports and high teas. Many of our people melted
under the heat of city lights into this whiteness, their Māoritanga
soon just a puddle from the past. A new life beckoned, offering
work, excitement and the English way. Ah, the English way.
Rugby, tennis and big brass bands. Pikelets, scones and wedges of
bright-orange cheese.*

How hard we strove to be citizens of this 'superior' world. We even went to war alongside our pale-faced compatriots to make real our intent, to fight for their Crown. Yet despite our bravery and the honours steeped upon us, we remained brown. Too brown.

Chapter Twenty-Eight

CARLA

Carla covered her head with a pillow. She couldn't say why she set an alarm, but she always did. It wasn't so much having to be somewhere – she rarely had to be anywhere – it was more about lending shape to the day. It also gave the weekend a point of difference; she never set an alarm on the weekend.

After a five-minute *snooze* respite, the beeping began again. She sat up and dropped her legs over the side of the bed, letting her toes brush the carpet. The coarse fibres prickled her soles. Slowly she stood up. It was important not to rush; the day had to be carefully filled.

After putting on her new slippers from the Two Dollar Shop – the old possum-fur ones had finally disintegrated – she reached for her dressing gown. As she tied a perfect bow in the mirror, she was mindful to keep her eyes on the task at hand and not allow them to explore the rest of her reflection.

In the kitchen, water spluttered out of the tap into an empty kettle, the pipes, like the day, still stiff and awkward. She placed an already used tea bag into her mug – her cue to now attend to the drapes and blinds. If timed correctly, the kettle would start to whistle just as she was opening the last blind.

She lifted the steaming jug and poured. The crumpled brown tea bag floated to the surface, releasing stingy ribbons of colour. Carla added a thimbleful of long-life milk, a spoonful of sugar, and stirred. Three rotations.

Mug in hand, she sank down into the chair at the window and watched Oteha Valley Road wake, cars gliding out from nowhere like disturbed woodlice.

At nine o'clock she stood up, prepared and ate a buttered slice of raisin toast, then placed two frozen sausages on the bench to defrost, before going to get dressed. Lunch, a ham sandwich, was at twelve. A midday nap would follow, then a trip into Browns Bay to visit Kevin. By five-thirty she'd be home again, seated in front of the television, with a glass of cheap sherry in hand. Sausages and mash were at six, and after that, the day could be allowed to seep into the long night. This order and routine was everything. It harnessed the flux.

She was having her afternoon nap when the telephone rang. Her mouth clunked shut, arresting her sleepy drool.

She reached for the receiver. 'Hello.'

'Mrs Reid?' A strong Australian accent.

'Speaking.'

'Bryce Deacon, Auckland Prison.'

Still drugged with sleep, Carla sat up.

'This is a courtesy call, really. Just to notify you that Ben Toroa's first parole hearing is coming up at the end of the month. You are invited to attend if you wish. You may, however, simply prefer to write a letter in opposition to, or support of, the prisoner's release. Should you elect not to attend in person, we will notify you of the outcome in writing.'

'Oh.' Carla's mind sluggishly made the relevant connections. Even the name Toroa was momentarily foreign. It had been over four years.

'I'll . . . Um . . . I'll have to think about it. I mean, I'm not sure whether I—'

'I understand. If you do decide to participate, you are entitled to bring a support person to accompany you into the hearing. We've posted you a letter and booklet outlining the process, but I'll give you a number to call in case you have any other queries.'

Carla scrambled for a pen and scribbled down the number on the back of a birthday card from Geoffrey and Mildred – a sunglasses-wearing baboon blowing out candles in the configuration of the number fifty.

'Between you and me, Mrs Reid, I don't expect parole to be granted, so probably no concerns there. Just a formality, really.'

'Yes . . . uh, right. Thank you.'

Then a click and the line went dead.

Carla chewed off a piece of nail and worked it between her teeth. Parole. Already? He'd barely served one-third of his sentence.

Everyone had said time would be a great healer, and in some respects they had been right. The passage of years had dulled her grief and faded the intensity of her pain. Yet now, like some cruel joke, she found herself back at the beginning, the anguish as acute as ever.

She fiddled with her wristwatch, flicking the clasp open and shut. Just before two. With her siesta interrupted, the day was in disarray. What would she do with the extra time? Kevin would still be asleep at the centre, and they wouldn't allow her to disturb him until three at the earliest.

* * *

The room for the parole hearing was bare – the walls, the whiteboard, even the waste-paper basket empty of any clues. The space reminded Carla of her old school science laboratory with its lifeless smell, rows of yellowed benches, and lone desk up front.

She made her way to the back of the room and sat down on a chair in the corner. She put her handbag at her feet and crossed her legs. Then she uncrossed them and picked up her bag. She rummaged through it for a mint. She shifted two seats along. Then one along from that.

A man in prison green put his head around the door. '*Kia ora*,' he said with a friendly grin. 'Won't be long now.'

She nodded.

No sooner had he left than the door swung open and four men in dark suits and a woman in a cherry-red two-piece filed in with all the gravity and solemnity of a funeral processional. They took up their seats at the front table and one of the men poured each of them a glass of water. A policewoman talking on her mobile wandered in and sat down in the front row, followed by a large, wheezing woman, who subsided into the chair right in front of Carla, obscuring her view completely. The woman's dandruff-sprinkled blouse ballooned in and out with each whistling breath.

Just like in a movie theatre, thought Carla irritably, people clumping together in tight pockets when there is an entire room of seats available. She stood up and moved back to her original corner.

Ten minutes elapsed. The members of the parole board shuffled documents and conferred in hushed tones. More people arrived. The noise level in the small room rose. Talking. Coughing. Sneezing. Chairs scraping.

After fidgeting and worrying at a scab on the back of her hand, it started to bleed. Carla dabbed at the raw skin with a tissue until the tiny spring of red dried up. When she looked up her throat constricted around a painful gulp of air. *He* was there. In the room. A dark, brooding shape. His back to her.

He was taller than she recalled, his black hair longer and wilder, and streaked with grease that glistened under the lights. His tracksuit bottoms hung low over his hollowed-out bottom and his shoulders curled away from her.

The man in green uniform stood up to open the session. Carla tried hard to concentrate on his words, but her eyes kept wandering to Jack's killer.

'And he has been involved in a number of violent outbursts,' the officer said in a plank-flat voice. He looked down at the notes on his clipboard. 'It is noted that the prisoner's behaviour has in fact deteriorated over the past two years of incarceration. He has shown little motivation to change, not signing up for any of the recommended rehabilitation classes. He has also been found with contraband on his person on several occasions and . . .'

A psychologist – the wheezy woman – was next. Her tight bra corrugated her outline.

'I would have grave concerns about the release of prisoner Toroa into the community at this time. As you have heard, his behaviour has often been aggressive and hostile towards staff, and his tendency to violence appears to have become more pronounced in the past eighteen months – an observation already outlined by my colleague. The prisoner is manipulative to his own ends, and it is my opinion that . . .'

Everyone was facing the front, their backs turned on Carla. They should have been addressing her, not five random people up front! Had the woman in red ever felt Toroa's hand over her mouth?

The man with a silver tiepin, had he smelt Toroa's fermented breath on his face? And the guy with a chisel-thin nose and absent chin, had he ever heard Toroa's soulless voice raging around him? The degrees that no doubt hung on their walls would attest to their qualifications and wisdom. But what of real life? She could tell them. She had the most important qualification of all.

She'd not been able to stay away from the hearing. She wanted something from the process. Perhaps the knowledge that Toroa was suffering. The security of seeing him shackled? A sign of repentance, maybe. An apology. At least an acknowledgement – if not from him, then from the others – of her grief, of the sense of hollowness inside that never abated. The law had forgotten about her and her family. To have simply written a letter would have been too academic, too abstract. She had come as Jack and Kevin's representative. She was there to remind the board that it was dealing with people, not a series of events and blood-soaked evidence already bleached by time.

The busyness of the small room suddenly overwhelmed her. The voices were too loud, the place too hot. She felt herself disengage; she'd become a master at it. Had she taken the chops out of the freezer in her hurry to catch the bus? She should stop on the way home to buy grapes for Kevin at the fruiterer – the black seedless ones he loved. She had to remember to also stop at the post office to pay her electricity bill. It was overdue. They would cut her off.

Toroa's voice was slow, slovenly – one word running into the next – and evil deep. He slouched there before the table of five, speaking indistinctly, sloppily. Carla shook with anger. His posture smacked of disinterest and irreverence. His demeanour was blatantly scuttling the civility such a proceeding demanded. She couldn't even see his face – his untidy mane concealing his profile from her. She had the right to see his face.

Bile shot into her mouth. He was asking to be released.

Hearing that word suddenly crystallised for Carla what the day was about. She had not allowed herself to even entertain the idea he might be freed. It was unthinkable. The man who'd telephoned had said the hearing was a mere formality. Yet the people on the panel seemed to be listening to him. Considering. Weighing up the possibility.

She swayed in her chair.

Then, it was over. Abruptly.

A brief explanation. No slow build to a climax. The parole board had announced its decision. Toroa had failed in his bid.

Carla was the first to leave, but as she hurried from the room, she in no way felt the victor.

Chapter Twenty-Nine

BEN

'Fuck 'em all!'

'Chill, Bennie boy. There's always next year.'

'Piss off, Randy! Anyway, you in this shithole for longer than me. Your mitt'll have fallen off by then from all the jacking off you do.'

'I thought you weren't in any hurry to get out of the boob, brotha? Wasn't that what you said last night? "Not like something special waiting for me out there." Your words, bro, not mine.'

'I know what I said. And I meant it. I won't give those pencil necks the satisfaction of thinking I'm desperate or nothin'. They just want the power to play with my fate. Well I'm gonna have the wood over them.'

'Sometimes your logic's all twisted, man. Anyway, we're tight.'

Ben ignored the mixed compliment. He was still reeling from the belated realisation that what he'd just missed out on was the one thing he actually wanted the most. He hadn't made any effort to present well, hadn't bothered to enrol in any courses in the lead-up to the hearing. He hadn't even brushed his hair for it.

Thought he didn't care. But standing there in front of those suits had vacuumed up all the interference in his life and clarified his thoughts. His freedom could have been just a signature away. Now he couldn't let go of the notion. In his mind he was already released and cruising the hood.

'I'd give anything for a proper piss-up, bro. A shit ton of DB draught, a tub of chicken wings from the Chinks. Smokes too. And bitches. As many as I can handle.'

They were standing in the corner of the yard, not easily visible to the bridge. Randy glanced over his shoulder, then put out a hand, his fist clenched tight. 'My shout.'

'Fuck me! Is this what I think it is?' Ben said, grabbing the small parcel. 'Where'd you get it?'

His friend tapped the side of his nose. 'Special delivery.'

'Jesus, you're the man,' Ben crooned, a proper smile spreading over his face.

'Stick with me, bro,' Randy grinned, slapping him on the back. Then he stepped behind the wall to shoot up.

'Hey,' Ben called after him.

'What?'

'I'm getting out of this hellhole next hearing.'

'Whatever you say, brother.'

'I got me a plan.'

Randy looked up, his eyes already glassy.

'I'm gonna meet with that Reid woman. I'm gonna r-e-f-o-r-m. Tell her I'm real sorry for what I did. Them parole dudes gonna be so impressed, it won't be long before Ben Toroa parties when he wants to party, and not just when his homie gets his paws on some!'

* * *

Dear Mrs Reid,

I am writing to you on behalf of Ben Toroa, who, as you are aware, is currently serving a fourteen-year prison term in Auckland Maximum Security Prison. You will no doubt recall his unwilling participation in the restorative justice meeting a few years ago. This is not uncommon in such cases. Frequently, it takes a significant amount of time before the offender will come to own his crime.

Recently, prisoner Toroa has expressed regret over the offence and vocalised a desire to meet with you again. We are encouraged by this gesture and are hopeful that it signifies a change in his attitude – a crucial step towards the reform of an offender. The prisoner was very young at the time he perpetrated the felony and with the maturity that comes with additional years under his belt, this may account for his recent transformation.

We understand if you no longer wish to have anything to do with him. A significant time has elapsed since the incident and we hope you have been able to move beyond the terrible events. If, however, this is something you would wish to participate in, we will provide every support. I encourage you to give the proposal due consideration. We must look beyond retribution towards rehabilitation, if we are to achieve a better society.

The meeting would be closely monitored, and counselling made available both before and after the session, should you so desire it.

I look forward to hearing from you.

Yours sincerely,

Jim Haslop

Manager

Auckland Maximum Security Prison

Chapter Thirty

CARLA

The morning was brisk, the sky a frost blue and the air taut. Carla welcomed the changing season, winter at least more congruent with her reclusiveness. It was acceptable to stay indoors when it was cold; shunning the sun of summer was altogether stranger.

Her Citroën complained at the early start, heading up The Avenue in lurches and pauses. She turned on the radio and dialled through the crackles to find a station. Soon a light melody filled the moment.

The road was steep as it wound up the hill to merge with Paremoremo Road, a once regular haunt of hers. She used to visit the Curly Cabbage on a weekly basis, the farm store boasting the freshest produce in town. Good old Roy with his polio-short leg and flaming-red hair, always throwing in something extra with her order, and never tiring of sourcing the unusual ingredients she needed for her Mediterranean meals. 'The Italian variety of parsley has a more subtle flavour, Roy. And the texture is altogether more pleasing than the curly-leafed variety.'

'I'll take your word for it, Mrs Reid,' he'd say with a chuckle, his ruddy cheeks dimpling into deep culverts. He'd eventually cultivated some for her from seed, in exchange for a jar of salsa verde whenever she made a batch.

She salivated now as she thought of the tangy blend of chopped parsley, anchovies, boiled egg yolks, garlic and olive oil – a condiment to be eaten alongside poached chicken or boiled meats. Roy just ate it by the spoonful!

A stack of taupe town houses now covered the slope where pumpkin vines had once rambled, the rows of affordable housing spreading greedily over the hills to transform the green curves into monotonous urban angles. The city had cast its net widely and without regard.

After a time, the landscape became more honest – the cabbage-tree skyline, orange-clay earth, and grey-green manuka, siding more closely with her memories.

Then she was on the brow of the hill. She slowed. Below her, crouching in the valley was Paremoremo Prison, dark and brooding.

'No mobiles allowed, love.' The guard's accent was pure Cockney. He was gaunt, with impossibly high cheekbones and close-set eyes. He stood behind the counter in regulation green, the last letters of a tattooed name poking out from under his uniform.

Carla tried not to stare at his nose – an unsettling violet colour.

'You can leave your bag in one of these lockers. You'll need a locker too, sir.'

Carla turned to see a young man standing behind her. He had an open face and a head of loose blonde curls. He smiled. An ID badge – Social Worker – was clipped to his brown jumper. She could imagine him working in such a role; his pleasant face fitted.

'I need to take this in with me,' he said to the guard, holding onto his small red rucksack. 'Got all my paperwork and that sort of stuff, mate.'

The other guard at the desk invited Carla through the metal detector.

'Have a seat, Mrs Reid,' he said, pointing to a wooden bench. 'Mr Haslop shouldn't be long. Just finishing up in a meeting.' He tipped his head towards a door marked *Manager*.

'Is there a toilet nearby?' Carla asked, her stomach a knot of nerves.

'That door there, love. Unisex.'

She closed the door to the windowless booth. Someone had sprayed the air freshener too generously and a cloying scent of frangipani hung heavily in the air. The margarine-yellow walls had been scrubbed so that they shone and Carla could catch a silhouetted shadow of herself in them. On the back of the door was a handwritten note: *Please remove any pubic hair from the toilet seat. It is only courtesy. Rachel.* Life beyond the security of Carla's daily routine was so surprisingly crude, so blatant.

Back outside, she sat down where the guard had first left her. The bench was hard, the bones of her bottom uncushioned by any extra flesh. She shifted, trying to get comfortable. It was cold and her jumper was thin. She should have brought a coat. She fiddled with her visitor's sticker, pulling it on and off until she'd blunted its stickiness altogether.

'Jesus, Bob. What we gonna do 'bout it?' It was the Cockney guard, in a loud whisper.

'Is . . . dog handler still . . . site?' It was the other guard. '. . . here this morning.'

Her interest piqued, Carla strained to follow the thread of conversation.

'I'll ring down to Rachel and see.'

'Stupid fella. What was he thinking?'

'Look, it's not our problem. Just wanna hand it over. Then me job's done.'

'Hiya. Rachel. Ross here. Good, yeah. Listen we got an incident at the gate. Is the dog handler still with you? Yup. Great. Can you send him up ASAP?'

Carla was deep in the intrigue when a door to her left swung open and several people emerged. One, a very tall man with a fluff of grey hair and dense black eyebrows, moved towards her, his hand outstretched in greeting.

'Mrs Reid? Sorry to have kept you waiting. Jim Haslop. Do come in.'

The prison manager had an easy smile, a strong handshake, and a warm office.

The room was frugally decorated with a wide wooden desk off to one side and a navy leather couch pushed up against the wall. A rubber plant, its leaves dulled by dust, stood under the window beside a fish tank, which was home to two sluggish goldfish.

Carla sat down on the couch. The seat, clearly just recently vacated, was still warm.

Haslop went over the procedure for the day, his manner a careful blend of kindliness and pragmatism. He didn't fit the Hollywood image of a truculent prison warden that she'd been expecting. This was no Karl Malden of Alcatraz.

Once the preliminaries had been dispensed with and the red tape cleared, walkie-talkie commands were relayed, and Haslop and Carla began their descent into the bowels of the building. They moved briskly through a warren of corridors, their progress clatteringly arrested as gates were electronically unlocked and then re-secured under the watchful eye of closed-circuit cameras. Carla had to move quickly to keep pace with Haslop's long strides.

The room set aside for the meeting was empty except for six blue chairs spaced evenly in a semicircle. A red plastic chair completed the ring. Déjà vu. How the intervening years fell away.

One by one, four other officials arrived: Toroa's unit manager, a caseworker, the prison psychologist, and a member of Victim Support – not Lorraine, though; she'd moved to Nelson.

There was much preliminary discussion about the format the meeting would take, with considerations diplomatically vocalised and recommendations made. Carla peeled off her jumper. Despite the group consisting of only a handful of people, the acoustics left the room feeling cluttered and overcrowded – too many words echoing around the room and already muddling her thoughts.

When the door off to her right finally opened, it came as a relief. She sucked in a stuttering breath. This time she could get a proper look at him. The boy had unfurled into a man, his teenage skin shed, his lankiness filled out, his Adam's apple absorbed into the thickness of manhood.

He walked across to the red chair, his boyish swagger replaced now with a steady stride.

Even when the caseworker opened with a *karakia*, Carla couldn't stop herself from staring at him – the three-day-old stubble, the jagged scar puckering his smooth brown cheek, the tattoo spreading out over his fingers like a spider's web – long, tapering fingers reminiscent of scrawnier days. Those fingers. That wrist. That fist.

'Ben has prepared a statement of regret.' Haslop's voice punctured Carla's stupor. 'Stacey will read it out.'

The caseworker opened the manila folder on her lap, swept a

strand of hair off her face and began to read. 'When I committed a crime against your family I had no thought for my actions. For this I am sorry. I have seen the errors of my ways. In prison I have found God. He has shown me the way. I hope you can find it in your heart to forgive me.'

'Thank you, Ben,' Haslop said. 'This is an encouraging first step. To ask for forgiveness, you have to first acknowledge wrongdoing, and today you have done that. Well done.'

Carla felt flat. Nothing about this 'momentous occasion' rung true. Toroa's words were simply words on a page and devoid of any depth. They were not even spoken by their author. Not even acknowledged with his eyes. Nothing about Toroa's demeanour, not even his exaggerated solemnity, suggested there was any sincerity behind them.

'Mrs Reid?'

The group looked on expectantly. Toroa was flicking his thumbs against his forefingers.

Haslop leant towards her, inviting her participation. 'Mrs Reid, is there something you would like to say in return?'

'Yes,' Carla said after a long pause.

Haslop's face relaxed. Toroa's tightened.

She bent down and picked up her handbag. Unhurried, she unfastened the clasp.

'I too have something to be read,' she said.

Haslop smiled.

'And since we are reading each other's words,' she continued, 'perhaps Ben could read it to us?'

The prison manager tilted his head uneasily, clearly uncertain as to whether it was sarcasm he'd detected in her voice. He fixed his eyes on the tatty mauve envelope in her hand.

Carla held it out. Toroa's eyes flicked up and down, but he made no attempt to reach for it. Haslop intercepted the delivery and cleared his throat. 'Is this your victim impact statement, Mrs Reid?'

'Of sorts,' she said. 'It's a card from my son, Jack, given to my husband and me on the day he moved out of home to go flatting in the city. I think it should give, uh, Mr Toroa, a clearer appreciation of the impact his actions had on my family.'

Haslop looked down at the floral design on the card. 'May I?' he asked, and on her nod, opened and perused it, then he held it out. 'Ben.'

Toroa looked up, but did not take the envelope.

'Ben?'

Stacey, the caseworker, touched Haslop on the elbow. 'Jim,' she whispered, 'Ben can't read.'

Carla thought she must have misheard.

Haslop flushed. 'Of course! I forgot.' Quickly, he passed the card back to Carla. 'Mrs Reid, Ben can't read. Perhaps you'd be so kind as to.'

'Can't read?' Carla blurted out in disbelief. Everyone could read! Toroa was a grown man. Was this yet another ploy on behalf of the thug to retain control of the situation and steer it in whichever direction he wished?

Ignoring Haslop's outstretched hand, Carla looked across at the prisoner. She was momentarily thrown; his self-satisfied eyes were now downcast and his brazen body had folded in on itself. His slouch spoke more of defeat, than disinterest. Confused, she hesitated, unsure of how to proceed.

Everyone was waiting.

Flustered, she left the envelope in Haslop's outstretched hand and began to recite the words from memory.

'"Mum and Dad",' her voice quivered. She clenched her teeth. '"Mum and Dad, you've always believed in me and made so many sacrifices on my behalf. Thank you! I leave the farm today with a rucksack full of your love. This is all I need to succeed. I hope to do you proud. Love Jack. PS. I'll be back, Mum. Don't worry".'

After a long pause, Carla looked slowly around the room at the six other faces.

'This is my loss.'

Ben Toroa's face was again set strong, his posture once more defiant. But Carla had glimpsed something else, and for the first time she felt a little less hostile towards him.

As she headed out of the prison that day, through the metal detector and past the British guards, she spotted the man who'd followed her in a few hours earlier – the social worker with a brown jumper and red rucksack. He was sitting glumly on the bench beside a policeman. His rucksack lay open on the counter beside a plastic bag, which seemed to be stuffed with dry green leaves.

Chapter Thirty-One

CARLA

The days following her visit to the prison freewheeled into chaos and Carla's carefully honed routine collapsed. Conflicting emotions, revisited memories, and puzzling thoughts had been stirred up in the cauldron of her mind.

Every morning for the rest of that week she drove up The Avenue, then down into the valley where the concrete and barbed-wire beast waited for her to slow, do a U-turn, and head home again.

One day, after returning from this pointless pilgrimage, she decided to drop in on Kevin. She always visited in the afternoon, but it had just gone ten o'clock when she pulled into the grounds of the facility, hopeful they'd let her in.

Kevin had graduated to the hospital wing, where he could receive more specialised nursing care. The previous few months had seen him suffer a series of setbacks: one bout of pneumonia after another, a deep-vein thrombosis, and recently, a bladder infection, which had spread to his kidneys and was still challenging the doctors.

However, regardless of what condition Carla found Kevin in, whether he was aggressive, in a drug-induced stupor, or simply slow and bewildered, her vigil was never less than a full three hours, the maximum allowed for a visit in the medical wing.

Mostly she knitted squares for Hospice while sitting beside his bed. Occasionally she paged through a magazine. Never a book. No longer able to engage with fictional characters, she hadn't read in a very long time.

'Oh, Mrs R, it is a surprise to see you so early,' Lisi, the kitchen aide, said as she rattled down the corridor with a tea trolley. Tucked into her sharp black curls was a salmon-coloured hibiscus bloom.

Carla smiled. 'Yes, Lisi. Just to keep you on your toes. Can I please slip in and see him?' She herself wasn't sure why she was there. Everything was out of kilter.

Lisi beamed, flashing her beautiful milk-white teeth. 'All good. You just in time for tea.'

'Oh, I'd love a cup.'

'You look good today, Mrs R. Something different?'

Carla shrugged. 'Washed my hair.'

Lisi chortled. 'No. Something else. White, one sugar, right?'

'I don't know how you remember everyone's preferences.'

'Just the special ones,' Lisi said with a wink and passed Carla a heavy-duty, thick-rimmed cup.

Kevin was snoring loudly when Carla opened the door to his room, a bubble of mucus ballooning from his left nostril each time he exhaled. She wiped his nose gently, careful not to wake him, then kissed his brow. He smelt of the fragrance-free, hypoallergenic hospital soap that swam in the soap dish of his small sink. She pulled up a chair. The whole wing had recently been redecorated, the tired pink decor making way for new beige walls and donkey-brown furnishings. The reflected light lent Kevin a more sallow hue. Or perhaps it wasn't the light.

Carla's tea was safely lukewarm with tiny globules of fat floating on the surface. Lisi had also smuggled her in a freshly baked scone. It was still warm and the knob of butter on top had melted, leaving a glistening smear of gold.

Carla opened the canvas bag she was carrying and cursed. She'd brought the wrong bag. In her mind's eye she could see her knitting lying beside the sofa where she'd fallen asleep the previous evening, *Campbell Live* swimming into *Firstline*.

Three hours stretched ahead of her, and of all days, today she needed some distraction.

She rearranged Kevin's toiletries, repositioned his slippers under the bed, and gave his basin a clean with a wet-wipe, removing the grey blobs of toothpaste that had hardened around the rim. She switched on his radio, quickly turning the volume down. Rock music! Every day she turned it to Concert FM, and every day someone changed it back.

She looked around. There was little left in the generic cubicle of space to link to Kevin. His few belongings had been further whittled down in the latest shift – a gradual paring back to naught.

She peered through the thick glass water carafe, screwing up her eyes and playing with the visual distortions it created of the photograph behind it. She reached for the frame, recapturing the clear lines of the three people in the picture. Moisture had crept under the glass and a milky stain now discoloured an already sun-faded family. In the centre stood the farmer – sun-brown, leathery skin, strong muscles, bright eyes – one hand resting on his young boy's shoulder, the other wrapped around his wife's tiny waist.

Carla put down the photograph and looked over at the wretched figure in bed – folds of transparent skin pleated over sunken eyes, a crumbling frame collapsed into the soft mattress . . . She sank back in the chair and closed her eyes.

'Carla?'

She started. No one else was in the room.

'Carly.'

It couldn't be. He hadn't called her that in ages.

Kevin's eyes were open and shining, as if cloudy cataracts had just been stripped away.

'Kev, you're – you're awake!'

'How are you?' he croaked, struggling to sit up.

She jerked into action, slipping an arm through the crook of his, and behind his back, pulling him in to her. He was so light. 'Here, let me help you.' She cradled his wafer of body against her while using her other hand to puff up the pillows. Then she lowered him gently back down.

He sighed and shut his eyes. 'How are you?'

'Me? Oh me? I'm – I'm fine.'

'That's good, snoeks.'

Snoeks! Was she losing her mind? Had she finally succumbed to the madness that ever hovered in the wings?

'Well, maybe not so good,' she found herself saying.

Kevin coughed, tenacious strings of phlegm netting across his airways. 'Not so good,' he repeated.

In an instant the years concertinaed and they were again sitting out on the deck at sundown, sharing a drink and the day's events.

'. . . and when I gave him Jack's card, he couldn't even read it. He can't read, Kev! How can he understand what he's taken from us when he can't even read? I mean, it's like he's a child in the body

226

of an adult. God, I almost felt sorry for him. Can you believe it? I must be mad.'

Kevin stretched out his hand – a web of raised purple veins and sunken furrows. Her heart swelled with the connection, the voluntary touch of his skin on hers.

'You are a teacher,' he said slowly.

'I *was* a teacher.'

He squeezed her hand tighter. 'You are a teacher,' he repeated. His hand was cold and bony and pulsed irregularly with life.

Tears ran down her cheeks. The relief of a problem shared after all this time.

She slipped her arms under him and lifted him again towards her, his frame like a wisp of air in her hungry embrace. 'Thank you, my love. Thank you.'

Then she felt his body gradually deflate and the breeze of his thin breath on her face grew still. She laid him back down. A faint smile pulled at the corners of his chapped lips.

She waited for the next bubble of mucus to balloon from his nose. It never came.

Jack's ashes were put alongside Kevin in the casket. Carla would not have her husband cremated like she'd done with their son. She wanted him to be laid to rest somewhere beautiful, surrounded by gracious old trees and an undulating lawn. She wanted him to be somewhere permanent – a rectangle of grass that resembled his exact height and girth, a patch in the sunshine she could tend, visit, talk to.

Chapter Thirty-Two

BEN

It is rising. Up to his neck. He can't swim and struggles to stay above the warm, red current. He's going to drown. It is waterfalling into his mouth. He can't breathe. It gushes into his ears, loud as thunder. He cries out, but the waves of blood swamp all sound.

'Jesus!' Ben sat bolt upright in bed. The walls, fractured by a web of fine cracks, came slowly into focus.

He wiped a hand across his face, then stared at his trembling palm. No red, just tears. Same dream. The same suffocating feeling he'd experienced the time he'd jumped off Kauri Point Wharf as a kid – all bravado, unable to admit to his friends he couldn't swim. Down, down, down, kicking and jerking, arms and legs flailing. Some big guy, an off-duty fireman, had jumped in to save him.

Too scared to fall asleep again, Ben got up. He'd had enough. Robbed of Zs yet again – the only way to use up fourteen hours of nothing. Ever since that woman had come to visit, he hadn't been able to sleep properly. She'd brought the spirits with her and they were playing noughts and crosses with his sanity.

His mum had started appearing in his dreams too – blood

trickling from her ears like the time Ryan burst her eardrum. Whenever Ryan and his mum used to fight, Ben and Lily would hide under the bed until the screaming stopped. It was horrid huddling there – their own reprieve marbled with fear. They were safe while Ryan was distracted, but they never knew what they'd find when they climbed out.

Ben wiped his nose on his sleeve. No place for tears in Pare. He hoped to hell nobody had heard anything. He could just imagine what would go down: 'Staunch Toroa bleating in his sleep like a fuckin' baby!'

Lockdown wasn't lifted till eight. Ben counted it out in his mind. Still ages to go. He was out of smokes and out of fun. He toyed with the idea of clanging on the metal pipe that ran along the back of his cell to the adjacent cell. He could call in a favour. Get a joint or something to tide him over till the muster. Then he thought better of waking the whole block. He wasn't up to a rumble. He felt too stink.

Looking around the cell, he let his eyes settle on one of the posters on his wall, then slid his hands into his pants. But after what seemed like forever, he abandoned the ritual; the topless slag had lost her magic.

He hauled himself out of bed and lay face down on the floor to do push-ups. 'One and two and three and four and—'

'Which dick is exercising in the middle of the fuckin' night?' Silver's voice hollered down the corridor.

No one messed with Silver unless they had a death wish. He was head of the Pare Chapter. He could get to people, whether they were inside or out. Rumour had it he'd recently arranged a hit on a narc who'd run off to Oz.

Silence.

'Well, listen up, brotha, whoever you are. I'll smash your lousy head in if you make another fuckin' peep.'

Others began to waken and stir, scratching about in their cells like rats in a roof. Ben slipped back under his blanket and closed his eyes. The next thing he knew, the bell was announcing first roll.

'Prisoner Toroa.'

'Here.'

'Prisoner Toroa.'

'I said here!'

'To Visits.'

'What?'

'To Visits,' the guard repeated impatiently.

Ben felt the surge of excitement that any change in routine imported. He wasn't expecting anyone, but if admin had got it wrong — and they sometimes did — just the walk to Visits and back was a sufficient change from the habitual boredom of each day. Then again, if by some stroke of luck someone had decided to visit, smokes, weed, chocolate, or even a bit of porn could be on the menu. So long as it wasn't his Bible-bashing sister, Lily, he'd be good.

Lily's latest foster family — the third 'permanent' placement since their mum had died — was better than the previous ones. Before that, she'd had it pretty rough, poor kid. The first time she was allowed to visit him in jail, he'd got a real shock. She looked awful, not like the pretty Lil he remembered. Her skin had broken out into angry red cysts and her beautiful hair had been peroxided and turned a greenish yellow. Yet it wasn't the physical changes that bothered Ben so much as the fact that the light inside of her seemed to have gone out. There was stuff going on she just couldn't talk about, not even to him.

After running away for the hundredth time, she'd been placed with this new family, hopefully the last before she was deemed an adult. Things were good for a while. When she visited, she seemed a bit more like her old self. But then she started going all weird on him. By the sounds of it, the family was into some fundamentalist religious stuff and soon Lily was caught up in it too. She became bent on prising Ben from the devil's clutches. Whenever she visited, which started becoming too often, she was on a mission to convert him to the ways of the Lord.

As for the rest of his brothers and sisters, well, they were sprinkled all over the North Island like freckles on a Pākehā's face. He'd lost touch with them all. Someone told him Anika had topped herself, but he never got it confirmed. Getting information in prison was like playing Chinese Whispers; and you didn't know how far down the line you were when someone passed on information.

Haslop was standing at the top of the stairs. 'Ben.'

No staff ever used Ben's first name inside Pare. Hearing it carried him back to a different place, a different time, a forgotten world.

He soon realised this was not some chance meeting. This was it. There would be no visit.

'Ben, after a pretty positive meeting with Mrs Reid a month back, I've had a request come down from Head Office for another visit, from the victim herself this time.'

Ben was floored. He thought he'd seen the last of the woman. He'd reckoned on restorative justice being one session and one session only. Enough to convince the parole board next time.

Haslop slipped his hands into his pockets and leant forward, his long body wavering in space. 'I think something good has been set in motion.'

Ben wasn't so sure.

'Are you agreeable to us setting up another meeting?'

Ben looked down at his feet and kicked at an imaginary dog, then looked up abruptly, straight in Haslop's eyes. He could play ball if it meant he'd get one step closer to getting out of this place.

Beyond

*Sometimes it seems as if you are even further away, Benjamin Toroa,
than when the wind first brought news of you that mild March night.
I have watched the hardening of your heart and I see the way you now
navigate the road ahead; you have packed for one.*

*I am not surprised. After all, it is the way of many. And I
understand some of what brought you to this place, and some of what
prison has wrought.*

*Which brings me to when many of our own shifted to the city
in pursuit of the elusive Pākehā ideal. Slowly our communal Māori
way of life collapsed. Iwi and hapū were carved up, quartered and
packaged into small, solitary families. Men and women became defined
by themselves alone, a tribal identity of little relevance in the concrete,
high-rise future. And as individuals – unsupported, uncounselled,
unaccountable – they made their way in this chosen world.*

*But what good were the skills of a shepherd, hunter, carver or
weaver? The urban way demanded different talents, and many of
our own found themselves deemed 'unskilled' and forced again to find
poorly paid jobs in the freezing works, factories, and fisheries – jobs*

that were the first to go when the economy dipped and dived. Others not even that fortunate were simply added to the swelling girth of the unemployed.

So you see how a new landscape was being painted for Māori. A blighted one of dislocation and deterioration showcasing poverty in all its splendour.

And the walls of your cultural kete *kept unravelling, until the most important building block of all – the* whānau *or family – finally fell apart. You were born into this unanchored flux, Benjamin Toroa, with little left to hold you firm once the umbilical cord had been cut.*

Do you see yet where I am headed, boy? Do you follow?

Chapter Thirty-Three

CARLA

Same room. Same chairs. Carla knew the drill. The only difference was that now the hall was full with people; it was a regular visiting day.

Orange jumpsuits on red chairs, mufti on blue, khaki patrolling the periphery. A child was crying, a woman too. A vending machine stood *Out of Order* in the corner, a lone packet of 'sour cream and chives' crisps wedged in limbo against the glass. A toddler ran round and round his parents while his father stroked his mother's hand and stared at her breasts. And an Indian mynah swooped and dived through the din.

There was something about birds in prison; Carla noticed them on every visit. Surely a taunt to the inmates, she thought, as the birds slipped between liberty and incarceration, some even choosing to nest within the crannies of the institution.

The door at the far end clanged open. A shot of acid refluxed into Carla's mouth. The surprise of that first moment was always so sharp.

He was standing in the doorway again: same face, same fingers, same black eyes.

'Your turn, Ben.'

'Fuck, Tate, I'm cool, man. Leave her. Let's get out of here.'

'What's wrong, Ben? You just a wannabe?'

Today those same eyes looked tired.

The toddler adjacent to them was now bouncing on his father's knee, the mother on her blue chair, laughing. Carla bit her lip. This was no time for distraction.

The arrangements for this second meeting were less formal; she and Toroa had successfully calmed the prison staff with their civilities. She could see right through Toroa's motivations for agreeing to the sessions, but could he see through hers?

'Bet you didn't think you'd see me back so soon?' she said, as he sat down.

The guard stepped back and the noise of the room stepped in.

'Look, lady, I'm real sorry I messed up. Nothing I can do about it now,' he said, his eyes focused on her forehead. 'I've made my peace with the Lord. You should do the sa—'

'I've thought a lot about you lately,' Carla said, refusing to be in the passenger seat of this conversation, 'and what I want from you.' She fixed him with an unflinching gaze. 'You took things from me by force.' Her voice was just low enough to be inaudible to the guard. 'But hey, I'll stick to the rules. We need to be on an even playing field first before I get what I want from you.'

Toroa sat back in his chair, hands gripping his thighs, legs spread wide. He threw back his head. Carla wasn't fooled by this show of nonchalance. His eyes were staying with her.

'There are a few inequalities we first need to rectify.'

'You speaking English, lady?'

She rolled her lips inwards. 'What I'm saying is, let's make the battle fair.'

236

'Who said anything about a battle? Thought we was doing peace this time round.'

'We had war on your terms four years ago. Now we'll do it on mine.' She leant forward. 'You can't read.'

'Fuck you,' he spat out under his breath.

'I'll teach you.'

'What . . . ?' His face was a contortion of surprise and stolen anger.

'I will teach you to read. Then we can talk more about pain.'

Ben pushed his tongue over his top teeth. 'I don't need no charity, lady. I did the crime, I'm doing the time.'

'Those phrases roll so easily off your tongue, don't they? Anyway, I'm not doing it for you . . . Ben.' There, she'd actually managed to say his name. She'd used it once before, at an earlier meeting, but it had felt wrong, pairing them too closely. It was easier to think of him in the third person. Language was powerful that way. Choosing between one word and another, how it altered reality. 'I'm doing this for someone else.'

He had nowhere left to go. She knew what he wanted out of these meetings, even if the prison staff were blind to his motivations. He was after a free pass to the outside world next time parole came up. Well, he was going to have to sing for his supper. She held that ticket and the power felt good.

'Okay then, Mrs Reid,' he said, enunciating her name with sneering exaggeration. 'You teach me to read.'

Round Two to her.

The kitchen was covered in a fine film of flour. It had got into and onto everything. Even the images on the TV of a flooded and battered New York were all pixelated and fuzzy; though the white coating did little to lessen the horror of Hurricane Sandy. Carla quickly changed channels, leaving doughy fingerprints on the remote control.

Then she stood back to appraise her handiwork. How had one person managed to make such a mess? Her nose itched. She rubbed it, leaving a long white scar across her cheek. Scooping up the remaining clump of dough from the bowl, she slapped it onto her floured bench top. One more batch and she'd be ready to cook.

She rolled the dough in a long thin cylinder, sliced it into inch-sized cubes, then proceeded to roll each cube off a fork, the adept flick of her thumb sending the indented shapes somersaulting across the bench.

The salted water was bubbling furiously when she tipped the first batch of potato dumplings into the pot. As the small pale spheres rose to the surface, she lifted them out with a slotted spoon and transferred them into a dish already doused with a generous lug of olive oil. Then she repeated the entire process, again and again, until all one hundred and eleven gnocchi had been cooked.

Finally finished, she opened the kitchen window, ushering in a welcome breeze. Half a day to create what had always been Jack's favourite dish! Mind you, it did look pretty impressive, the pile of glistening golden orbs steeped in a rich bolognaise sauce.

The lengthy preparation hadn't blunted her hunger in the least, and Carla dished herself up a big bowlful. She had forgotten the urgency that came with a real appetite, that gnawing mix of anticipation and discomfort. For so long, food had been merely incidental.

It had all started the night before, when she'd dreamt about preparing gnocchi out on the farm. It was a wonderful dream – the first happy dream in such a long time. But just as she was about to savour her first mouthful, she'd woken up. The disappointment! So the next morning had seen her waiting impatiently outside the Four Square store for Virender to open up. She'd bought potatoes, eggs, flour, a tin of tomatoes, a bulb of garlic, mince, an exorbitantly expensive bottle of extra virgin olive oil, and a dinky bottle of Shiraz, spending more money in ten minutes than she usually did on groceries for a week. On her walk home she also nicked a stem of fresh rosemary from a garden backing onto the reserve.

Carla had forgotten just how long it took to make the dish. Strangely, though, despite her labours, she wasn't weary. In fact, for the first time in years, she felt alive. The concentration and creativity of the process had been more therapeutic than any counselling session she'd attended, carrying her beyond the confines of her very small life. It was as if her thoughts, along with the dough, had been kneaded and pummelled and reshaped.

The gnocchi were perfect, each little pillow of potato melting in her mouth. The potatoes had been just floury enough to yield exactly the right consistency. She smiled as she thought back to the evening Jack's friends had come over to learn how to make the iconic Italian dish. The boys had added far too much flour to the mashed potato mixture and the end product had been solid, indigestible little bricks.

She removed the napkin she'd tucked into her collar, undid the top button of her slacks, and sank onto the sofa with a deep, satisfied sigh.

There was still two-thirds of the dish left. What on earth was she going to do with the rest? Mingyu was away for a fortnight in China, and really, there was no one else. Even if she divided the leftovers into single portions to freeze, there wasn't enough space in her token freezer. The recipe was for eight – eight substantial eaters. In her other life, willing diners had always miraculously appeared, teenage boys demolishing however much she prepared.

Then an idea came to her, and ten minutes later she was placing a basket in the footwell of her Citroën. She had triple-wrapped the tub in tinfoil, then wads of newspaper, to keep the dish warm, but still the aroma of garlic and rosemary filled the car. At a red traffic light she leant over and carefully lifted the dishcloth covering her cargo, as if checking on a sleeping baby. No sign of leakage.

It was a gorgeous day, the winter air thin and silvery. She turned onto the old highway and wove through Albany Village, passing the cafes and car yards, the pub and the park, then down over the narrow bridge and left into The Avenue.

As she started to climb the hill, a burst of blue and red light filled her rear-view mirror and the screeching wail of a siren pierced her calm. She pulled over to let the patrol car pass. Police cars always managed to tamper with her mood and trigger unwelcome memories.

To her surprise, the police car pulled over too. Carla cursed. She'd meant to get the Citroën serviced. It was most likely a faulty brake light or a malfunctioning indicator. She switched off the ignition and waited. Hopefully, it wouldn't take long. She didn't want the gnocchi getting cold.

The officer took his time donning his hat and climbing slowly and deliberately out of his car.

Carla wound down her window. 'Morning, Officer,' she said, still bathed in the insouciance of her kitchen exploits. 'Is something amiss?'

'Is something amiss?' he said in staged disbelief. 'You've just lost your licence, madam. That's what's amiss.'

A cold sweat swept over Carla. 'Lost my licence?' she repeated incredulously. 'But . . .' Policemen were her friends, her confidants. She was the one on the right side of the law.

'What speed are you supposed to do coming out of Albany?' he demanded.

'Fifty.'

'Correct. Ninety-five is what you were doing. Ninety-five! That's a six-hundred-dollar fine and suspension of your licence for twenty-eight days. May I see your driver's licence?'

In a daze, Carla fumbled in her bag and retrieved her purse. Her hands were shaking and her fingers clumsy as she withdrew the card from its plastic sheath. Tears welled, blurring her vision. She passed it over, a record of happier days smiling back at her.

'I'm so sorry,' she began. 'I can't believe I was travelling that fast. I'm usually a very responsible driver, Officer. I'm not a criminal. It's just that I had to get this dish up to the prison and . . .' Her tears, now loosened, streamed down her face, arresting any further intelligible speech.

The cop shifted uneasily, then took her licence and headed back to his car to check on her details. The wait seemed interminable, confusion and humiliation spinning through Carla's mind. In one moment, her status as 'good citizen' had changed. She'd unwittingly crossed the line.

'Look, lady, I feel bad making you so upset.' The officer was back at her window. 'I hate to see a woman cry.' He forced a laugh. 'It's usually the boy racers we catch speeding up the Albany hill.'

'No, I understand,' she stuttered, a second wave of tears spilling. 'You're just doing your job.'

'I tell you what – I'll just make it an eighty-dollar fine and twenty demerit points.'

'So I'm not going to lose my licence?'

'No. But let this be a warning. You want to get to your destination in one piece, don't you?'

She nodded, then shot a glance at the basket of food on the floor. 'Officer, could I interest you in a plate of gnocchi?'

'Excuse me?'

'Italian dumplings.'

He gave her a bemused stare.

Carla flushed. 'Right then, I'll be getting along,' she said hurriedly, and headed off, driving the rest of the way at forty kilometres an hour, and gathering a line of impatient drivers behind her. And by the time she reached the prison, the gnocchi were completely cold.

Chapter Thirty-Four

CARLA

Carla agonised for days over how to teach Toroa to read. She knew that so much rested on the first lesson. She would have just one hour to gain his trust, engage and relate to him on a level he understood. Trust. Relate. Engage. Words that were world's apart from how she felt towards him. That he had robbed her of everything she valued had to be set aside. Her focus was to teach him to read. Her motivation for doing this was still not entirely clear to herself. Perhaps it sprang from a desire to convert something so evil into a more positive energy and thereby give a measure of purpose to her existence. It probably also arose from a more basic desire to reclaim control and not allow Toroa to 'win'. Words were her fists. And Kevin had sanctioned the initiative. Given his blessing. That was all the directive she needed.

The challenge became everything, consuming her every moment and importing depth into her one-dimensional days. Like an old cushion filled with new innards, so Carla's life took on a more robust shape. She borrowed books from the library on innovative ways to teach adults to read, spoke with Haslop about Toroa's family history, and trawled through newspaper archives for stories of disaffected youths. She read Alan Duff's *Once Were Warriors*,[5] learning something of the horror of domestic violence in an urban Māori family, and *Life Is So Good* [6] by Afro-American George Dawson, the grandson of slaves who'd learnt to read at the age of ninety-eight. Carla bought coloured paper to make flashcards, bars of chocolate for rewards, and a lever arch file, which she labelled TOROA. She fell asleep with books in her lap and dreamt about alphabet zoos, giant Milky Bars, and pages without print. She trialled teaching techniques on Mingyu, her willing and ever-patient guinea pig, and she read poems to the bathroom mirror, until it was all fogged up and her bath cold.

Finally, the first lesson was upon her.

BEN

He was seated opposite the Reid woman in a small meeting room adjacent to the prison chapel. The authorities had put an oil heater in the room, which was a plus. At least it promised an hour of warmth, if nothing else. In prison, the cold lived permanently in your bones.

The Reid woman had surprised him by asking the screws to remove his handcuffs. They'd had to get the okay from above, but eventually his hands had been freed. Now she was pulling things out of a large basket. He eyed it suspiciously.

'Did you get the meal I dropped in last month?' she asked, pulling out a chipped blue bowl and a spoon, and placing it on the table in front of him.

What was she up to?

'You did or didn't get it?' She was persistent; he'd give her that.

Yes, he had received the tub of cold little balls, but he hadn't touched them. They'd smelt good, but he wasn't about to get poisoned or anything. He nodded.

'You know I got a speeding ticket bringing that here.'

Ben raised an eyebrow.

'An eighty-dollar fine.'

Was she blaming him?

She smiled. The wire coiled around his insides gave a little.

'I still can't believe it. I nearly lost my licence,' she said, continuing to unpack the wicker basket. 'Forty kilometres over the limit. Forty-five, actually. It's no fun seeing those red and blue lights flashing in your rear-view mirror, I can tell you.'

Ben's lips twitched, holding onto a grin that wanted to break free.

'Anyway, I hope it was worth it. It used to be . . .' She swallowed. 'It used to be my son's favourite dish.'

Ben looked away. There was no easy place to leave his eyes in this small room.

The woman lifted four ice cream tubs out of her basket. He was seriously confused. Some literacy class!

She arranged them in a row in front of him. Vanilla. Vanilla. Vanilla. Vanilla. He could tell by the picture on the lid, the same on each, a scoop of the creamy white stuff. He hadn't had ice cream in the longest time. He missed it. Not so much the sweetness, as the texture and temperature on your tongue. All the food in prison had the same feel. Lukewarm and slop-soft.

'Mr Haslop tells me you've been given a job in kitchens.'

Jeez, was the woman stalking him?

'We've been impressed with your progress recently,' Haslop had said to him. 'That left hook of yours at last behaving itself, Ben. In fact, I note you've not been involved in any disruptive behaviour for some months now.' Ben had yawned. 'So we've decided to trial you in the kitchens.'

Working in the kitchens came with serious perks. Kitchen workers had their own gym. There was no lockdown in the daytime. You got first choice of *kai*. And perhaps the greatest benefit was that it quickened the slow creep of time.

'As you know, this comes with privileges and responsibilities,' Haslop had continued. 'What we're saying to you, Ben, is that we are placing our trust in you. I hope you'll not disappoint us. This could be the next step to getting out of here, the next step towards reclaiming your life.'

Ben looked at the Reid woman now sitting in front of him. The light was coming from behind her. She was wearing a baby-blue jumper with fine hairs of wool that stood out in a soft, fuzzy aura. Bizarrely, something about it reminded him of the big mustard-coloured sweater his mum used to wear on cold, rainy days. As a kid, he'd loved snuggling up to her, the soft sweater enveloping him in big folds of woolly skin. He shifted in his chair.

'I hear kitchen work is one of the most sought-after jobs.'

'Yeah,' Ben said in a really loud voice, trying to scare her off. Her face stayed the same – calm. He looked around for a clock. He wanted the hour over and done with.

She placed an oblong piece of card down on the table. 'Know what this is?'

Ben knew. He couldn't read the writing, but recognised it immediately. It got pinned up in the kitchen at the start of each week. The prison menu planner.

'Can you read any of it?'

Suddenly he was back in Mr Roberts's class and everyone was laughing at him.

'Ben?'

He hardened his jaw and his eyes.

'It can't be a good feeling,' she said, 'not being able to read. Being reliant on others to interpret the world for you.'

'I don't need no one to interpret my world,' he said with a sneer.

She pulled out a yellow book with the face of an old guy on the cover. 'See this man?' She held out the book.

He jerked backwards. She was invading his space.

She kept her arm outstretched. Her fingers were long, just like his mum's.

'This man learnt to read at the age of ninety-eight.' she said. 'Ninety-eight! Can you believe that?'

Ben took the book just to get her off his back. It felt weird. The weight of it. He thought it would've been lighter. The cover was smooth.

Strangely, holding it made him feel important, like he was one of those legals dressed in a suit, who always smelt super clean. He'd never held a book before, not a real book. Sure, he'd had A4 exercise books at school, but not one with lots of pages filled with perfectly square black writing.

He brought it in closer. The old guy on the cover's eyes momentarily trapped him – straight-looking, bright eyes.

'You can learn too, Ben. You're smart enough, that's for sure.'

He dug his feet into the ground to stop himself from being sucked into this woman's world. Words like 'smart' and 'I know how hard' were drawing him in.

'So today I thought we'd begin with fruit salad.'

Far out! Never mind fruit salad, this woman was a fucking fruit cake.

'A recipe for fruit salad. One you can use in the kitchens.' She started to open the ice cream tubs.

Ben peered inside. No ice cream.

'Unfortunately, they wouldn't let me bring in a knife,' she said with a tilt of her head. 'So I had to cut up all the fruit beforehand.'

He snorted. Just the thought of this woman bringing a knife into prison. He made his face serious again.

She passed him the spoon. 'Now tip the apples into the big bowl.'

He leant forward and found the tub of cubed apples. They were browning at the edges. In they went. Then the woman was holding up a piece of card.

'Apple. See how it's spelt: A-P-P-L-E. Follow my finger as I say it.'

Did she think he was five years old or something?

He made a cursory show of looking at the card.

'Next, bananas.'

It seemed like forever since he had eaten a solid, sweet banana. There was no banana in any fruit salad he'd eaten inside. Once a month, at breakfast, they might get a cup of 'fruit salad', but it was just cubes of tinned peaches with a few pieces of floury apple floating on top.

'B-A-N-A-N-A.'

He rolled his eyes. 'Fruit salad,' he hissed between pursed lips.

'Good. Now for the peaches and pears.'

Peaches and pears. He was getting hungry. He'd not tasted a fresh pear, or a peach for that matter, before.

He nonchalantly tipped out the contents of the last two tubs. They smelt like some other life, of green grass, blue sky and sunshine.

'See how both these words begin with the same three letters?' she said. 'We say them a bit differently, though. We say . . .' She twisted her mouth up as she repeated them. 'I know it's confusing, but that's English for you. Always playing tricks on us.'

Us. Ben's body prickled.

The woman unrolled a big piece of paper. As she smoothed it out, he saw that there were hundreds of crazy cartoons jumbled all over it, the page packed with pictures. Some of the drawings were so minute he could barely make them out. He couldn't take in the whole picture at once it was so busy.

'Use this magnifying glass,' she said, handing him a thick circle of glass stuck to the end of a stick.

Ben sighed and grabbed it. It would have some uses inside. He'd try and snaffle it when she wasn't looking.

'Hold it over the poster.'

He made an exaggerated show of doing this. The pictures behind the glass grew bigger. There was a dog sitting inside an orange kennel. A pink house in the clouds. Loads of *korus*. A rugby ball. Some square black words.

'Now see if you can find the fruit salad words.'

He knew there was a catch. The stupid woman was just trying to humiliate him. He dropped the magnifying glass.

'Hidden somewhere on this page are those four fruit words,' she said, seemingly oblivious to his protest.

Ben's heart knocked against his ribs. So she wanted to show him up, well he wouldn't give her the satisfaction.

Then he saw it, tucked up under SpongeBob SquarePants. 'PEACH!' he cried, jumping up.

She laughed.

She looked different. She had the whitest teeth he'd ever seen, packed in two tidy rows like notes on a piano keyboard.

He sat down and made his face serious again.

'How about you find "banana",' she said, her smile dying too. 'Then we can eat some fruit salad to finish off. You'll be eating your words,' she said with a smile.

Beyond

Stand tall, I shout! This is an important moment, Benjamin Toroa. You cannot yet hear me, so why do I raise my voice? Even when I find you unguarded in your sleep, your dreams still thwart me. Though I suppose one cannot dream about things of which one is ignorant. You do not yet know what great people you are descended from. Do not realise that their blood runs through your veins, and their aspirations lie buried within you – seeds that can be cultivated.

So much has changed for our people. Sometimes even I feel the walls of my story bow under the pressure of all that has changed. Our people have been corralled so far down this new road that at my lowest I wonder if we can ever go back. If you look over your shoulder, Benjamin, it is now hard to see what was left behind.

You inhabit a world where too many children die. And not just from the pox. Too many women cower in corners and accept. There are those who drink till they cannot remember, the fuzz and fury of alcohol changing who they are. And those who smoke the small glass pipe, corroding their conscience . . . It was not always like this. Violence finds an easy home living with the poor, the dislocated, the isolated.

And like yeast left unattended, swells and grows, spilling into and onto everything.

But give up? Never! What mother gives up on her child? And you are my child. Our child. All of Māoridom's child.

We cannot only watch over the good. I persist with you, Benjamin, for every day brings a new sunrise, just as every winter is surely followed by a spring, and just as today this Pākehā *woman chose to look forward. I will never give up, because I have spied something that sparkles like gold dust within you, and it waits to be found . . . by you.*

Chapter Thirty-Five

BEN

Gravy trickled down Ben's chin. He speared another chunk of beef. Music pounded. It was Sunday. He was hanging with Owen and Marvelle in Marvelle's crib, the three enjoying a communal feed and sharing what their respective visitors had brought them. Marvelle's tongue searched for a greasy noodle stuck to his cheek, then he crammed another forkful of chop suey into his mouth, before passing Owen the plastic container.

Marvelle's lag was eight years. Ben didn't know for what – Marvelle never said – but he liked hanging with the guy. He was a choice card player and had a wicked sense of humour. He also had a great voice and could do an awesome impersonation of Vanilla Ice. It helped that Marvelle was built like a powerhouse. Since Ben had been invited into Marvelle's inner circle, no one bothered picking a fight with him any more.

'What you got there, bro?' Marvelle asked, pointing to Ben's tub.

'Osso bucco,' Ben said, his tongue wrapping itself carefully around the words.

'Ozo fucking what?'

'Ossss-o buuu-co, dumbo,' Ben repeated. 'It's bray . . . uh . . . braised veal. Osso means "bone" in Italian and buco means "hole". "Hole-in-the-bone", 'cos the best bit's the marrow, man.' And with a loud slurp, he sucked up the pocket of jelly hiding in the centre of the bone. 'Want some?' He held out his tub.

'You've lost the plot, cuz,' Marvelle said, pulling a face. 'Gone soft in the head ever since that woman came calling. She's sucked out your bloody marrow, that's what.' He tapped his skull.

Owen, who'd been lying on the bunk, burst out laughing, his saliva spraying across the room. 'Next thing, you'll be asking the screws for conjugal favours with the ho,' he said, chortling. 'Mr and Mrs Ozo Buko.'

Ben lunged across the room and grabbed Owen by the throat. 'Shut the fuck up.'

Owen's face darkened.

'Get off him!' Marvelle shouted. 'You're strangling him.' He grabbed a handful of Ben's track top. Ben looked down at Owen's dusky face. Marvelle brought his elbow up around Ben's neck and pulled, and they both fell backwards onto the floor.

Owen stood up, coughing and gasping for breath. He stumbled, steadied himself, then staggered out of the cell.

Marvelle pointed to the door. 'Get out!' he said to Ben. 'Get the fuck out of my crib. You've changed, man. Gone fuckin' weird, you have.'

Back in his own cell, Ben cursed, his fists clenched and his eyes screwed up. What was happening to him? It was like some spirit had set up shop in his brain. Who was he? He didn't know any more. Why had he got so upset with them for dissing the stupid Reid woman?

It had started out as a ploy, part of a greater plan to get out of prison. He'd forced himself not to be rude to her, pushing out politeness and acting like he was concerned. Then she'd begun arriving with food. At first, he reckoned she was trying to poison him, but after testing it on some of the newbies, he'd been won over. Free *kai* was free *kai*, and you could never get enough inside. Plus, it was food like he'd not tasted before. Seriously good food.

The sham had become easier over time, and occasionally he'd had to remind himself it was all bogus. Like an actor had started living his role and couldn't confidently pin down who Ben Toroa was any more.

But it was when he started learning to read, that weird things really began to happen. His anger sort of burnt down like a candle, till there was only a short wick drowned in a pool of melted resentment. Rumbles didn't interest him much any more, while learning a new word gave him the same high a left hook used to do.

'Stupid bitch!' He punched the wall, his fingers crunching against the concrete. He grimaced, but it wasn't pain he felt, just fury. All to do with that ho. She'd enticed him into her web and wrapped him up in her sticky string, and he'd been blind to it. Now he'd pissed off his two best mates. That was it! He'd tell her next week. No more visits.

Chapter Thirty-Six

CARLA

She'd stop at Albany library en route to Paremoremo. An email had arrived notifying her that a book she'd requested – *Grammar 101* – had finally come in. The librarian had recommended it. Carla's grammar was rusty, and needed some revision, before she attempted to teach it.

Cupping her hands to shut out the morning glare, she peered through the wall of glass. A figure was moving about inside, switching on lights and computers, and readying the room for the day. Four minutes till opening.

The library and courtyard still looked new, standing out against the tired village backdrop. Tree roots had not yet disturbed the concrete pavers, and the powder-coated joinery surrounding the wide-paned windows was still pristine. A life-size bronze rooster balanced in the middle of the courtyard on a tippling chair, the sculpture tidily encased in a square of buxus hedging. Carla stroked the bronze bird, running her fingers over the scalloped feathers and outstretched wings. She pushed her hand hard up against the bird's open beak. The sharpness was real, the discomfort almost pleasurable. It was a beautiful piece of art, capturing real life so honestly.

Nine o'clock. The library doors swooshed open.

Inside, traces of the librarian's perfume confused the familiar and comforting smell Carla so relished – that musty, sweet mix of aged bindings, page-trapped air, and old ink.

She collected the book she'd requested and headed out into the morning. With still an hour before she was due at the prison, she headed for the bakery across the way, wooed there by the aroma of freshly ground coffee beans and warm bread.

Carla rarely bought coffee out. For nearly the same price, she could buy a jar of instant at the supermarket, and it would last her a month. Lately, though, she'd become more reckless, challenging the rules she'd prescribed herself.

'Morning.' A wrinkly Chinese man peered out from behind a cabinet of sticky buns, Louise slice, and apricot shortcake.

'A half-strength flat-white please and a Chelsea bun.'

Many businesses were now owned by Asian people. So much had changed over recent years, and not only in Carla's small life. The very fabric of New Zealand was being rewoven, with more and more foreigners settling in the country. The influx of Chinese people, in particular, had seen a swell of animosity amongst New Zealanders, many resenting the expensive cars and designer clothes flaunted in the face of tough economic times. Carla herself had harboured some prejudice. It was only after meeting Mingyu, her delightful neighbour, that her preconceptions had been split wide open.

With a steaming paper cup in hand, she strolled over to Kell Park and sat down on a bench. With one hand, she paged through the library book. It was just what she was after – simple explanations, bold print, and multiple examples. However, she wouldn't be showing it to Ben just yet; she had something else planned for the day's lesson. The time was right.

A lone rooster ventured closer and began scratching in the dust at Carla's feet. It was a mangy old thing, with dull, moth-eaten feathers and a scarred crest. Perhaps a remnant of the bantam population that once roamed the park.

Some years back there'd been much debate in the local gazette about the Albany 'chook problem'. To cull or not to cull? Nearby residents had voiced their frustration over the noise and mess created by the ever-increasing avian population, while media reports highlighted the desperate lengths some 'fowl-mouthed' residents had gone to in order to ensure a peaceful night's sleep. The grisly discovery of a dismembered bird had caused outrage amongst animal lovers, and further fuelled the call to action. At the time Carla couldn't have envisaged an Albany without chickens. For as long as she could remember, they'd been a part of the landscape – before restaurant, supermarket, house, or highway. In fact, the rooster was a symbol of Albany village and even on its logo, dating back to when it was just paddocks, orchards, and a ramshackle old dairy that served the biggest scoops of hokey-pokey ice cream around.

Carla sighed. Nothing remained the same. To survive meant to adapt.

As the sun stripped back the cloud cover, she found herself bathed in its gentle morning heat. What a ride the past months had been. The prison lessons had progressed at a stuttering and unpredictable pace. Some days she'd return home energised by the advances she and her student had made. Other times she felt despondent and frustrated by Ben's belligerent and wilful stagnation. Then there was the day he managed to make an instant chocolate pudding on his own by following the simple instructions she'd taped to the back of the box. That was a high point – a glimmer of hope breaking through the cracks in his act. That day had diluted her hatred of him, and her cynicism. For the first time she'd felt as if she was possibly succeeding in her mission.

But her excitement was short-lived, the weeks that followed seeing him again broody and resistant. And the headway she'd worked so hard to achieve seemed to quickly slip through her fingers.

She continued to take him in meals – risottos, lamb stew, bowls of minestrone – Ben accepting her food more easily than her instruction. The planning and execution of these dishes consumed most of Carla's waking hours, providing her days with a focus, and her own body with the sustenance and nourishment it had been starved of for so long. With every meal she made, her spirit and body grew stronger.

After some months, though, she realised that the cooking theme had palled, and she was forced to explore new and relevant ways to engage her now twenty-one-year-old pupil.

She thought back to Jack's schoolboy years, to when he too had shown little interest in reading. With a dearth of books suitable for boys, she'd had to trawl through second-hand bookstores and libraries searching for stories that could compete with catapults, river crossings and tree huts. Now she was similarly determined to keep her student's interest ignited.

This meant sometimes spending their allocated hour just talking about what was happening in the prison. Over time the stilted question-and-monosyllabic-answer sessions gave way to more spontaneous dialogue, in which Ben permitted her glimpses of his world – what incident had 'gone down' in the yard the previous day; which inmate was most likely a 'nark'. It was a world so foreign to her, and yet at times strangely familiar. She had reared a son, after all, and 'boys', whether in prison or out, pale-skinned or brown, were not very different. She still thought of Ben as a boy, even though he was now very much a man. Despite all their interactions, the picture she held in her mind was of the teen she'd met on that March night – the night when time had stopped.

If she felt dubious about their progress, Haslop was ever encouraging. Staff had noted definite changes in Ben's behaviour – he had become less aggressive, calmer, more motivated. And while he continued to pretend he was indifferent to the lessons, he apparently got very upset if anything or anyone got in the way of one.

Carla held onto these tenuous threads of hope, paring back her expectations and tempering her impatience. She was committed to success, whatever that was.

They were four months into the lessons, when she started to read aloud to Ben from *Life Is So Good*, about the man who'd learnt to read at the age of ninety-eight. She reserved the last ten minutes of every session for this.

As the story progressed, Carla found that she looked forward to this brief pocket of time, the act of her reading and Ben listening importing a new intimacy between them. She'd chosen the story to demonstrate to Ben that he was not alone in his struggle, and that it was never too late to learn. Yet reading aloud George Dawson's insights and reflections on the hardships of life, affected Carla deeply too. That this man who'd suffered at the hands of entrenched racism could still be so positive about humanity stirred something deep within her.

* * *

Now, she tore off a piece of Chelsea bun and tossed it towards the cockerel. A flurry of dust and feathers erupted. Mynah's dived, the rooster squawked, and sparrows shot through the mayhem.

She leapt up, spilling her coffee and dropping her bun in the dirt, where it was instantly devoured. Shaken, Carla dabbed pointlessly at the unsightly brown stain on her blouse. She couldn't possibly go to the prison like that. She'd have to go home and change.

Forty minutes later, she found herself out of breath in the familiar visiting hall. Their usual venue for the lesson, the meeting room beside the chapel, was unavailable. The authorities had become a lot more relaxed; Ben had proved himself and was no longer considered as much of a risk.

Carla looked around, recognising some of the faces. The big fellow with a facial *moko* was there with his now very pregnant girlfriend. They both smiled in greeting.

10.40 a.m. She smoothed out her linen skirt. Several months back it would have slipped right off her, but with all the cooking and baking she'd been doing, was now quite tight at the waist. Even her shrunken breasts had swelled and pushed out against her grey silk blouse.

10.45 a.m. Ben was late.

It was Tuesday. Usual time. Perhaps he had not been informed of the change in venue. Perhaps he was ill or had been hurt by another inmate. Maybe . . .

Then with relief she heard the recognisable clang of steel on steel.

Ben walked in.

She gasped. His right arm was in a sling.

'What – what happened?'

261

He sat down and fixed her with a stare.

Carla felt strangely awkward. He was probably preoccupied. Had been in a fight. Was . . . But his eyes. They were *those* eyes – the *shut-up-cunt*, *fuck-you-bitch* eyes. The eyes she had come to know over the previous six months were gone.

She smiled nervously, her calm evaporating. Suddenly she felt ridiculously overdressed.

'Your arm. What have you done to your arm, Ben?'

He looked down, as though just reminded of it, then pushed back the white sling. She saw that his hand and part of his forearm were encased in an already grubby cast.

'This,' he said in a fierce whisper, 'is because of you!' He jerked the triangle of arm threateningly toward her.

She jolted backwards.

'You,' he reiterated. 'Don't come here no more. You're getting on my wick!'

Carla sat completely still, the Tupperware container of lemon slice, the books, the other thing, at her feet. All at once she was again trembling on the farm floor.

She pulled herself out of her stupor, hastily gathered her belongings and stood up. She had to get out, hurry back to her flat, put out two sausages for dinner, and then take a nap from one until two-thirty.

The previous night she'd opened the door to the spare room, the hallway light trapping motes of dust in its pale beam. The room smelt of locked-away years and decaying mothballs. A cockroach scuttled under the cupboard door. She'd selected a box from the neatly stacked tower, and slipped a Stanley knife under the cross of masking tape. What would it hold? Lucky dip.

A set of photo albums. Perfectly preserved.

She'd dragged the box into the lounge, where she unpacked it, lining up seven photo albums across the floor. Tentatively, she'd opened the first, a red album with a faded filigree border, and pored over it. Then a hunger had overtaken her and she'd begun turning the pages faster and faster, snapshots of another time knitted haphazardly back into her life like dropped stitches . . . The kingfisher perched on a branch of the chestnut tree in the Taylors' Christmas lunch photo . . . The rowboat moored on the lake edge. It was yellow inside and white out. She'd always thought it was all white. Russell trying to feed his cake to the cat at Jack's seventh birthday party. Her sister-in-law posing with the Governor General. Mildred actually had quite thick ankles. Carla had never noticed them before.

She'd finally put out the light just after midnight, and slept soundly, without even the rustle of a dream. On her bedside table lay a blue album.

Now, a wave of heat surged through her. Would she never learn? She was cursed. Nothing could ever remain good for long.

She kicked the Tupperware aside, sending it planing across the floor, then curled her fingers around the blue photo album and lifted it up like a placard.

'Let me tell you what's getting on my wick, you . . . you low life, good-for-nothing scum of the earth!' Her voice plunged into the room, rage wound around each syllable, fury streaked through every word. The big guy and his girlfriend looked up, their faces all surprise. 'You sit in this cage, as you call it, eating three meals a day, sleeping and exercising and demanding and defecating, while my son, *my son*, has been reduced to a canister of ash, and my husband lies in a box in the ground. You . . . you bastard! You took them away from me. How dare you!'

The background hum in the visitors' room evaporated into a gaping silence.

Two guards approached.

Carla ignored them. 'Look here!' she screamed at Ben. 'I said, look here!' She opened the album and turned it to him. 'My family are gone because you and your sick mate surfed through a night on drugs, satisfying the animal in you. You complain, poor boy, because the scabies you caught from the prison blankets is itchy and keeps you awake. Oh dear! While I still endure the crops of pus-filled blisters that burn my insides out, a sweet memento left me by your friend. What am I doing bringing you food and teaching you to read? Stupid, stupid woman! Well, good riddance. I hope you rot in hell, you illiterate . . .'

She got up and strode toward the approaching warders, tripping over *Life is So Good* and ripping the cover.

Chapter Thirty-Seven

CARLA

Carla lifted the book off the trolley, checked the number on the spine, then slotted the classic in beside Frame's other works.

'Carla, you haven't taken a tea break yet,' Diana, the head librarian, called after her. 'I brought in a carrot cake for my birthday. You'll be lucky to still get some.'

The tea room was empty. Carla flicked on the kettle, cut herself a slice of cake from the remaining wedge and sank into a lime-green chair shaped like a pudding bowl.

It had been seven months since her last visit to the prison. So much had happened since the day she'd sped away from the grey monolith, her hands trembling, her tears mixing with outrage. When she'd stopped off at the library to return the book she'd borrowed only that morning, Diana was there behind the desk.

'That was quick, Mrs Reid. Any good?'

Carla had burst into tears, causing quite a stir and leaving the astonished librarian no option but to usher her to a backroom, away from a gathering of curious eyes. An hour later, and Carla's story told, Diana was offering her a temporary position assisting at the library.

'We're very short-staffed,' she'd said, running a finger down the weekly roster. 'One librarian is away on maternity leave, another on extended sick leave. It's only for a few months, but should keep you out of mischief and us out of a tight spot.'

Carla was signed on for two mornings a week, but turned up for five. She loved being there, the large windows that invited the outside in; the floor-to-ceiling shelves crammed with books; the buzz, the energy, the purpose.

Her new colleagues – Diana, Zoe, Bunty, and Paul – were good people, and gradually, Carla dropped her guard, allowing easy friendships to flourish.

She banished Toroa from her mind. Yes, she'd made similar resolutions before, but this time was different. She wondered whether a fatal bond existed between them. Sometimes it felt as if an invisible thread kept them orbiting each other, with ever the promise of another collision.

She had not seen his latest outburst coming. The Geoffreys and Veras would no doubt have said, 'I told you so!' and 'When will you learn?', reminding her that Ben Toroa was rotten through and through, and beyond redemption. Yet things had been going so well.

Chapter Thirty-Eight

BEN

Trays of lamb chops spat and hissed behind the hot yellow glass; spirals of steam twisted towards a giant range hood, as if caught in a powerful rip; and mammoth stainless-steel pans of sliced pumpkin rested on a bench waiting their turn under the grill.

Ben stood peeling the last of a mound of potatoes, his paring knife removing a thick layer of yellow flesh with each peel. His hand had been out of plaster for months now, but he was still clumsy with the fine work, his last two fingers clawing permanently into his palm. The surgeons had recommended daily physiotherapy. Like that was going to happen in prison!

'Prisoner Toroa.' Lawrence, an ex-SAS guard, put his head round the door of the galley kitchen.

Ben's nickname in prison was Bull, while the guards called him either by his number or surname. It was really only Haslop who'd ever used his first name. Sometimes Ben almost forgot that he was Ben.

He laid down the knife. 'Hey, Skunk, can you put the spuds into the oven in five, if I'm not back?'

As far as Ben was concerned, kitchen duty was alright. It could get noisy and explosively hot when they were working full ball to get a meal out. But he liked the perks that came with the job; kitchen hands were treated differently. The screws trusted them more. They had to, considering the guys were working with knives and boiling water every day. Anyway, you didn't need to be able to access the kitchen if you were after a weapon; most were fashioned from the unlikeliest of things – pegs, paperclips, toilet flushers. Inmates were a resourceful bunch. A toothbrush filed to a point could inflict as much damage as any knife if rammed under the ribs with enough force.

The kitchen guys wielded a different sort of weapon. Food. With little to break the monotony of every twenty-four-hour day, what was on the menu and the size of a prisoner's portion were serious matters. *Kai* was a currency for trade and stand overs, coming in a close second to contraband.

Lawrence handed Ben a long white envelope. 'Your transfer.'

'Transfer?'

'Ngawha, Friday.'

Ben was bewildered. 'What? How come? Suddenly, after how many fucking years?'

'Maybe they moving you closer to your *whānau* or something?'

'*Whānau*? Yeah, right!' Ben laughed. What family did he have? Even Lily hadn't visited in months. She must have finally realised he was beyond salvation.

Lawrence shrugged. 'I'm only the messenger, mate. Anyway, you should be stoked. It's a holiday camp up there. Cushier than the real world, I can tell you.'

'Not interested,' Ben said, turning away and heading back into the kitchen. 'I'll see out my bid here. This is my crib.'

'Gimme a break, Toroa,' the guard said, exasperated. 'Report to your unit manager at nine, Friday morning, cell packed, ready to go.'

Ben stopped in the doorway. Coldplay's song 'Paradise', was blasting through the clouds of steam. It had been nearly seven years. They couldn't just move him. His heart started running in his chest, running away from the news. He knew the facility north of Whangarei was a cushy number, but his mates were at Pare and they were his *whānau*. There was no one else. He knew Pare, knew the rules. He understood the guys, who not to mess with . . .

Sure, he sometimes complained, but it was a safe sort of complaining, with no expectation of change. Routine regulated his life, each day practically predictable. Now, without warning, they wanted to mess up everything.

Something else was also bothering Ben as he stood there in the doorway chewing on his new fate, but he quashed the thought before it could breathe any oxygen.

He stepped back into the stifling kitchen. 'I thought I told you to fuckin' put the potatoes on,' he barked at Skunk.

'What's with you?' the big guy replied. 'It's only five minutes now.'

Ben's eyes scanned the bench and stopped at the butcher's block. The pumpkin knife lay there, glinting under the 100 watt bulbs, its grey handle thick and greasy.

Ben moved towards the bench, towards his ticket to a longer stay, towards his handle on a different outcome.

'You okay, bro?' his mate's voice echoed through the fog in his mind. 'Something happen out there?'

Skunk was a big fellow, a solid crate of flesh with a gentle teddy bear face and ears that stuck out at right angles. He'd worked for the council driving a garbage truck, before landing himself in prison. He was in for manslaughter, killing his cousin in a drunken brawl. It wasn't hard to see how Skunk could have killed the bloke; he didn't seem to appreciate his own strength. With a casual swipe of his hand he could easily drop someone.

It tore Skunk apart being away from his five kids and all, but he'd 'found God' since being inside. He loved working in the kitchen and planned to get a job as a chef when he got out.

Skunk was your model prisoner – repentant, motivated, always toeing the line. The guy had even been granted special permission to use the workshop out of hours so he could build his youngest kid a go-kart. And it wasn't just any old go-kart; it was a sight to behold, with suspension, proper steering, and a jazzy purple paint job. Skunk really wanted to be a good dad. From what Ben could tell, he already was one.

But Ben couldn't be getting sentimental about his homie. Skunk wasn't his problem. When it came down to it, it was every man for himself.

He shook his head, trying to reshuffle his thoughts, but the tunnel in his mind kept closing in, until just one thought ruled.

Skunk turned to check on the chops.

Ben picked up the knife, his pinkie and ring finger curling around the handle with deformed ease, the other fingers quickly following.

He moved towards the big man who was peering into the oven.

They'd think twice about shipping Ben up north if he picked up another sentence.

As Ben lifted the knife, Skunk spun round in a rap manoeuvre, his lumbering body bending in time to the music. He stopped, confusion streaked across his face. 'Jeez, man?'

Then something happened; the eyes in front of Ben were no longer Skunk's but his mother's, wide with fear as Ryan laid into her.

Switch.

They were the farm kid's surprised stare when he spotted them crouching in the shadows.

Switch.

Now the Reid woman's.

Ben squeezed his eyes shut as if someone had put them out with a red-hot poker. Then he dropped the knife and ran from the kitchen, out into the quadrangle, where he spewed all over his feet.

He hovered over the mess – strings of saliva hanging from his mouth, water dripping from his nose, his whole body shaking. Then he slid down the wall and dropped his head onto his knees.

After a time he felt a hand on his shoulder – a strong, warm hand sucking up some of his pain. It was Skunk.

Skunk didn't say anything, but Ben knew the big guy understood. It felt as if Skunk *was* the Lord he was always droning on about.

As the van pulled away from Paremoremo, Ben felt as empty as the vehicle in which he was travelling.

He was tired. If only he could sleep for a hundred years. Even the drugs had started to pall, flattening his mind into a collage of nothing.

He thought he'd learnt not to cling onto stuff. With no control over anything, it was best to skim across the surface of your lag, and form no attachments to people or place. So why was he so eaten up over the move?

Prison was a riddle. Everything seemed so certain – your sentence, your timetable, your space – yet everything was also completely uncertain – your placement, friendships, your privileges, and safety, your very next day. The endless constant always threatened to change. A bombshell around the next corner? Hide and Seek.

Strangely, Ben wasn't that scared of what lay ahead. Not like when he'd moved from remand to Paremoremo as a newbie. He wasn't so worried about starting at the bottom of the pack again, obliged to forge fresh connections, find new protection, set new precedents. He was sort of indifferent to all of that. It would happen. He'd most likely survive. But there was this other thing tugging at him and churning his innards. He'd lost something, and by travelling farther away from where he'd lost it, he had even less chance of ever getting it back.

In Whangarei they stopped for fuel. One of the guards bought him a doughnut. It was greasy and delicious, the yellow icing alone a novelty. Colour, after the monochrome existence that was Pare. Then they were on the road again.

For a time, Ben crouched beside the back window, watching the landscape slip by. Despite his legs going into cramp, he wouldn't give up his position. From it, he could see green. Life green. Bursting bright green. Calm green. Frog and frond and grass green. Peace green. He'd forgotten the whole damn colour.

'Transfer from Pare,' someone called out.

They'd stopped. Ben pressed his face up against the grill. Surely they weren't there. They were in the middle of the countryside, green grass rolling away in every direction.

The van door opened.

'Morning, Ben.' A tall screw with an accent, not Kiwi, stretched out a hand. His grip was strong and surprising.

Ben . . . Ben . . . Ben. The name. It ripped through him.

A breeze. The air smelt different. Tasted different. It blew him into a memory. *He is small. Someone, Debs maybe, is teaching him to fly a kite on Bastion Point. The picture is hazy but at the same time sharp. Sweet wind. Green grass dipping into a basin of blue sea and sky. Triangular colours soaring. A yellow tail trailing fun and possibility.*

Processing at the Northern Regions Correction Facility was routine, with all the usual – strip-search, kit, medical. The difference was that the guards kept addressing him by his first name.

He was given lunch in the kit room because he'd missed out – a polony roll with no gristle, and a carton of cold, full-cream milk. Then he was led to his cell.

They had to walk some way from the main admin block along a gravel path that curved through park-like grounds. A haunch of laggers was weeding the lawn.

'Why you fuckin' pulling them out?' Ben asked as he passed. Any green was good.

His cell was in a pod: a closed circle of booths around a concrete yard. In the centre of the yard was a small rectangle of lawn with a basketball hoop planted in the middle. The cells were all unlocked, the doors opening onto the communal area. Inmates hung around in clusters, listening to music, lazing in the sun, playing cards. A grey-haired guy was doing weights.

Ben's cell looked clean and bright, but he didn't linger long. Impatiently he removed his shoes and headed out into the yard to the small patch of kikuyu lawn. He stepped onto it and let out a slow sigh as the cool sponginess pushed up between his toes, making its way through his body to his head, where it unlocked years of grey. Years of no grass could kill a man.

'Today we welcome a new brother to our family.'

A scrawny guy with brown hair gathered in a thin ponytail stood in front of his seated audience, tattoos inking all of his visible skin.

Ben looked around. Almost everyone in the room was brown and young, some still with the baby-faced freshness of first-timers, their expressions not yet tightened, their newness not yet decayed.

'Ben arrived yesterday from Pare. He's classified AB and is up the hill, but has been granted daytime leave to be with us in the *whare* till we have a vacant crib.' The man nodded at Ben and smiled, showing off two rows of broken teeth. 'We begin the day with a *karakia*. August, please.'

A lanky fellow stood up and bowed his head. Ben checked him out with a side-on glance. After the prayer, each of the guys came up to shake hands with him. One even tried to treat him to a *hongi*, but Ben pulled away; he wasn't about to press noses with some random stranger. Then the meeting broke up and the guys headed off to their work programmes, leaving Ben alone in the room with the main man.

A thin blue carpet covered the floor. A whiteboard with red scrawl rested on an easel at the front of the room. Big windows took in the grass outside. Cream prefab buildings broke up the view.

The scrawny fellow was as straight as a needle, his shoulders pulled right back to make a proud platform for his head. He oozed mana.

'I'm Chalkie. I'm a lifer. I run this joint. While you are in this unit you answer to me, you understand. And the screws, of course.'

Ben raised an eyebrow.

'You've come to a crossroads in your bid, mate. The prison service has decided to give you a chance, you lucky bastard. You've been selected to join this unit as part of a trial. Everyone high up is watching. The fate of other laggers will depend on you. Which path you choose.'

Ben looked at him.

'So, which house you prefer to live in – a jailhouse or a marae?'

Ben frowned.

Chalkie scribbled something on the whiteboard with the red marker, drawing two squiggly lines. One joined up where it started; the other went off the board.

'Two different routes, bro. One starts in a marae,' he said pointing to the ground, 'and ends out there in the real world. The other route starts in prison and ends in prison. A revolving door. You get my drift?'

Ben stared at the board to avoid the guy's eyes, all-seeing eyes that left him feeling naked.

'Your choice. Here we run things like on a marae. Same rules. Same customs. Same comforts. By now you'll know the boob ain't such a cool place to be.'

Ben shifted from one foot to the other. Why had he been put in a youth unit? It was like going backwards. In a strange way it also felt kind of good. Like someone had lifted adulthood off his shoulders.

'You can say "fuck society" or you can embrace it,' the guy continued, his voice growing intense and loud. 'You can go back there' – he pointed across the green lawns to the pod – 'and get stabbed, or maybe even get to see a mate hang himself with his bedding on his cell door handle. Perhaps someone'll fuck you over in the shower. I'm guessing that after, what, six, seven years, you've seen it all. It ain't a pretty place, is it?'

Ben found himself shaking his head, hypnotised by the guy's words.

'It's not so cool to have a screw strip-search you at random just 'cos he wants to teach you a lesson. It isn't such a cool thing to be told when and where you can shit, and whether or not you're allowed more bog roll. Alone for fourteen hours a day with just the cold walls for company is no party neither. Boredom and hatred fester like school sores. I've been inside a long time. I've lived it. I know.'

Chalkie's face was yellowy brown. The tips of two of his fingers on his left hand were missing. His eyes were thin, his nose bent.

'You can keep on this road,' he said, pointing to the line on the board that fed back to itself, 'or you can do the right thing – *tikanga*.' He pointed to the other drawing where the red line ran off the board to freedom.

Ben didn't know what to say. This was a different sort of stand over to any he'd experienced before. Things were definitely weird in the north of New Zealand. Experience told him to smirk and toss his chin, flip off this guy's hold. But he couldn't. The brown guy's words had hijacked his attention and were demanding his respect.

'I'm not playing high and mighty with you neither,' Chalkie said. 'I been where you been, boy. I've murdered dudes. Been president of a chapter. You could say I've lived a little. Got blood on my hands, just like you, and every night I sleep with my victims, swimming through their red.'

Ben swallowed. Same dreams! His eyes started to sting and his vision blurred. How did this dude know he surfed on waves of gore every night?

'I still got at least eight years in here,' Chalkie continued, 'before they even consider me for parole. But one thing I know is that I'm not coming back after I been released. I got a life to live.' He pointed to the line that led to freedom. 'I've chosen this route, brother.'

The word 'brother', the way Chalkie said it, lassoed Ben and was pulling him in. He ground his teeth, trying to keep tears at bay.

'And don't abuse the staff here, neither, 'cos all they doing is their job,' Chalkie added, 'to pay for food and a roof over their family's head. You gotta girlfriend outside?'

Ben shook his head.

'Okay, then, a mother?' It was a rhetorical question and Chalkie didn't wait for Ben to reply. 'Say someone broke into her house and was going to rape her. Who's she gonna call for protection? You're inside and can't do nothing to help. It's the police who will come to her rescue. The police! So don't slag them off.'

Ben's mind was spinning, his emotions tumbling.

'Who the screws gonna call if you get stabbed in your crib? The ambulance officers, that's who. People just doing their job. They deserve our respect, don't you think?'

Ben wiped his nose on his sleeve.

'Now some basic rules.' Chalkie turned to the board. 'No drugs, no drink, no bashings, and in my unit you'll be sweet.'

Beyond

Who would have thought you would find tūrangawaewae *in a prison of all places – a secure and safe place to stand right in the midst of other prison inmates. Ha! Such is the wonder of life and the reach of* tikanga Māori. *But I am cautious, so for now I say no more, but watch and wait with hope.*

Chapter Thirty-Nine

CARLA

It was early December and the pohutukawa trees were in full crimson flush. Shop windows boasted brash Christmas displays and postboxes overflowed with advertorials promising the world and guaranteeing a summer of stupid prices.

Carla leant against her front door, a pile of post and papers wedged under her arm. Suddenly the jammed key turned in the lock, catapulting her into her apartment.

Thirty seconds later, Mingyu was standing at Carla's door. 'Carla! What happen?'

'I keep meaning to get the damn lock replaced,' Carla cursed, collecting her post on all fours.

Mingyu helped her up. 'You got time for a cup of tea?' she asked, placing a packet of strawberry-cream biscuits on the counter.

Carla was about to decline, but her friend was already ferreting around in the cupboard for tea bags. 'Where you move the tea, Carla?'

'Behind the jam jars. Yes, there.'

Mingyu was in the habit of popping in every evening as soon as she heard Carla's latch.

Carla sneaked a look at her watch. Paul would be arriving in less than an hour and she still wanted to have a bath. 'I won't be able to make it a long one,' Carla began. 'I'm expecting a colleague shortly.'

Mingyu raised her eyebrows. 'Colly?'

'A col-league. One of the people who works with me at the library. He's asked me to teach him Italian.'

A knowing smile crept across Mingyu's face. '*He*,' she repeated. 'Very good, Carla. About time.'

Carla felt herself blushing. 'No, no. It's not like that at all.'

'Too bad. I'm think a man is what you need.'

Carla bit her lip to hide her embarrassment. The whistling kettle rescued her.

'Oh, I mean to give you,' Mingyu said, rummaging in her trouser pocket. 'Yesterday I am find a letter in dustbin outside. Not yet open. It is lucky. I am looking in bin because I lose my pearl earring. I'm not find the earring, but I find this.' She unrolled a crumpled blue envelope.

Carla had become ruthless about tossing out unsolicited mail and advertorials, sometimes without first sifting through them properly.

She peered through the bottom of her glasses. The faint postmark came into focus. A crest. The Department of Corrections.

'Oh,' she said. 'Thanks, Ming.'

'That postie, I'm never like him,' her friend said indignantly. 'I think I complain. He throw them in the bin. Too lazy, that man!'

Carla was only half-listening, the letter already toying with her equanimity.

Mingyu picked up the TV remote. '*Who Wants to be a Millionaire* is already start. We watch with our tea?'

'Would you mind actually if we don't tonight?' Carla said. 'It's just that I've got a lot to do before my visitor—'

'Oh, okay. No tea today. I see you tomorrow.' Mingyu said, retreating towards the door, the tea left unmade. On the threshold, she turned. 'You not open the letter?'

'Later. I will later, thank you,' Carla said, slipping it into the pocket of her cardigan.

Not long after Mingyu's departure, the doorbell rang, reverberating through Carla's tiny flat.

Muttering under her breath, Carla looked through the peephole. The distorted frame of Paul came into view. He was twenty minutes early. She was still in her dressing gown and had not yet dried her hair.

'One minute!' she called out, darting back to her room to pull on a dress.

When she opened the door, there he was with his wide smile, a bunch of proteas in one hand and a bottle of red in the other.

'Sorry, Paul. I'm running a bit late,' she blurted out. 'Excuse my attire.'

He eyed her towelling turban. 'Very fetching headgear,' he said in his thick South African accent. 'I am early. My apologies. But I wasn't sure how long it would take to get here in the traffic.'

A noise in the stairwell distracted Carla. She peered out into the lobby to see Mingyu standing in her doorway. On being spotted, her neighbour gave Carla the thumbs up. Carla hurried her visitor inside.

The masculine smell of sandalwood filled the living room. Carla realised she'd not entertained a man in the apartment before.

Feeling suddenly awkward, she excused herself and went to finish getting ready.

By the time she re-emerged, hair blow-dried and make-up applied, the curtains had been drawn, the flowers arranged in a vase, and two glasses of red wine poured.

She stopped in the doorway to catch her breath. It was a giddy feeling having someone attend to such things for her.

'Wow, you've managed to make my small box of a place look good,' she said.

'You look good,' Paul said with a skew smile. Paul had suffered from Bell's palsy a few weeks back and his facial muscles had yet to regain their full function. Disconcertingly, the creaseless left side of his face still drooped.

Carla's mind went blank.

'Proteas!' she suddenly blurted out, jumpstarting the conversation again. 'I haven't seen them in years. We used to stop at a protea farm on the way up north. Such dramatic flowers. I tried to grow them once, but the Auckland climate – it's too wet, and the soil too clayey. Not everyone likes them, mind you. The flowers, they're quite different. I do. I mean, I like them.' Words tumbled out of her mouth.

We used to stop . . . We used to stop. She and Kevin used to stop . . . Kevin . . . She was being highjacked by her own words. She felt like a traitor.

'I hope you drink Pino,' Paul said, proffering her a glass. 'It's a Pinotage from Stellenbosch. I still have a bit of a thing for the reds of my homeland.'

'I drink anything and everything.' Oh Carla! Now he'd think she was a lush. She was behaving like a schoolgirl – gauche, inept, tongue-tied. And this wasn't even a date. What was she thinking?

Paul worked at the library. He was a quiet man, which she'd initially mistaken for aloofness, but over time had come to realise was simply a manifestation of his shyness. Buried beneath this reserve was a delightful, dry sense of humour.

The other librarians had filled Carla in on all the gossip. Paul was a retired publisher who'd worked in Durban until he and his wife followed their only daughter to New Zealand. Soon after arriving, however, Paul's wife was diagnosed with a brain tumour, and eight months later died. Not long after this, Paul's daughter was headhunted for a job in Germany, and after much agonising, decided to make another shift. This time Paul did not follow. He couldn't face relocating again, or leaving his late wife behind; she was buried in New Zealand.

Now, a year later, he planned to visit his daughter in Berlin and had decided to combine this with a trip to Italy. When he learnt of Carla's heritage, he'd asked if she might teach him some basic conversational Italian. And so it was that she'd come to invite him over.

He was a tall man, in his late fifties, with haywire grey eyebrows. Their prominence lent him a serious demeanour and belied his playful eyes, which sloped away gently to disappear in deeply rutted crow's feet. He usually wore cashmere jumpers and baggy trousers.

'Mmm. Something smells good,' Paul said, breaking another awkward silence.

Preparation for the Italian-themed meal had taken Carla the entire weekend. Parma ham and melon to start, home-made ravioli filled with spinach, ricotta cheese and porcini mushrooms to follow, and Tiramisu to finish.

Carla squeezed her eyes shut, trying to blot out the intrusive thoughts about Kevin. She'd never had trouble working alongside Paul. Yet somehow allowing him into her home had altered the dynamic. It was all Mingyu's fault for putting a different spin on what was going to be an innocent evening. This had been a bad idea.

'To Italy,' Paul said, clinking his glass with hers. 'It was a long-held wish of my late wife, Veronica, to visit Italy. I guess I'm doing this for her.'

The mention of Paul's wife came as a welcome relief, immediately redefining the boundaries of the evening.

Carla took a gulp of wine. 'Mmh, *molto buono*,' she said with a nod. 'Which means "very good".'

'*Molto buono*,' Paul repeated slowly.

'I see you're a natural.' She took another swig. 'This will be easy.'

'Let's not get ahead of ourselves,' he said with an engaging smile.

They sat down to dinner at eight. At eleven o'clock they were still at the table; three hours had effortlessly elapsed.

Paul poured the last of the wine into Carla's glass. 'The way Kiwis say "see you later" is confusing too,' he said. 'Veronica and I held a dinner party soon after arriving in New Zealand. The guests left around midnight, and as they were departing, one chap said "see you later". We thought he was coming back later that night. We didn't dare go to bed till after one.'

Carla laughed. 'You South Africans have some strange words too. I mean, calling traffic lights, robots!'

'And?'

'A robot is an automaton! You know, Star Wars and all.'

'I guess, but—'

'And what about "hold thumbs",' she said, watching Paul scrape at the last smudge of tiramisu, 'instead of "fingers crossed". A South African friend of mine once said to an electrician who'd just repaired her faulty telephone, "Let's hold thumbs." She couldn't understand why he suddenly started to flirt with her.'

Paul's laughter was contagious. It had been a long time since Carla had laughed. It felt so good.

When he finally got up to take his leave, they hadn't covered much Italian.

'Consider this a taster,' Carla said as she walked out with him to his car. 'An introduction to the proper course.'

The blue night air was sharp against her face. 'Next time, the real work begins.'

'Carla.' Paul stopped, his jovial eyes suddenly still. 'I haven't enjoyed myself so much in a long time.' He took her hands in his. They were big and warm, like Kevin's. 'Thank you. Or should I say *grazia*?'

'*Grazie*,' she corrected.

He leant forward and kissed her lightly on the cheek. Carla's body melted, and a hungry ache hollowed out her insides.

Then he climbed into his old Saab convertible and reversed into the darkness.

Chapter Forty

CARLA

Paul squeezed her breasts and kissed her in the gulley beneath her collarbone. Carla's head was ringing. He fingered the space behind her knees. Ringing. Kissed her inner thighs. Ringing. Blasted ringing! Carla sat up and slammed her hand down on the snooze button of her alarm clock, then collapsed back onto her pillow in the hope of landing again in the dream. But it was gone and she was awake, Kevin watching her from the photograph on the bedside table. She turned it face down.

She hauled herself out of bed and traipsed through to the kitchen to brew herself a strong black coffee, even though a migraine was threatening. Then she began to tidy up the mess from the previous night. Her cardigan hung abandoned over a dining room chair, the corner of an envelope poking out of the pocket. A letter. The one Mingyu had retrieved from the rubbish bin.

A large yellow stain on the envelope had dried, wrinkling the paper into a contracted scar. Carla brought it up to her nose. It had the putrid smell of garbage.

She didn't want to open it. It felt as if all her yesterdays were chained to her, dragging behind like the Ghost of Christmases Past. Could she never break free?

Finally, she took a sharp knife out of the drawer and sliced open the envelope.

Neat pencil print.

To Mrs Reid,

I am writing to you about one man we both know. Ben Toroa. He is now transferred to Ngawha and I think you should have this important information. I have seen the change you bring in him when you visit. I witnessed good growth where there before had been hard ground. Ben Toroa needs you, even if he does not have the words to say it. I hope you will not abandon him. His bad words come from confusion. I know Ben is very regretful for messing with your life. He liked learning to read and your very excellent cooking.

With greatest sincerity,
A friend,
Skunk.

Carla's skin had risen into hundreds of tiny bumps. She slipped the letter into the bottom drawer of her desk, concealing it with other papers.

'You are full of surprises,' she said out loud, then put a hand over her mouth, surprised by her own words. It had been so long since she had spoken to Him. It had been so long since she had believed.

Paul was arranging a book display at the front door of the library when she hurried past him. He made a show of looking at his watch.

'*Buongiorno, Signora Reid*. Fine time to arrive! Did you have a late night or something?'

Carla laughed.

'Thanks again for a great evening,' he said, following behind her like an overenergetic puppy.

She stopped and turned. His eyes were shining. She looked away – coy, clumsy and confused, and with a serious hangover. Then hurried on.

'I'd like to reciprocate,' he called after her. 'I know this fabulous little trattoria in Birkenhead. My shout Saturday?'

'Talk to you later,' she mouthed, as Diana at front desk looked up.

They went out the following Saturday night, and the one after that. Then Carla started to decline Paul's keen invitations. It was an attempt to ring-fence her emotions. For the first time in years she had felt alive and sexual, both emotions she'd thought had died on that fateful autumn night. However, along with these wonderful feelings had come guilt, overwhelming guilt. She didn't feel entitled to happiness. By engaging in the frivolity of living, she was surely dishonouring the memory of her son and husband. She had survived. They hadn't.

Paul took the hint and backed off.

When his visits dwindled, Mingyu was the first to notice. One afternoon she sat Carla down. 'Carla, you love Jack. You love Kevin.'

'Of course!'

'You love beautiful sunset?'

Carla nodded.

'You love my pork dumpling?'

'Where is this going, Ming?'

'You can love many thing, Carla. The love for one is not

undo the love for the other. There is much room in your heart.'

'Mingyu's pragmatic philosophies to the fore,' Carla said, brushing off her neighbour's advice with an air of nonchalance. However, she found herself pondering the words, and with time the struggle inside her heart began to ease.

She started seeing more of Paul again outside of work hours, and slowly began sharing bits of her biography with him. However, it was a censored and abridged version she shared; she wasn't going to allow the past to tarnish what she had this time.

They had been seeing each other for several months when he stopped her in the Reference Section one day, somewhere between the letters N and P, and asked if she'd consider joining him for a weekend in Wellington, where he'd be attending the Readers and Writers Festival.

The prospect of going to Wellington was both exciting and daunting. It had been forever since she'd even travelled over the Harbour Bridge. Her life had shrunk down to a circumscribed coin of safety. To test the boundaries was terrifying.

The day they arrived in the capital, Wellington put on quite a show. Its notorious wind settled and the sun's rays cast the ocean in a stunning Pacific-blue hue. The mewling cry of seagulls overhead, the sun-baked boulders and the mineral-scented air were all so marked in their difference from Carla's familiar landscape. Nature had opened a window and helped her step outside.

The day was theirs to enjoy before the festival's opening that evening, so after depositing their bags at the hotel, they hailed a taxi and headed for the national museum.

A few hours proved hopelessly inadequate to do justice to Te Papa, and by the time they emerged from the bold building of block and glass it was three o'clock and they were ravenous. They grabbed a belated pub lunch on the waterfront, then headed back to their hotel to ready for the evening.

Carla had just climbed out of the shower when she heard someone knocking at the door. Swathing herself in one of the luxuriously thick hotel gowns, she pulled the door ajar.

Paul was standing there, all polished and spruce.

'Hey, Speedy Gonzalez,' she said, laughing, 'a woman needs time to get tarted up.'

Paul looked sheepish. 'It's just that it has been such a great day and I wanted to . . . I had to tell you something.'

She opened the door wider.

'*Ti amo.*'

The words caught her off guard.

'Did I get it right?' he asked anxiously. 'I mean, *ti amo*. Is that the way you say "I love you"?'

'Yes. Yes. I . . . Yes. Absolutely. Corre—'

Without waiting for her to finish, he leant in, his mouth trapping her words. They stumbled backwards into the room, Paul kicking the door shut with his foot, and they landed on the king-size bed with a thump.

He untied the belt of her dressing gown and parted the thick white cloth. Her breathing was loud in her ears, her whole body an extension of this rhythm – anticipation, anguish and excitement all distilled into each noisy breath.

Paul ran a finger down her middle, dividing her in two. She groaned as he lingered at the end of this imaginary line, then began pulling at his shirt buttons, her fingers clumsy and impatient. He slipped his hands behind her ears and out through her curls, returning to massage her earlobes. Her body loosened. He stroked her spongy belly, detailing every crease. She clasped the back of his neck, digging into the strong ridges that ran down his back. Gently he parted her thighs.

Then he was leaning over her, his eyes . . .

All of a sudden they were those eyes staring at her – the black, angry, mocking eyes. Too close. Taunting. Hot breath . . .

'No! Get off me! Get off!' Carla screamed.

Paul pulled back, the colour draining from his face, confusion spinning through his pallor.

She sat up, panting. 'I'm sorry. I'm so sorry.'

She began to cry.

Paul was on all fours at the end of the bed, his arms trembling. 'I . . . I don't—'

Loud knocking at the door interrupted them.

'Everything all right in there? Open the door, please!'

Paul jumped up, buttoned his shirt and stumbled towards the door. A freckly lad stood in the corridor, a shiny brass *Concierge* badge pinned to his lapel and a keycard in hand.

'Is everything okay, sir? I was passing and heard a woman s-screaming.' He craned his neck, trying to see around Paul.

Carla was now lying in the foetal position on the bed, the bedspread pulled over her. 'Yes. All fine.'

The concierge hesitated.

'The lady . . . uh, my friend, just saw a mouse,' Paul added quickly.

'A mouse?' The lad was now on tiptoes, trying to get a better look at Carla. Paul coloured.

'Would you like to be moved to another room then, sir?'

'Oh no, that won't be necessary. I've killed it.'

The boy's eyes grew round. 'Killed it?'

'Yes. With the Bible in the bedside drawer. That book sure

comes in handy. Anyway, I've flushed it down the toilet,' Paul said, pre-empting the next question.

Before the boy could move beyond a stutter, Paul thanked him again and closed the door.

He peered through the spyglass. The young man was still there, ear to the door.

Paul waited until he had gone, then walked back over to the bed and passed Carla her gown.

'I'm sorry,' he said. 'I don't know what to say. I didn't mean to ruin things. I misread the moment, thought you—'

She shook her head. She didn't know where to begin, or what to say, but she couldn't stall her history any longer.

They never got to the festival opening. She told him everything – about Jack and Kevin, and about Toroa. Everything. Even that she had herpes, and if they ever made love he would need to use a condom.

Chapter Forty-One

BEN

'A Ka mate! Ka mate! Ka ora! Ka ora!
Ka mate! Ka mate! Ka ora! Ka ora!
Tēnei te tangata pūhuru huru,
Nāna nei i tiki mai
Whakawhiti te rā!
A upa . . . ne! ka upa . . . ne!
A upane kaupane whiti te rā!'[7]

Twelve bodies, chests bare, thighs spread solid, arms reaching up to the heavens to pull down the ancestors. The chant, hands slapping, tongues protruding, eyes ablaze. Ben could feel a formidable force pulsing as he moved in unison with his brothers. Sweat ran down his body, and inside, something was exploding. It was hard to describe. He wondered if the spirits Chalkie so often talked about were in fact real. Perhaps they were in the room with him right now.

At the front, standing apart from everyone, was August. Chalkie moved up beside him.

'August Honatana,' he said, his voice deep and strong. 'You have heard the words. You have heard the pre-battle challenge:

> *I die! I die! I live! I live!*
> *I die! I die! I live! I live!*
> *This is the hairy man*
> *Who fetched the sun*
> *And caused it to shine again*
> *One upward step! Another upward step!*
> *An upward step, another . . . the sun shines!'*[7]

His voice held the entire room in its reach.

'Today, as you leave prison, the real battle begins. Your enemies are out there.' Chalkie pointed into the distance. 'Drink, drugs, all the temptations . . . They are lying in wait for you. Be strong. Hold your head up high. It won't be easy, but you *can* come through.' He paused. Looked about the room.

Perspiration was pouring off Ben's forehead, and not just because of the war dance. It had been over a month since he'd been high – six weeks without weed, ice, or even glue – and he was still edgy. Tears came for no reason and irritability crawled over him like a disturbed nest of ants.

'Remember, stay with your people, stick with your history, and make your ancestors proud.' Chalkie was speaking to August as if no one else was in the room. He had that way of directing his attention so absolutely. Like a searchlight, he'd find you and hold you in his gaze, making you feel special, but at the same time sprung.

'And don't come back! We don't want to see you here no more.

Not unless you come back as a teacher, or a warden.' He laughed. 'Or maybe a policeman.'

August shifted uneasily.

'God watch over you, man.' Then he pulled August into him, nose to nose, eye to eye, and they held each other with the strength of equal men. Both August and Chalkie's staunch eyes were shining with tears.

'Now for the best part,' Chalkie said, his sternness breaking into a grin. '*Kai*!'

Everyone clapped.

'August's *whānau* has provided us with a mean feed.' Chalkie bowed his head to the elderly couple. 'Thank you.'

August's mother's serious expression unfurled. Like a ball of paper set alight, happiness and tears curled the edges of her wizened face.

What would his own mother have looked like now? Ben wondered. He didn't have a single photograph of her.

Recently, she'd been showing up in his head at random times. Just the other day a memory pitched up of the time she took him and Lily with her to work. Ryan had been drinking at the house with his crew and she didn't trust leaving Ben and his sister alone with him. After she had more kids, she became less vigilant. Or maybe she just grew tired, because she started leaving them alone with Ryan a lot, even after he broke a chair over Cody for soiling his pants.

It was a long night traipsing after their mother as she moved through the office blocks on Wellesley Street, vacuuming and dusting and emptying bins. He and Lily had found a carpeted corner where they'd dozed for a while, Lily curled up beside him, sucking her thumb.

They were all heading out of the building into the grey light of dawn when his mum spotted a fifty-dollar note lying in the crease of the concrete steps. She couldn't believe it, laughing and whooping all the way down Queen Street. 'What about I treat you to a special breakfast, kids,' she'd said, leading them into a proper sit-down cafe. 'Our little secret, okay?'

As Ben moved through the memory, he could again taste the smoky sweet maple syrup on the hotcakes and smell the strips of bacon grilled all wavy and crisp. His mum asked the waitress for a beer, but the place didn't serve alcohol, which Ben was pleased about; his mum was nicer off the booze. After she'd paid for the breakfast, there was still enough money for ice cream. Fifty dollars felt like a fortune. It was the best day ever.

Then Lily went and ruined it all. It wasn't really her fault; she was too small to understand the keep-a-secret bit. Their mum got smacked about by Ryan for not bringing home the cash and spewed up all her breakfast, the ice cream too. So it was a proper waste of the money.

August's father now waddled over to Chalkie to shake his hand. He was short and round, with a shiny brown scalp and a circular smile that looked like he was saying the letter O . . . He kept saying over and over again. 'Thank you. Thank you, sir. Thank you for saving our son.'

Ben wondered if August had been saved. Most of his mates at Pare would usually be back inside within a year of their release. The only reason Ben ever used to watch *One News* was to see who was coming back.

'Before we eat,' Chalkie said, raising his voice above the din. 'I nearly forgot. Ben, our newest arrival at the unit, has composed a rap for the occasion. Danny helped write it.'

The room with the blue carpet and big windows went quiet. Ben's legs went bendy. He held up the paper, pretending to read it even though he'd memorised most of the words. The sheet shook in his hands. He started to move to the beat in his head.

> Hey, August, you lea–ving us,
> That's too bad,
> We've become family,
> We gonna be sad.
> Now hear our cry, before you fly –
> No dope, no booze, don't even try.
> You'll mess it all up if you waste this
> chance,
> So take your talent bro, and advance.
> Tikanga.

Then everyone was clapping and whistling, and shouting. 'Choice!'

'You da man!'

'Cheers, bro.' It was a good feeling.

Ben dunked a sausage roll into a bowl of tomato sauce and stuffed it into his mouth. He was sad to be losing August – over the past six weeks they'd become tight – but at least he could move down to the unit permanently into the dude's vacated cell.

Beyond

I feel the excitement that comes with the anticipation of something new. The same excitement I feel seeing small flecks of green on the skeletons of wintered trees. You have reached the waka, *and can surely feel the embrace of* kaupapa Māori. *But my eagerness must be tempered; you are not yet on board, and there is still such a long way to haul you home. So much can happen in between.*

Home, Benjamin, will not be the world of before, the place I told you about. That no longer exists. Such is the nature of life; nothing remains the same for ever. Colonisation wrought changes, both good and bad, changes which cannot be undone; time moves in one direction only. However, you can still carry with you packages from the past. Take with you the best of your people's beliefs and weave them together with the peculiarities of others that you will meet.

Just now I am looking down on Te Noho Kotahitanga Marae and see a central brass pole around which two brass vines intertwine. The great master carver, Dr Lyonel Grant, depicted these as two individual plants with separate roots that come together around one central pole. *They twist over and under each other until you cannot discern their separateness. Yet still they must be tended individually, or else one might die and the other grow rampant.*[8] *True unity embraces separateness.*

Chapter Forty-Two

BEN

Chalkie knocked on the open cell door. Ben was lounging on his bunk.

'What's going down, Chalkie?'

'You got a visitor.'

Ben swung his legs over the side of the bed. 'Not expecting no one.'

'I've persuaded the screws to drop some of the formalities,' Chalkie said. 'Kinda turn a blind eye to the paperwork and all that shit. Don't let me down.'

Ben stood up, his interest hooked. 'So you gonna tell me who it is?'

Chalkie paused. 'Carla Reid.' The words dropped into the room like a corpse.

'Driven all the way up from Auckland to see you, she has.'

Ben stood fixed to the spot and stared at Chalkie's two short fingers.

Neil, the warder, appeared in the doorway swinging a pair of handcuffs. 'Sorry, Ben, but gotta stick to the rules.'

Ben put out his hands. 'It's okay, Neil. I'm cool with it.'

* * *

She was standing near one of the windows in the meeting room, her back to him, light pouring in around her. Someone had left a plastic water bottle on the window ledge and the sun drove straight through it, coming out the other end split up into colours, which trapped her inside the rainbow.

She turned.

He stopped.

Then she was walking towards him, her hands outstretched. He lifted up his manacled wrists. They both smiled at his predicament. She brushed her hands momentarily over his, the touch running through him like an electrical current.

She smelt nice. Of the outside.

Suddenly he was a kid again. *He's fallen out of a tree and is bleating like a baby. His mother wraps him in her arms – skin on skin, the smell of shampoo, her warm words.*

'Good to see you, Ben' the Reid woman said, her voice a gentle catapult bumping him back into the room.

He didn't know what to say.

'I thought it was time to continue with our lessons.' Her tone was matter-of-fact, as if they'd just seen each other the previous week. 'Chalkie tells me you're managing to read quite a bit on your own now.'

Ben looked across the room at his mentor, then back to her. 'Sort of.'

'So I've brought some of Jack's old books with me.' She pointed to two chairs. He sat down slowly. It was weird sitting next to her.

'I brought something else too.'

He looked away. He couldn't handle any more stuff. No games. No more record of his badness. He already knew what an evil bastard he was.

'Neil and Chalkie have turned themselves inside out to make this happen,' she said, bending down to take something out of her canvas carrier bag.

He frowned. He understood the unspoken warning: *Don't fuck this up*. But what was she on about?

It was a brown cardboard box with the picture of a food processor on the side.

A food processor? What on earth was he going to do with one of those? Not another cooking story!

The box was punctured with hundreds of holes, as if someone had sprayed it with an air rifle.

'What the . . . ?'

'Aren't you going to take a look inside?' she said, putting the box in his lap.

It was lighter than he'd expected. He lifted the cardboard leaves. 'Jesus!'

Inside was a grey bundle of fur with ears as sharp as the corners of a page. Two big round eyes looked up at him.

'*Please, Ma, can't we have a cat? Pania's cat's borne kittens. Six of 'em. Just one. Please.*'

Pania was Ben's girlfriend from when he was just six years old. She'd lived next door.

'*Ask Ryan.*'

'*A cat? You gotta be joking. The only fuckin' cat coming in this house will be a feed for Diesel.*'

Ben opened his hands, which were still joined at the wrist, and closed them round the small creature. It was soft. Nothing in prison was soft. His fingers fizzed as the softness seeped into him, and negatives that had been in a dark room of his mind for so long were instantly developed.

Pania's heavy black hair falling to her shoulders . . .

Driving the clapped-out wreck in the garden — Pania in the front, Lily in the back, laughing and laughing till Lily spewed . . .

Pania holding his hand in the playground . . .

Pania reading to him behind the dairy, spinning long, silky words around him . . . Pania and her family moving away.

'I'll bring her with me each time I visit,' the Reid woman said, 'but she's yours.'

She's yours. Ben hadn't owned anything important ever.

'She doesn't have a name yet.'

'Pania,' Ben said. 'Her name is Pania.'

CARLA

'So how did it go?' Paul asked, folding away the newspaper and pulling his car seat into the upright position. The convertible's hood was down, inviting the glorious day in.

Carla kissed him. 'Well the kitten was a hit,' she said, carefully lifting Pania out of the box and putting her into the cat cage on the back seat. 'He didn't want me to take her away again.'

She opened the passenger door and dropped into the seat with a sigh. 'Hey, thank you, Paul. For everything.'

'All I did was play chauffeur,' he said, starting the engine. 'The rest has been your doing, and don't you forget it.'

As they drove back to Auckland, she recounted the events of the morning. Finally she fell silent, her mind coasting in neutral as the breeze rifled her hair. She was tired, but in a good way. She'd worried all week about how the visit would go.

Next thing she knew, Paul was stroking her head.

'That was quick,' she said dreamily, looking around. They were parked under a giant pohutakawa tree, its gnarled limbs dipping down to finger an expansive stretch of grass that sloped down to a river. Yellow umbrellas dotted the lawn like buttercups.

'Not home yet, but I thought we could stop for a bite. I don't know about you, but I could eat a horse.'

So they ordered lunch from the nearby cafe and found a free table close to the car, so that they could keep an eye on Pania.

The cafe was busy for a weekday and she and Paul people-watched as they ate their lunch.

A baby girl, all strawberry-blonde curls and cherub cheeks, was crawling along the grass under the watchful eye of an older child, who intermittently reprimanded her in an exaggerated, grown-up tone. 'No, no, no. Not that way, young lady!'

Carla saw who she thought was likely the mother sitting some distance away, a large straw hat canopying her face.

'Bit too much chilli on the squid,' Paul said, washing down a mouthful with a swig of ale. 'Nice, none the less. Want to taste?'

As Carla leant towards his outstretched fork, she saw that the toddler had ventured right down to the water's edge. Its distracted young minder was scaling the branches of a tree.

'Careful!' Carla cried, knocking over Paul's beer as she jumped up and raced down the slope.

As Carla scooped up the child, the wee girl let out an ear-piercing yowl, which brought her mother running.

'Thank you!' she said breathlessly, lifting the bawling child out of Carla's embrace. 'I'm so sorry!'

Hearing the commotion, the boy dropped down from the tree, but hung back.

'I asked you to look after your sister!' his mother shouted. 'She could have drowned.'

'It can happen so easily,' Carla said, trying to calm the moment. Her eyes met the mother's. They were unmistakable in their hue. Carla knew those eyes. That face. The long auburn hair.

'Don't I know you? I . . .'

The woman flushed.

'Weren't you at Jack's funeral?' Carla said slowly.

The woman nodded.

Then Paul was upon them, a large ale stain down the front of his shirt. 'Everyone OK?'

There was an awkward pause, filled only by the little girl's whimpering.

'Mrs Reid?' the woman finally said.

Carla nodded.

'You two know each other?' Paul asked, bemused.

His intrusion was suddenly an irritation for Carla.

The woman stretched out her long, pale hand. 'I'm Myra.'

'We never got to talk that day,' Carla began. 'I . . . I wanted to ask . . . I always wondered. You were his girlfriend, weren't you?'

Myra's teary eyes answered Carla's question.

'Why don't you join us for a drink?' Paul suggested.

The woman hesitated. 'Olivia is due for her nap, and—'

'Olivia,' Carla repeated, with a smile. 'She's very sweet. How old?'

The mother smoothed her little girl's hair. 'Twenty-three months and quite a handful.'

Carla looked over at the youngster still skulking behind the tree. 'And your boy?'

'Seven,' Myra replied briskly.

'Don't be too angry with him,' Carla said. 'Boys can be quite oblivious to what's going on around them.'

The young woman's smile did not camouflage her tense expression.

'*Do* join us,' Carla said, gesturing to their table.

'We really must be on our way. Olivia needs her nap and—'

'Not even a quick drink?' Paul chimed in. 'I'm going to get another beer.'

Myra faltered. Then her son was running towards her, his hands cupped against his chest. 'Mum, look what I've found!'

Carla felt the colour drain from her face as the lad approached. Her gums tingled.

'You alright, Carl?' Paul said as she leant against him.

Swimming-pool-blue eyes. Long lashes. A craze of blue-black hair. A wide grin. *That* grin.

'A praying mantis, Mum! I think it's hurt,' the boy said, cautiously opening his hands.

'Oh dear,' his mother replied distractedly.

'Can we take it home and make it better?'

'Josh, uh . . .'

Carla kept staring.

'Muuuum, are you listening?'

'We should talk,' Myra said quickly. 'But not now. Sometime when we can be alone.'

'I could take the kids for an ice cream, if that would be easier,' Paul said.

The woman looked around, panicked.

'You'll be able to see us from where you're sitting,' he reassured.

So the kids ran up the slope to the cafe with Paul, and the two women sat down.

'Is he . . . ?' Carla finally said, her voice faltering.

Myra nodded, the rims of her eyes reddening.

'I don't understand. How? I mean, when?'

'Mrs Reid,' Myra said, stretching across the wooden table to grasp Carla's hands.

'Call me Carla, please.'

'Carla. I only found out I was pregnant the week before Jack died. I was in a terrible way. I couldn't believe it. First discovering I was pregnant and then losing Jack.' Her words spilt out. 'I couldn't tell you. I'd never even met you before. And my parents – they're Catholic. Jack was my first boyfriend. I asked Jack's friend, Russell, for help.'

'Russell? You mean Russell Catchpole?'

'Yes. Of course you'd know him. Jack's best mate. We were kind of like the Three Musketeers that year – him, Jack, and me. We did everything together. Anyway, Russell offered more than I could ever have hoped for. He offered to marry me.'

'*Marry* you?' Carla repeated, incredulously.

'And Josh was born seven months later.'

Russell, who had practically lived at the farm for most of Jack's school years. The lad they would collect from the school hostel almost every weekend after his parents moved to Kerikeri. The Russell, who'd gone flatting with Jack.

As if travelling through some theme-park maze, Carla's bewildered thoughts careered around her head. 'So he . . . So Joshua is *my grandson*?'

Myra closed her eyes and tears spilt onto her cheeks.

She had a grandson! No one had told her. Jack's son! How dare Russell have kept it from her. How dare sh—?

'Mrs Reid. Carla. Josh doesn't know about Jack. Not yet. Russ has always been so good. A great father to him. It's easier this way. Less complicated. We plan to tell him when he's older.

He's only seven; you understand.' Her blue eyes were pleading.

'Did Jack know?' Carla asked, her mind trawling through the fragments of memories leading up to Jack's death, searching for the clues she had missed.

Myra nodded. 'And his GP. No one else. Jack was planning to talk to his dad about it, but I know he didn't want to worry you until we had proper plans in place. I'm so sorry. Then everything changed.'

Carla stroked the surface of the table, her eyes navigating the dark grooves running between the strips of wood.

'What a terrible thing to have to cope with,' she finally said. 'I can't imagine what it must have been like for you, unable to share a secret like that on top of all your grief. You poor girl.'

Myra's face momentarily loosened. She blew her nose and cast an anxious look towards the cafe.

'He's the spitting image of Jack, you know,' Carla said, shaking her head. 'The spitting image.'

Myra nodded.

Jack's boy. Jack's boy. Jack's boy.

'Mama, look! Twiple chocolate!' Olivia waddled across the lawn towards them.

The boy hung back. He was talking with Paul. He walked with a slow sort of Jack lollop.

'Mum, Paul owns a Ferrari Testarossa. He's restoring it,' he said, out of breath, just an arm's length from Carla.

'Is he indeed?' Myra said, trying to smile.

'Can we go see it one day? Can we? Please.'

'Josh is car mad at the moment,' Myra said apologetically, taking her son by the hand. 'We'll speak to Dad. He'd be jealous if he couldn't go too, wouldn't he?'

Carla flushed. *Dad.* The word stung.

'We really should be going,' Myra said, her clipped tone ring-fencing any emotion. 'I'll be in touch.' She touched Carla on the shoulder. 'You still out in Dairy Flat?'

'Oh no!' Carla said, scrambling for a pen in her bag and jotting down her phone number on the back of a supermarket docket. 'How do I get hold of you? Do you live nearby?'

'I'll give you a call,' Myra said, gently. 'Nice to meet you, Kevin.'

'Paul,' he corrected, with a perplexed smile.

Chapter Forty-Three

CARLA

The tennis ball rolled across the carpet. Pania pounced, sinking her claws into the fluorescent fuzz.

Ben let out a snort. 'Puss, puss, come here, you.'

But the kitten had other ideas, all of which involved the ball.

'She's got heaps bigger.'

Carla smiled. 'She has, which is pretty surprising considering what a fussy eater she is. Only the very best for Miss Pania.'

'Did Jack have a cat?'

These days, Ben's questions arrived without warning. There was no guessing what he'd toss next into the ring. Sometimes his enquiries were too intrusive, too familiar, and she instantly repelled them, still scared that Ben would in some way wreak more havoc, even if only on her memories. She alone would determine what to share. Yet despite her resistance, deep down she believed that these unpredictable enquiries actually sprung more from a genuine interest in her life than an expedient gathering of information – his interest in her life in fact a measure of their kinship.

Kinship? Something had happened between her and this young man – something bewildering and frightening and good all at the same time.

She swam back to the surface of her thoughts.

'He did, Ben. In fact he could have filled Noah's Ark entirely on his own! He had everything from a Bearded Dragon to a family of twenty-six mice. Then there was Sinbad the parrot, a Siamese cat called Cleopatra, and Tutti the guinea pig. He even used to catch frogs in the pond on the farm and smuggle them inside under his cap.'

Ben sniggered at the thought of Jack sneaking them past his mother. 'Chancer!'

Carla laughed. 'Yup, he was full of mischief. And you, Ben? Did you have pets?'

Ben looked down at his shoes. 'Nah. Well, yeah. I mean, we had this mongrel called Diesel, but he wasn't really a pet, like. We also had a bitch called Tequila. She had puppies, but I don't remember what happened to them.' He paused, his face darkening. Then the wave passed and his eyes lit up again. 'Once, my friend Pania gave me this bottle of silkworms. I used to go over to her place to get leaves, special swan plant leaves, 'cos that's what they live off, you know.'

'They sound more like the caterpillars of Monarch butterflies.'

'Anyway, Pania and me—'

'Pania and I,' Carla corrected.

'Pania and I had these stupid plans to set up our own silk factory and get rich.' Ben laughed with embarrassment. 'But Ryan threw the jar at Cody when he shat—I mean pooed in his pants, and that was the end of that – Cody crying like a

312

baby and all my munted worms sliding down the wall.'

'Had any got to the cocoon stage?' Carla asked, trying to steer the conversation away from the darkness.

'Nah.'

Ben's face lit up as Pania somersaulted into view and he bent down and picked the kitten up.

'I'll try to get hold of some for you,' Carla said. 'It's an amazing thing to watch – their lifecycle from tiny black egg stuck to the back of a leaf, to caterpillar, cocoon and then butterfly.'

He nodded. She could tell he didn't believe her. No expectation, no disappointment. Or maybe he just didn't care. He was a grown man, after all, and she was still treating him like a teen. Yet at times he seemed almost half-formed and vulnerable, and she felt the urge to mother him.

'Actually,' Carla said, thinking out loud, 'there's a great short story by a New Zealand author. Her name just eludes me. My memory! Anyway . . . Oh, I know. Patricia Grace. The story is called "Butterflies". I'll try to get a copy for you from the library. Yes, that's what I'll do.'

Ben shrugged.

'So, tell me, how's that writing of yours coming along?'

He opened his exercise book, his face retreating behind a curtain of long hair. 'I'm rubbish at it.'

She scanned the rows of letters tracking down the page. 'No. This is good, Ben.'

He looked up slowly.

'It's good. Really. Just make sure that when you write the letter r, you start from the top of the little stem and keep your pen on the page all the time.' She traced one of the letters with her finger.

''Kay.'

Someone coughed. Carla looked up and was surprised to see three youngsters slouching in the doorway. Two darted away as soon as their cover was blown. The third – a thin fellow with purple-brown acne scars pitting his forehead remained. 'Can we sit in, miss?'

'Sit in? On the lesson?'

'Yeah.'

The other two reappeared behind their spokesman.

'Where are you meant to be?' she asked.

'Nowhere, miss,' they replied in unison.

'Sorry, guys, but—'

'C'mon. How come Ben gets to learn to write and all?'

'But you guys know how to, don't you?'

Silence.

'All right, then. Pull up a chair. Let's see if I've got a few more pens.'

Later that week, Carla came home to a message from the prison manager asking if she would consider helping with the literacy programme at the unit. They'd had a surge of interest in the course since she'd been teaching Ben. She accepted.

The rollercoaster ride she'd been on for so many years finally felt less of an ordeal – the dips not as drastic, the ascents not as steep. When Paul visited his daughter in Germany for six weeks, Carla coped. And when the anniversaries of Jack and Kevin's deaths came round, she did not crumble.

One thing, however, continued to tamper with her equilibrium, and plague her new-found evenness; she had not heard back from Myra. It had been months. Paul cautioned her against trying to track the woman down, and it took all Carla's willpower to adhere to his advice. She had a grandson. Somewhere in Auckland was Jack's son. It had been easier not knowing.

Chapter Forty-Four

BEN

'Ben! Hey, Ben!' Isaac's voice boomed through the space.

'Sounds like you in for a hiding,' Rusty, a new inmate on the block, snorted, cornflakes and spittle spraying from his mouth.

Ben stood up from the breakfast table, preparing for a rumble. In the boob he was always prepared.

Isaac burst into the canteen. 'Jesus, you motherfucker,' he panted. 'I be-be-been calling you for ages.'

Chalkie walked in behind him, drawn by the commotion. He laid a hand on Isaac's arm. 'What's up?'

'It's them— I mean, it's them c—' He couldn't get the words out. In the end, he just pointed to the door.

The canteen cleared faster than in an emergency drill, the promise of excitement spicing up the day. They ran down the corridor, their numbers swelling till all twelve of them, plus Chalkie, were headed for the meeting room. They careened round the corners like a freight train in the night – all muscle, steel and noise.

Neil, the unit guard, was at the end of the passage when they rounded the last corner. He took one look at the entire muster heading his way and slammed the gate shut just in time to bring all thirteen to a clanging halt. Then he was shouting into his radio. 'Incident on Fourteen! Incident on Fourteen!'

'What's up, Neil?' Ben puffed, pressing himself against the cold bars.

'On the floor,' Neil shouted. 'On the floor!'

'But what we done?' Wiki hollered.

'Yeah. What we done?'

Chalkie pushed through the hunch of guys. Neil spotted him, and his expression relaxed a little. 'Chalkie, you got to get down too.'

Chalkie nodded and sank to the ground. He knew the drill.

Ben pulled himself along the floor until his face was right up next to Isaac's, the guy's hot, agitated breath blowing over his face. 'So you wanna tell me what's going down, Isaac? Slowwwly.'

Isaac's bad stammer could drive a man mental. The only words he never struggled with were swear words; they rolled off his tongue as easily as a morning piss.

Isaac sucked in a deep breath. 'It's . . . it's them chr . . . chr . . . chrysalis things. There's fuckin' b-butterflies ev . . . ev . . . everywhere.'

Ben started to laugh. A snicker at first, that grew into a shaking howl.

'What's so funny, bookman?' Rusty sneered.

Ben ignored him, tears of laughter running down his cheeks. He could these days ignore most taunts. His anger had gradually burnt down to cooling embers.

When backup arrived, the guards found thirteen inmates on the floor hollering with laughter. It took a bit of explaining, but finally the gate was unlocked and a more subdued crew spilt into the meeting room.

Isaac went in first, his grin stretched taut across his teeth.

'See! S-S-See!' He was spinning round and round – a hairy, hulking ballerina pointing at the ceiling.

Floating above them, like autumn leaves swept up in a gust, were monarch butterflies, their orange paper wings ignited by the sun.

Then the room was still, except for the faintest, perhaps imagined sound of beating wings. Everyone was looking up. Up was different.

So the caterpillars the Reid woman had brought in had done good, mused Ben. Silly little critters . . .

Isaac counted them. 'Five chrysalises. F-f-four b-b-butterflies.'

The guys pushed past Ben to check out the two potted swan plants drooping in the corner. Four torn balls of burst silk hung there like emptied pockets. Only one perfect package remained. It was no longer cucumber green with golden pimples, but almost see-through – a window onto a folded world of orange and black.

'Let's see!'

'Hey, give us a look!'

'Don't push, you cunt!'

'Fuck you!'

They pushed and shoved and jostled to get closer. Ben didn't react. Once he would have thumped anyone who tried thrusting him out of the way.

The regular old room was like some giant popcorn machine spewing out excitement. All twelve of them refused to budge for the rest of the day in case the final pouch popped. They even missed out on lunch because Neil wouldn't let them eat in the meeting room. In the end, a screw's a screw, no matter what's going down, thought Ben. However, it didn't escape his notice that Neil hung around for a lot of the day too – finding one excuse or another to put his head in and check on the guys (and that last cocoon).

Ben was just glad that no one from outside could see him now – hanging around a plant waiting for some butterfly to hatch. How mental was that!

By late afternoon, the guys were bored, and Ben was starting to think that the last chrysalis was a dud. Then at ten past four, as the sun was painting fat yellow stripes across the carpet, the chrysalis shuddered . . . A faint tremble that swallowed the attention of the entire room. And, after some serious vibrating, something wriggled out.

It was misshapen – nothing like what Ben had been expecting. All long body.

It hung from the ripped sheaf for what seemed like forever, the creased and crumpled wings slowly opening like one of those capsules he and Lily used to buy from the corner store which, when dropped in water, morphed into some super cool shape – an octopus, a fish, a star.

Ironed-smooth. Flexing. A quivering sort of grace.

Then lift off!

Ben had never seen anything so awesome in his whole life.

Beyond

The woman's feet are bare, and her long hair is twisted into a knot. A cluster of speckled feathers drives through the thick, greying bundle. Her face is a calm crease of age. She lifts her hands; they tremble with life. Her voice, like the call of a tui, reaches high in welcome. She is one of the tangata whenua – *the hosts. Behind her the timber walls of the meeting house stand strong – the pitched roof an embrace; the carvings a record of time and tale; the blue eyes* pāua-*wide with seeing.*

A kaikaranga comes in reply. The messenger is once again a woman. Her voice is both strong and sweet like the honey of manuka, and she chants a retort. Her hands quiver too, and her feet are also bare. She is of the manuhiri – *the visitors.*

So continues this exchange, back and forth, back and forth, until the call comes inviting these guests to enter the sacred house.

They move slowly towards the sanctuary, this place with ribs and backbone, pillar and post, with its sturdy flax-woven walls.

Listen out for the karanga, *Benjamin Toroa. It will invite you to take off your shoes and enter your ancestors'* wharenui. *The meeting*

320

house still exists despite all that has transpired. Some of your people have kept it strong.

When the time comes, though, I will leave you on the threshold. I cannot push you inside. It will be for you to accept the challenge.

Chapter Forty-Five

CARLA

The grandmother plaited the granddaughter's hair and then said, 'Get your lunch. Put it in your bag. Get your apple. You come back straight after school, straight home here. Listen to your teacher,' she said. 'Do what she say.' [9]

Carla paused in her reading and looked up from the book. The room was still. Even the butterflies. Thirteen faces – brown, scarred, and dented – listening intently.

She'd got an urgent message from Neil at the prison. He told her the butterflies had hatched, and she had to come up. It wasn't Thursday, her usual day, but she was needed. So she'd taken leave from the library and headed north, Patricia Grace's short story tucked into her bag.

Carla continued. *Her grandfather was out on the step. He walked down the path with her and out onto the footpath. He said to a neighbour, 'Our granddaughter goes to school. She lives with us now.'*

'She's fine,' the neighbour said. 'She's terrific with her two plaits in her hair.'

'And clever,' the grandfather said. 'Writes every day in her book.'

'She's fine,' the neighbour said.

The grandfather waited with his granddaughter by the crossing and then said, 'Go to school. Listen to the teacher. Do what she say.'

When the granddaughter came home from school her grandfather was hoeing round the cabbages. Her grandmother was picking beans. They stopped their work.

'You bring your book home?' the grandmother asked.

'Yes.'

'You write your story?'

'Yes.'

'What's your story?'

'About the butterflies.'

Isaac let out a guffaw. 'It's about b-b-butter—'

'Shut your gob,' Rusty shouted.

'Hey, you shut it!' Wiki snapped.

'Shhh.' Ten voices in unison.

Carla dropped her voice to re-enlist her audience. 'Get your book, then. Read your story.'

The granddaughter took her book from her schoolbag and opened it.

'I killed all the butterflies,' she read. 'This is me and this is all the butterflies.'

The audience was suddenly restless. Ben stroked Pania's ears.

'And your teacher like the story, did she?'

'I don't know.'

'What your teacher say?'

'She said butterflies are beautiful creatures. They hatch out and fly in the sun. The butterflies visit all the pretty flowers, she said. They lay their eggs and then they die. You don't kill a butterfly, that's what she said.'

The grandmother and grandfather were quiet for a long time, and their granddaughter, holding the book, stood quite still in the warm garden.

'Because you see,' the grandfather said, 'your teacher, she buy all her cabbages from the supermarket and that's why.'

No one moved. Carla lowered the book slowly. She smiled. Faces glowered back. 'So what do you think?'

'It sucks,' Wiki said. 'That kid killed the butterflies.'

'Yeah,' another piped up indignantly.

'Well, yes,' Carla said, choosing her words with care. 'And if someone killed these butterflies ' – she pointed to the orange arcs dotted around the room – 'you'd be angry and hurt too.' The men had invested over six weeks in these creatures – setting up, watching and waiting, preparing, nurturing, even photographing.

Heads nodded.

'It's painful to lose something you love and treasure, something beautiful.'

Ben looked down.

'But I think Patricia Grace was telling us something else. Life is a lot about how you look at things,' she went on. 'To understand how someone thinks, how they feel and behave, you need to understand who they are. Need to walk for a time in their shoes.'

She took a swig from her water bottle. No one in the room moved. A man she'd not seen before, was standing at the back of the room.

'For the girl and her grandparents, the butterflies were pests, eating holes in the family's carefully tended cabbages and destroying the crop. The teacher didn't understand that when she read the girl's story.'

Some nods and gradual smiles.

'These are monarch butterflies,' Carla continued.

'*Kahuku*, in Māori,' interjected Chalkie.

'The Aztecs, people from an ancient civilisation, believed monarch butterflies were the spirits of their fallen warriors, their colourful wings the colours of battle. But the butterflies in *this* story were probably cabbage butterflies,' Carla said. 'They're different. Also beautiful, with white wings and powdery black markings. But they lay their eggs inside cabbages, and the caterpillars that hatch chew huge holes in the leaves. They can decimate an entire crop.'

'I hate fuckin' cabbage,' Rusty blurted out.

No one paid him any heed. Carla was impressed. The others were getting used to his attempts to sabotage the calm. And even though he could clearly drive them crazy, they seemed to understand; he was, after all, the newest on the unit. They'd once been in the same dark place themselves – in that abyss of purpose, where there was only room for anger.

'So are we ready to release them?' Carla asked, after a time.

'Release them?' the guys shouted incredulously.

'There's nothing for them to feed on,' she said above the protests. 'Just a few wilting pot plants and a dish of water. You can't hold them prisoner.'

That word hit hard, quashing all protest instantly.

'The butterflies need to eat and mate and carry pollen from plant to plant,' she continued. 'That's their job.'

Rusty gurgled and thrust his hips back and forth.

'Do you know,' Carla said, 'that butterflies taste their food by standing on it?'

'Fuckin' hell!'

'Rusty! Remember the rules of this unit,' Chalkie cautioned.

'They do this because they have taste sensors, sort of tongues, on their feet.'

This induced a wave of hilarity, Ben promising to walk over his porridge in the morning and Wiki declaring he'd lick his toes. The face of the mysterious man at the back of the room also dissolved into a grin.

'So it's freedom to the little buggers,' Ben muttered.

'I've brought some nets with me,' Carla said, standing up. 'You'll need to group in two or threes, as there are only five butterflies. You *can* catch them with your hands, but you have to be very gentle; a butterfly's wings are really delicate. Fingertips can easily rub off their scales.'

Outside in the yard, the setting sun had bordered the day in a carmine hue. Carla looked on at the youngsters standing on the small square of lawn – tough men with big hands guarding their fragile cargo. Who would be the first to release their charge?

'Miss Carla.' It was Ben, he was standing next to her, his hands empty. He'd let Roach hold a butterfly instead.

'Yes Ben.'

'You live in Albany, hey?'

'Yes,' she said warily, her defensive instincts kicking in. 'Why do you ask?'

He shook his head.

'What?'

'I learnt something yesterday. Do you know what Albany was called before?'

The others were becoming restless. Everyone was waiting for someone else to make the first move and let a butterfly go.

'Lucas Creek. I think it used to be called Lucas Creek,' she said.

Ben shook his head. 'Nah. I mean in Māori, the name for the whole area.'

Carla was getting a little impatient. This was an important moment for everyone in the unit, and she didn't want to distract from it. 'Ben, can we pick this up lat—'

'*Okahukura*,' he said. '*Okahukura*. It means "place of butterflies" or "place of rainbows". Cool, huh?'

Carla's skin rose into goosebumps.

'That *is* pretty cool.'

Then there was a gust of wind. A host of hands opened spontaneously and butterflies were tossed into the air like orange confetti. They hung there momentarily, suspended in the air as if on a wall frieze in a child's bedroom, before scattering across the evening sky.

'Carla, I'd like you to meet someone.'

She turned. Next to Neil stood the mystery man.

'Mike Adams,' the man said, his hand outstretched, a collection of copper bracelets on his wrist jangling.

Carla tried to place him. He looked too casual in his jeans and corduroy jacket to be part of the staff. And his ponytail was definitely not regulation.

'Mr Adams is a freelance journalist,' Neil said. 'He's heard about the work you're doing with literacy here.'

'Word does gets around,' Carla said, with a brittle smile. 'I thought only bad news travelled that fast.'

'Mr Adams was keen to meet with you and Ben to learn more of your stories. Maybe write a piece about the two of you.'

'No!'

Both men looked startled.

'No more written about me, or Ben,' Carla said starting to walk towards the building.

'He's gonna fry! He's gonna fry!' Rusty shouted. One of the butterflies was balancing on top of the electric fence.

'Come to our tea room,' Neil said, quickly following. 'We can talk more easily there.'

Carla helped herself to a gingernut and dunked it in her coffee. 'You see, Mr Adams—' she began.

He leant earnestly over his elbows. 'Please, call me Mike.'

'Mr Adams,' she began again. He had warm eyes and an open face, she'd give him that. 'I'll be honest with you. I don't have much time for you people. Journalists, I mean. I once believed in good journalism, but have come to realise that the truth usually gets in the way of a good story.'

Mike Adams opened his mouth to talk.

'I've nothing against you personally,' she went on quickly, affording him no opportunity to interrupt. 'You look like a decent chap. It's just that reporters these days seem to have forgotten that it's people they are dealing with. Real people, real lives, real pain. They have a moral responsibility to those they are writing about. They need to carefully consider the impact their words have on the world.'

The end of Carla's biscuit broke off and sank. She fished for it with a teaspoon. 'It's my experience that words used carelessly remodel reality, sometimes wreaking as much damage and pain as the knife, bullet, or baseball bat.'

Adams looked out of the small window. She followed his gaze. The inmates were still watching the last remaining butterfly perched atop of the security fence.

328

'Freedom of speech does not translate into a free-for-all. It is not an absolute freedom to trawl through other people's lives, and write without thought for the consequences.'

Adams bit his lip. She should stop. Just say no. Move on. But she couldn't. The extraordinary lengths some had gone to to get her story had only heightened the suffering she'd had to endure. The lies. The violations. The unremitting attention. And then, when her life had been sucked dry of all sensation, when there was nothing more to keep the story spinning, she had been discarded like a piece of garbage.

Neil cleared his throat. 'Carla, I'm sorry to have put you in this position. Perhaps Mr Adams can talk with Ben alone and not bother you again.'

Carla jumped up. 'Absolutely not! You will not speak with him!' She rested her palms on the table. 'He . . . He . . . Just don't.' She wouldn't let Ben's progress be thwarted, nor measured and confined by words. She would not risk anyone damaging what they had.

'I think that should be Ben's decision,' Neil interjected.

Mike Adams held up his hand in a gesture of peace. 'I should explain.'

Carla clenched her jaw and shook her head. She would not be persuaded. Enough reporters had hidden in the shrubs on her farm with their long lenses, to cement a permanent distrust for the media. Money changed hands when news was reported. That corrupted the integrity of the process.

He stood up. 'I'm sorry to have disturbed you,' he said. 'I'll leave your story intact. I think the work you are doing is incredible.'

He ran a hand through his hair. As he did so his shirtsleeve rode up to reveal the green patterned ink of a traditional

Māori tattoo. Carla was surprised. He didn't look Māori.

'You know, I tried to write about Ben and you a long time ago,' he said, his hand gripping hers in a handshake. 'For a number of reasons, I couldn't. The story refused to be tamed into a one-page article. Perhaps I got a sense, then, of its depth, and the onus on the one who would try to tell it.'

Carla swallowed.

'Eight years on I thought I'd give it another crack.'

Carla looked down at his hand; his fingernails were all chewed. 'So you're a biter too.'

Adams blushed, curling his fingers into a fist.

'Anyway,' she said, 'you know what they say: *Fact writes stranger than fiction*. Who would ever believe that a bunch of hoodlums could be bewitched by butterflies?'

Adams laughed. A genuine, endearing laugh.

He walked towards the door.

'I've got a proposition for you,' Carla said.

He turned, his expression a little wary now.

'Why don't you come up to the prison when time permits and assist me in my classes. I could do with a helper. Being the wordsmith that you are, I'm sure you'd be a great asset.'

Adams' eyes grew wide.

'Maybe after a while you'll be better equipped to write the kind of story I think Ben and I deserve.'

Chapter Forty-Six

CARLA

The sun pushed through a crack in the curtains, casting a skew of light across Carla's dreams. She stirred and slid her feet towards Paul's heat, wheedling her legs in and around him until she was enveloped by their warmth and weight.

'What must a man do to get some sleep?' he protested groggily, trapping her between his thighs. 'Isn't it Sunday?'

She moved her hand down his torso until it reached the rise in his boxers. 'Why sir, it appears you've been expecting me.'

'Carla Reid,' he said in mock chastisement. 'No rest for the wicked, eh?' He rolled onto his back, yielding to her attentions.

Carla loved him first thing in the morning when he was still doused in the earthy smell of sleep, his face crumpled, his hair all tousled and wild.

A ringing telephone interrupted their play.

'Has everyone forgotten what day it is?' he grumbled, hauling himself up and rubbing his eyes.

Paul reached for the handset, fumbled with the receiver, then passed it over to Carla. He was good that way, still respecting her place after all this time, and not allowing familiarity to blur boundaries.

'Hello,' she said in a husky morning voice.

'Is Mrs Reid there?'

'Speaking.'

'Sorry, I didn't recognise your voice for a moment. It's Myra. Myra Catchpole. I hope I haven't woken you?'

'Myra!' Carla's voice sprang forward in anticipation. 'Not at all. Been up for ages.'

Paul yanked the sheets over his head.

'I was wondering . . .' Myra paused. 'Russell and I wondered whether you were going to be in Auckland in two weeks' time. We're coming down for the weekend and—'

'Yes. Yes, we're free.'

'The fourteenth. It's a Sunday. Perhaps we could meet up?'

Carla's mind sighed and whooped and started to spin. 'Of course!'

'Where would be a good place to meet?' Myra sounded tense.

'Here, of course! Come for a meal. Lunch. Does that suit?'

'We really don't want to intrude; a cup of tea will be fine.'

'Don't be silly,' Carla said, hopping out of bed and starting to pace around the room. 'You must come for a meal. I insist. It won't be a problem at all. We're on the Shore, about five kilometres from—'

Paul popped his head out from under the sheet and mouthed, 'Slow down.'

When she put down the phone, Carla stared into space.

'So . . . What's up?' Paul said, relieving her of the telephone receiver.

'It was Myra. You know, Jack's girlfriend. She, I mean they, are

332

coming for lunch. I don't know if the boy is too. I should have asked. I don't know if Joshua is coming too. Oh, I hope he is!' She climbed onto the bed and started jumping up and down, the springs creaking under her excitement.

'Slow down, Mrs Reid, or you'll blow a gasket,' Paul said, tackling her at the legs and dropping her.

The following week dragged, refusing to be hurried. At the library Carla forgot to swipe books out and shelved a whole trolley of returned ones incorrectly. At home, she added salt to her tea, sprayed hairspray under her arms, and located her lost tube of toothpaste in the fridge.

Paul tried his best to anchor her enthusiasm, anxious about what the reunion would bring. In the end he gave up; Carla's mood was too contagious.

Every evening after dinner she scoured recipe books, planning what to prepare for the approaching lunch date. First it was to be a slow-roast leg of lamb, Greek style, the meat marinated in lemon juice and stuffed with feta cheese and anchovies. Then she opted for roast chicken rubbed with a paste of rosemary, garlic, and olive oil. Finally, she settled on pasta with a simple sauce of bacon, egg yolks and Parmesan cheese.

'Probably more suited to a child's palate,' Paul agreed wearily. 'That's if they decide to bring the children along. I don't want you getting your hopes up.'

The week of the impending visit finally arrived. On the Tuesday, Carla could feel a cold coming on. The thought of even a minor ailment ambushing the upcoming Sunday was too much to contemplate, and she dosed herself up on vitamin C and zinc,

Panadol and echinacea. But on the Thursday she still felt virally. Paul was spending the night out of town at a book fair, so she didn't bother to make dinner for herself, instead climbing into bed just after six.

When her bedside alarm went off the following morning, she struggled to muster the energy to silence it. Paul was her usual alarm, waking her each morning with a mug of freshly brewed coffee and South African rusk to dunk. Carla couldn't have stomached either now; her whole head was aching and the yellow taste of nausea coated her tongue.

Hauling herself out of bed, she headed for the kitchen to make a cup of hot lemon water, but then left it untouched.

She stumbled through her morning routine with limbs like logs and her head in a fug that was intermittently punctured by a painful spear of sunlight. By the time she got to making the bed, she was already half an hour late for her shift at the library. As she bent down to tuck in the sheets, a wave of heat swept over her and the room listed. She teetered there for a moment, then slid to the ground and crawled on all fours towards the telephone.

Chapter Forty-Seven

PAUL

Paul stood impatiently at the information desk. The woman's perfume was very sweet.

Her long fuschia fingernails clicked away on the keyboard.

'What you say the name is again, love?'

'Carla Reid,' he repeated slowly.

She scrolled down the computer screen. 'Not in this hospital, pet. Sure you got the name right?'

'Look, I was phoned this afternoon by a medical registrar to say she'd been admitted. I've driven all the way up from Taupo.'

'Sure it was on the Shore?'

Paul panicked. 'The registrar said Waitemata Health, I think. I mean—'

'What's her address, love?'

Paul repeated it robotically.

'Hmm.' She pursed her lips. Lines of crimson had bled into the creases around her mouth. 'The only other thing I can think might have happened is . . . if she, um . . . Oh dear. Just a minute while I check.'

Paul froze, the world around him suddenly on pause. He knew what she was suggesting.

'How do you spell that surname again, hon? Two "E"s or an "E" and an "I"?'

Paul spelt it slowly and deliberately, his impatience tempered by fear.

The woman shook her concreted curls. 'Silly me, love! There are so many variations these days. Here we go. She's in intensive care on the fifth floor. Poor sweet. Must be awful sick.'

BEN

A gloom had settled over Unit 14, mirroring the day outside. The canteen was like a morgue, the meeting room an empty school hall. Ben missed breakfast and lunch, spending the day in his crib staring at the ceiling.

By evening, the walls had started to close in around him and the ceiling seemed lower. He was suffocating. He jumped up, trying to shake off the heaviness, and cussed so loudly the whole corridor heard.

Neil put his head in. Ben searched the screw's face for news. Neil shook his head.

The other laggers mooched about too, occasionally snapping at one another and lashing out. Two fistfights went down, and Rusty was sent to solitary for booting Isaac in the balls. It was calmer once he'd been locked away.

Finally, Chalkie called a meeting.

Outside the sky was black. The wind thumped at the windows and messed with the rain, sending sheets of water colliding into the glass. The room was cold and the floor hard. Eleven of them sat on the worn blue carpet waiting to hear what the tattooed lifer had to say.

'I'm disappointed in you,' he began. 'Not only have you let me down, you've let Miss Carla down, too.' The group stirred. 'So her visits, they've been in vain, have they?' Chalkie looked at Isaac. Isaac shrugged. 'Can you only be cool when she's around?' Chalkie's eyes landed on Ben. Ben glowered.

'She was trying to set you free, don't you see? Just like them butterflies. Teach you to read and write, so that one day you'd be able to make something of your lives. How'd you think she'd feel if she knew that the first thing you do when she's not here is sink back into old habits, into a vacuum of meaningless shit?'

Ben let his head collapse onto his chest.

'Look, I know you're worried. Angry. At the randomness of it. Me too. Sometimes life is just plain unfair. But the best thing we can do is keep working. Miss Carla believed in you. I believe in you. Do her proud, boys. Keep up with your writing. Your reading. That way you respect her.'

Ben looked up from under his fringe.

Chalkie pointed a thin finger at him. 'I want you to take charge of the lessons in her absence.'

Ben shook his head. 'But—'

'No bloody buts.'

Beyond

I must leave you, Benjamin Toroa, even though your story is not yet finished. The wind has brought me news of another who has fallen from our people's embrace. I must go in that direction. But I will never really leave you, boy, for I am the mountains and valleys, the sea and the sky. I am everywhere and everything. Recognising me is what takes time. You are just at the beginning of understanding. I am hopeful. I have seen the early buds of change.

I leave you with this one thought. Time stacks each generation upon the one that has gone before, just like layers of rock. What is built today depends on the strength of what was laid down yesterday. Your life, Benjamin, forms the foundation for those who come after. What you do now, son, will determine whether the platform stands strong or crumbles under the weight of new lives. Live well, for this story is about more than just you. It has always been about your people.

Haere mai.

PAUL

Paul pushed open the heavy swing door, leaving the metal-cold air of ICU behind him. A vending machine lit up the dingy corridor, offering a selection of hot drinks. Paul scrutinised the menu, then rammed a gold coin into the slot and pressed *Coffee black no sugar*. The money rattled, clunked, then dropped into the hollow belly of the dispenser. Nothing. The screen fluoresced: *$2.00. $2.00. $2.00.*

Paul cursed and fumbled in his pocket for another coin. Finally, a plastic cup dropped down and the machine spat out a treacly brew.

He hadn't eaten for eleven hours. His mouth felt dry and his tongue furry. He held a hand over his mouth; his breath smelt foul. He took a swig of the scalding liquid. Pleasure and pain.

Meningitis. Just like that. Normal one day, near death the next. Carla had already had her fair share of suffering. Was there no balance or even-handedness to what life dished out? Was fate really so capricious?

'Jeez, Carla, don't do this to me!' he said out loud, his words echoing down the corridor.

He thought about ringing his daughter in Germany, then dismissed the idea. It would be the middle of the night there. And she hadn't even met Carla.

What he needed was a cigarette. He hadn't touched one in years. Now he'd sell his soul for a smoke.

He headed down the long green corridor, stopping just short of the window at the end. A huddle of humans was gathered there, their pain silhouetted against the milky light of dawn. In just a handful of hours Paul had got to know these strangers so intimately. People were more real in the face of tragedy, the hindrances of pretence and polite restraint stripped away in the face of grief. They were about to switch off their child's life support machine. The teen had 'come out' that he was gay then jumped off a bridge, breaking his body and his parents' hearts. The tubes were still in place, the machines whirred and beeped, and the lad's chest heaved and fell fifteen times a minute. But the papers had been signed. The kid's life had already been lost. His body was just tricking the eye.

In that moment the essence of human existence was distilled for Paul – the need to belong and the need to be loved.

JOSHUA

'Dear God, my new granny is very sick. I was supposed to have lunch with her today. I hope she won't die, because . . . uh . . . because she's my father's . . . my other father's mother.'

'Amen. Okay, boy, into bed,' Myra said, tousling his hair.

'Mum?'

'Yes, Josh?' she said, sitting down on the edge of the bed and smoothing the creases in the duvet cover.

'Did my other dad like cars too?'

'Sure he did,' she said pulling the sheet up under his pudge of chin. 'His first car was a VW Beetle – an old turquoise one with cream-coloured seats and an indicator light that flicked out from the side. I helped your dad sew the seat covers, you know. We called it his love bug, after a movie we'd seen.'

'That's a funny name. Love bug. Love bug. Love bug.'

Myra smiled.

'Ma?'

'Yes, my boy.'

'Was it sore for my other dad when he died?'

She swallowed. 'I think God reached down very quickly and took him before he had time to feel sore.'

'Mum, don't turn off the light. I'm scared. What if God reaches down and takes me or my new granny.'

CARLA

The blackness was solid – an impenetrable nothingness.

Slivers of light poked in around the edges.

Cool floating fabric. Rigid. Plastic. Dry wet bubbling. A prickling. Smell.

Beep, beep, beep.

Sandalwood and Dettol.

Grey turned to white, then yellow. Light.

'Carla.'

'Carla.'

'Carla, can you hear me?'

Yes, I can hear you!

But the voice kept asking. Kept asking. Kept asking. 'Carla, can you hear me?'

The light was now expansive, whole and round. A mood. An understanding. A golden comprehension.

Her father is stooped over his desk. He looks up, brown eyes dancing as he spins the globe on his desk. Her mother stands at the kitchen bench in her purple slippers. She wipes floured hands on her housecoat and smiles a smile that shares a childhood. Dana wags her tail and trots under the table in search of scraps. Jack leaps down off the school bus and lollops towards her, a stick of cherry-red sherbet in his hand.

341

Kevin winks a no-worries-Carl wink, and there is Gabby, pin-size petite in the incubator.

A kauri tree drives through a cerulean blue sky. A tui calls. Clouds settle. A carver kneels over a long beam of wood and chisels a story. Fronds unfurl. A moa pushes through the undergrowth disturbing a hedgehog's stuttering passage. One young man holds a book in his hands and reads, his posture all pride. Another cradles his baby and makes promises. Butterflies capture magic. An elderly woman, her chin patterned with ink, weaves fingers of flax into a coat of great beauty. A farm fence divides one place into two.

Carla wraps herself in these images, all seamlessly sewn into one enormous quilt. She is comforted by the colours and stories it tells.

Suddenly lights, metal, a windowpane, blue curtain, white sheets, twists of tube, a graph, a vase of freesias, a face . . .

'Carla, you're awake!'

A familiar face.

'She's awake. Nurse, she's awake! Oh my God, you're awake.'

Too much. Too fast. She shut her eyes.

Trembling lips touched her cheek. Cool water ran down her face.

She opened her eyes slowly this time.

It was Paul.

Paul.

And Carla smiled, for she was still on the same side of the fence.

Permissions

Hunt, Sam. N.d. 'Winter Solstice Song'. In *JAAM 21 'Greatest Hits': An Anthology of Writing 1984–2004*, ed. Mark Pirie and Mike O'Leary. Wellington, NZ: JAAM in association with HeadworkX publishers and ESAW. With grateful thanks to Sam Hunt for permitting me to quote his poem in my work.

Grace, Patricia. 1987. 'Butterflies'. In *Electric City and Other Stories*. NZ: Penguin. With grateful thanks to Patricia Grace for permitting me to use her short story in my work.

Endnotes

[1] *Genesis 2.24* The Official King James Bible Online, Authorised version KJV. < http://www.kingjamesbible.org/1611_Genesis 2-24/ >

[2] Hunt, Sam. N.d. '*Winter Solstice Song.*' In JAAM 21 '*Greatest Hits': An Anthology of Writing 1984–2004*, ed. Mark Pirie and Mike O'Leary. Wellington, NZ: JAAM in association with HeadworkX publishers and ESAW.

[3] King, Michael, p. 156 *The Penguin History of New Zealand* (New Zealand: 2003).

[4] On plaque on wall at Paremoremo prison. Also in Foreword by Robson, Matt p. vi *About Time*: *Turning people away from a life of crime and reducing re-offending. Report from the Department of Corrections to the Minister of Corrections* (New Zealand 2001). http://www.corrections.govt.nz/ data/assets/ pdf file/0011/666218/abouttime.pdf

[5] Duff, Alan, *Once Were Warriors* (New Zealand, 1990).

[6] Glaubman, Richard, *Life is So Good* (USA, 2000).

[7] Haka Ka Mate http://www.kawhia.maori.nz/haka.html.

[8] Information from a talk I attended at the wharenui Ngākau Māhaki, Unitec Mt Albert campus, May 2015, as part of the Auckland Writers Festival and handout: *A Vision Beyond Its Time: Moemoea Kei Tua I Tōnā Wā* (UNITEC, New Zealand).

[9] Grace, Patricia. 1987. 'Butterflies'. In Electric City and Other Stories (New Zealand:1987).

Research Bibliography

With thanks to all the authors and individuals below whose works enlightened me, and enriched my understanding of the world my characters would inhabit.

Anderson Atholl, Binney Judith, Harris Aroha. 2015. *Tangata Whenua. An Illustrated History*. NZ: Bridget Williams Books.

Capote, Truman. 2000. *In Cold Blood*. UK: Penguin Classics.

Compain, Glen. 2008. *Street-Wise Parenting*. NZ: Harper Collins.

Duff, Alan. 2004. *Once Were Warriors*. NZ: Vintage, Random House NZ.

Ihimaera, Witi. 2014. *Māori Boy*. NZ: Random House.

Isaac Tuhoe 'Bruno' with Haami Bradford. 2007. *True Red –*

The Life of an Ex-Mongrel Mob Gang Leader. NZ: True Red.

King, Michael. 2003. *The Penguin History of New Zealand*. NZ: Penguin Books.

Lashlie, Celia. 2005. *He'll Be OK – Growing Gorgeous Boys into Good Men*. NZ: Harper Collins.

Lashlie, Celia. 2003. *The Journey to Prison – Who Goes and Why?*, revised edition. NZ: Harper Collins.

Latte, Nigel. 2007. *Into The Darklands and Beyond – Unveiling the Predators Among Us*. NZ: Harper Collins.

Picoult, Jodi. 2008. *Change of Heart*. Australia: Allen and Unwin.

Scott, Owen. 2004. *Deep Beyond the Reef – A True Story of Madness and Murder in the South Pacific*. London: Penguin Books.

Wishart, Ian. 2001. *Breaking Silence. The Kahui Case*. NZ: Howling at the Moon.

Radio NZ. 2008. Sat 16 August. 09.05hrs Kim Hill interview with JJ Joseph and Celia Lashlie. *Male Violence*.

Radio New Zealand. 2008. Sunday 18 May. 13.35hrs. Lynn Freeman interview with Isaac Marsh.

TVNZ. 2009. *The Outsiders*. Greenstone Pictures.com. Director: Reuben Pillsbury. Producer: Cass Avery.

TV 3. 2008. Thursday 19th June 21.30hrs. *Inside New Zealand: The Gangs*: Part One. Top Shelf Productions Ltd. Producer/director: Laurie Clarke.

TV 3. 2008. Thursday 14th August 21.30hrs. *Inside New Zealand: First Time in Prison*. Ponsonby Productions Ltd, Director: Te Arepa Kahi, Producer: John Keir.

Acknowledgements

Writing *The Last Time We Spoke* has been a long and fascinating journey for me. It was a work in its infancy during my Masters of Creative Writing year at AUT in 2009 and grew to adulthood over eight subsequent years. I grew alongside it.

Many people have impacted on its evolution – to all, a big thank you.

Special mention to:

John Cranna, Tina Shaw and fellow colleagues of the MCW Class of 2008 for your early encouragement and feedback;

Renae Maihi for your invaluable honesty, guidance and support;

Amali Fonseka, John Quirk, Rob Tuwhare, Steph Van Meulen and Murray Darroch for your time, enthusiasm, interest and input;

Inspector Gary Davey and Constable Glen Compain for assisting in my research around violent youth offending in New Zealand, as well as police protocol; and Catherine Lawla of Victim Support North Shore;

Those in the NZ prison service who facilitated my research into prisons: Warren Cummings, Kelly Pouhotau, Annie Tausi, Chris Burns, Tom Sherlock, Peter Phelan, Ranga Hohai, inmates at The Northern Correctional Facility Ngawha; and Dr Julian Fuller for assisting in the above introductions;

Alan Ringwood for your time and expertise;   Lesley Marshall for your sharp editorial skills of the very first draft, and for so generously sharing some of your life experiences with me;

And The New Zealand Society of Authors and Kobo for your endorsement through the Kobo/NZ Author Publishing Prize 2014.

A huge thank you to the A-team – my wonderful agent, Hannah Ferguson, and all the terrific people at Allison & Busby – for your unerring support and hard work.

Finally, thank you to my dearest Nadia, Andrew and Luigi for your endless patience, unconditional love, and might I say, supreme editorial skills. I'm keeping you all on!